VANISHED!

Dusk had descended as Kane and his companion has-tened through the streets, and darkness was creeping across the deserted silence of Saxe-Coburg Square when they arrived.

They halted then, staring into the shadows, seeking the spot where the shop nestled between the residences looming on either side. The shadows were deeper here and they moved closer, only to stare at the empty gap between the two buildings.

The shop was gone.

—From "A Most Unusual Murder" by Robert Bloch

THE HAUNTED HOUR

. . . includes stories from these celebrated authors:

• Richard Matheson • Simon P. McCaffery • Bram Stoker
• David Dean • Ray Bradbury • Jo Bannister
• Robert Bloch • Stephen F. Wilcox • Robert Campbell
• David Braly • Patricia Highsmith
• Richard F. McGonegal • Patricia McGerr
• John C. Boland • Marjorie Bowen • Tim Myers
• M. R. James • Gregor Robinson • Bill Pronzini
• Nora H. Caplan

D1413469

MORE MYSTERIES FROM THE
BERKLEY PUBLISHING GROUP . . .

THE HERON CARVIC MISS SEETON MYSTERIES: Retired art
teacher Miss Seeton steps in where Scotland Yard stumbles. "A most be-
guiling protagonist!"—*New York Times*

by Heron Carvic	*by Hamilton Crane*
MISS SEETON SINGS	HANDS UP, MISS SEETON
MISS SEETON DRAWS THE LINE	MISS SEETON CRACKS THE CASE
WITCH MISS SEETON	MISS SEETON PAINTS THE TOWN
PICTURE MISS SEETON	MISS SEETON BY MOONLIGHT
ODDS ON MISS SEETON	MISS SEETON ROCKS THE CRADLE
	MISS SEETON GOES TO BAT
by Hampton Charles	MISS SEETON PLANTS SUSPICION
ADVANTAGE MISS SEETON	STARRING MISS SEETON
MISS SEETON AT THE HELM	MISS SEETON UNDERCOVER
MISS SEETON, BY APPOINTMENT	MISS SEETON RULES
	SOLD TO MISS SEETON

SISTERS IN CRIME: Criminally entertaining short stories from the top
women of mystery and suspense. "Excellent!"—*Newsweek*

edited by Marilyn Wallace

SISTERS IN CRIME	SISTERS IN CRIME 4
SISTERS IN CRIME 2	SISTERS IN CRIME 5
SISTERS IN CRIME 3	

KATE SHUGAK MYSTERIES: A former D.A. solves crimes in the far
Alaska north . . .

by Dana Stabenow

A COLD DAY FOR MURDER	A COLD-BLOODED BUSINESS
DEAD IN THE WATER	PLAY WITH FIRE
A FATAL THAW	

FORREST EVERS MYSTERIES: A former race-car driver solves the
high-speed crimes of world-class racing . . . "A Dick Francis on wheels!"
—Jackie Stewart

by Bob Judd

BURN	SPIN
CURVE	

INSPECTOR BANKS MYSTERIES: Award-winning British detective
fiction at its finest . . . "Robinson's novels are habit-forming!"—*West
Coast Review of Books*

by Peter Robinson

THE HANGING VALLEY	PAST REASON HATED
WEDNESDAY'S CHILD	FINAL ACCOUNT

CASS JAMESON MYSTERIES: Lawyer Cass Jameson seeks justice in
the criminal courts of New York City in this highly acclaimed series . . . "A witty, gritty heroine."—*New York Post*

by Carolyn Wheat

FRESH KILLS	DEAD MAN'S THOUGHTS

THE HAUNTED HOUR

Edited by Cynthia Manson and Constance Scarborough

BERKLEY PRIME CRIME, NEW YORK

THE HAUNTED HOUR

A Berkley Prime Crime Book / published by arrangement with
Dell Magazines

PRINTING HISTORY
Berkley Prime Crime edition/October 1995

ISBN: 0-425-15010-0

Berkley Prime Crime Books are published by
The Berkley Publishing Group,
200 Madison Avenue, New York, NY 10016.
The name BERKLEY PRIME CRIME
and the BERKLEY PRIME CRIME design
are trademarks belonging to Berkley Publishing Corporation.

PRINTED IN THE UNITED STATES OF AMERICA

10 9 8 7 6 5 4 3 2 1

CONTENTS

INTRODUCTION

All Hallows Eve, otherwise known as Halloween, is one of the most fancied yet feared days of the year. It is a day when tricks are played, spells are cast, and all the dead walk the earth.

In this ghoulish collection of tales from *Ellery Queen's Mystery Magazine* and *Alfred Hitchcock Mystery Magazine*, prepare yourself for a nail-biting journey down terror lane as you experience the madness of voodoo in Richard Matheson's "Needle in the Heart," or the ghost of Jack the Ripper in Robert Bloch's "A Most Unusual Murder." For those of you a little harder to chill, we are sure that you will find the visitor in Richard F. McGonegal's "The Grin Reaper" someone who will make even your heart stop beating. Add to those tales of terror stories by such masters as Ray Bradbury, Robert Campbell, Patricia Highsmith, Patricia McGerr, Bill Pronzini, Marjorie Bowen, and the great Bram Stoker, you will have all of the ingredients for a hellish witches' brew.

As another Halloween approaches, be sure that before you begin reading this collection of spine-tingling tales you close all the shades, turn on all the lights, lock all the doors, and settle in for a Halloween treat that will surely keep your heart racing.

One final word of caution: If you hear something in the other room, don't check to see what it is. It could be a "Black Wind" blowing!

NEEDLE IN THE HEART

RICHARD MATHESON

April 23: at last I have found a way to kill Therese. I am so happy I could cry. To end that vile dominion after all these years! What is the phrase?—" 'tis a consummation devoutly to be wish'd." Well, I have wished it long enough. Now it is time to act. I will destroy Therese and regain my peace of mind. I will!

What distresses me is that the book has been here in our library all these years. Why, I could have done it ages ago!—avoiding all the agonies and cruel humiliations I have borne. Still, I must not think like that. I must be grateful I found it at all. *And* amused—how droll it really is!—that Therese was actually in the library with me when I came across the book.

She, of course, was poring avidly over one of the many volumes of pornography left by Father. I shall burn them all after I have killed Therese. Thank God our mother died before he started to collect them. Vile man that he was. Therese loved him to the end, of course. She is just like him really—brutish, carnal, and disgusting. Oh, I will sing for joy the day she dies.

Yes, there she was, below, darkly flushed with sensuality while I, attempting to avoid the sight of her, moved about on the balcony where the older volumes were kept. And there I found it on an upper shelf, a film of gray dust on its pages. *Voodoo: An Authentic Study* by Dr. William Moriarity. It had been printed privately. The Lord only knows where or when Father acquired it.

The astounding thing: I perused it, bored, then actually put it back in place! It was not until I had walked away from it and glanced through many other books that, suddenly, it came to me.

I could kill Therese by use of voodoo!

April 25: My hand is trembling as I write this. I have almost completed the doll which represents Therese—yes, almost completed it. I have made it from the cloth of one of her old dresses which I found in the attic. I have used two tiny jeweled buttons for its eyes. There is more to do, of course, but the project is at last under way.

I am amused to consider what Dr. Ramsay would say if he discovered my plans. What would his initial reaction be? That I am foolish to believe in voodoo? Or that I must learn to live with Therese if not to love her. Love that *pig*? Never! How I despise her! If I could—believe me—I would happily surrender my half of Father's estate if it would mean that I would never have to see her dissipated face again, never have to listen to her drunken swearing, to her tales of lewd adventuring.

But this is quite impossible. She will not leave me be. I have but one course left to me—to destroy her. And I shall. I *shall*.

Therese has only one more day to live.

April 26: I have it all now—all! Therese took a bath before she left tonight—to Lord knows what debaucheries. After the bath she cut her nails. And now I have them fastened to the doll with thread. And I have made the doll a head of hair from the strands I laboriously combed from Therese's brush. Now the doll truly *is* Therese. That is the beauty of voodoo. I hold Therese's life in my hands, free to choose, for myself, the moment of her destruction. I will wait and savor that delicious freedom.

What will Dr. Ramsey say when Therese is dead? What *can* he say? That I am mad to think voodoo had killed her? (Not that I will ever tell him.) But it will! I will not lay a hand on her—as much as I would like to do it personally, crushing the breath from her throat. But no. I will survive.

That is the joy of it—to kill Therese willfully and yet to live! That is the utter ecstasy of it!

Tomorrow night. Let her enjoy her last adventure. No more will she stagger in, her breath a reeking fume of whiskey, to regale me in lurid detail with the foul obscenities she had committed and enjoyed. No more will she— Oh, I cannot wait! I shall thrust a needle deep into the doll's heart, rid myself of her forever. Damn Therese, *damn* her! I shall kill her now!

From the notebook of John H. Ramsay, M.D.

April 27: Poor Millicent is dead. Her housekeeper found her crumpled on the floor of her bedroom this morning, clutching at her heart, a look of shock and agony frozen on her face. A heart attack, no doubt. No marks on her. Beside her, on the floor, was a tiny cloth doll with a needle piercing it. Poor Millicent. Had she some brain-sick notions of destroying me with voodoo? I had hoped she trusted me. Still, why should she have? I could never have helped her really. Hers was a hopeless situation. Millicent Therese Marlow suffered from the most advanced case of multiple personality it has ever been my misfortune to observe. . . .

THE DEEP END

SIMON P. McCAFFERY

Darren was perched high atop the pool in the orange plastic lifeguard chair, the one overlooking the deep end, when he noticed with a jolt the shape suspended beneath the wavering surface.

Something lay sunken in ten feet of water, out near the center above the drain vent.

It was the second weekend of July, and the Glenwood city pool had been overrun by heat-crazed kids who splashed and frothed the water like piranhas. The L-shaped pool swarmed with airmats and schools of swimmers. Others donned diving masks to explore the light-speckled bottom for glittering coins. A straggled train of swimmers waited to scale the aluminum ladder to the high dive boards, jostling and heckling one another. The girls jack-knifed in with precision while the boys, many of whom Darren knew from Glenwood High, performed various gyrating belly flops, smacking the water like stones and sending columns of spray into the air. Summer voices buzzed across the hot air, and the sky burned so shockingly blue that the preceding winter's gray ice and sleety rain seemed as remote as the last ice age. A Dr Pepper thermometer hanging above the snack bar window registered the mercury pushing ninety-eight, and the concrete deck shimmered like a desert highway.

Darren had been daydreaming of improbable schemes to buy a high-rise manifold for his '66 Mustang without tipping his parents to the missing chunk from his college sav-

ings account. The sight of the rippling, distorted shape on
the pool's bottom snapped him out of this heat haze like the
end of a wet-tipped towel in a locker room shower.

He leaned forward, his brows knitting themselves together in puzzlement.

The commotion on the surface made it difficult to see
anything clearly that far down. It looked too big to be a waterlogged beach towel or discarded T-shirt. Probably one of
the penny-diving boys waiting for a girl to knife down from
the high dive and lose her top. There was a skinny seventh
grader, Kyle Berryman, who spent most of the summer
submerged off the six foot mark like a Russian sub, squinting intently through his Kmart Aqua-Adventure diving
mask, his cheeks bulging like a blowfish. A lot of the girls
would flip him the bird on their way to the surface, but this
seemed only to excite Kyle further.

Slow seconds passed and Darren's heart began kicking
harder beneath his ribs. His right hand strayed to the
chrome whistle hanging above his bare chest.

The kid wouldn't come up.

While fresh sweat popped out on his relatively zit-free
forehead, Darren made two quick deductions. Either this
young Cousteau could hold his breath longer than Houdini
(or even Kyle Berryman) or he was in the process of
drowning right before Darren's eyes.

Smack in the middle of Glenwood's modern, Olympic-
size public pool.

Darren stood, ready to blow his whistle, and two very
strange things happened.

For a moment the surface cleared like crystal, just long
enough for Darren to see what was hanging down there: a
redhaired girl in a sleek black tank suit, not a boy. She
seemed to stare straight up at Darren with eyes greener than
seawater, her long hair floating around her face like a flaming veil. Darren was assaulted by a laserlike sense of déjà
vu.

Pamela Hartman?

A tubby kid named Doogan bounded off the diving
board and hit the water atop the submerged girl in an explosive cannonball (of course, when you're shaped like ten-

year-old Jerry Doogan it is damn near impossible *not* to cannonball). Darren lost sight of the girl (drowning?) as a miniature tidal wave swept across the pool's surface.

The ripples smoothed themselves a few moments later but the girl in the deep end had vanished. Except for a fleeting second when Darren imagined he saw a black and orange shadow slip down through the drain vent.

Darren blinked behind his RayBans. The overpowering feeling of déjà vu was replaced by vertigo as he stared at the pool bottom. Nothing there but wavering light dancing on cobalt concrete.

The girl must have darted away and surfaced after the Doogan kid hit the water. Darren scanned the surface but didn't see any redheads. Still, there were a lot of heads and shoulders bobbing around. False alarm. His heart gradually slowed to a trot.

He was about to sit down when the other two lifeguards simultaneously blew their whistles in a shrill double scream.

Darren jerked, leaned out beyond the point of balance, and barely caught himself by grabbing the edge of the tower, white-knuckled. His heart slammed into his throat like an icy cannonball. For one terrifying second he really expected to look down and see the flame-haired girl's water-choked body floating in the pool, dead eyes bulging up at him in accusation.

But it was only the signal for the first fifteen-minute break of the afternoon: everybody out of the pool.

Darren climbed down from his chair, ignoring the swimmers—mostly fellow white suburban kids—who dripped wet trails back to scattered towels. Boom boxes blared to life, bombarding the still air with heavy-metal percussion. Coppertoned hands counted wet coins, and a new line formed at the snack counter. The Glenwood crowd knew that fizzy soda and deliciously frozen candy bars were a sure way to keep the blood spiked with sugar. On the baking deck, rows of cliquish girls began the ritual of combing wet hair and applying suntan accelerator before arranging themselves as splayed, willing sacrifices to the sun.

Darren, the tallest of the lifeguards with legs made to run down tennis balls, padded to the edge of the pool, feeling the concrete under his soles like a blowtorch. He watched the water bend the sunlight into ribbons that wiggled across the deep end's bottom in hypnotic, inviting patterns. During breaks he usually stepped off into that sapphire coolness to wash away the sweat and boredom. He stared at the water, unsure. How long could he hold *his* breath? Ninety seconds, two minutes maybe, if he had a chance to tank up.

A hand touched his shoulder, and he flinched. Turning, he saw his square jawed, tanned face reflected twice in Steph's chrome Boss-man shades. His eyes looked distant, spaced out. And tired; he hadn't been sleeping well. The unrelenting heat made him feel like a zombie. Darren the Undead.

"Time," she said, then sauntered back to he tower. On the far bank of the pool, Marc was already seated on his orange throne, looking like a Soloflex ad. Climbing into his chair like a sleepwalker, Darren wondered where the fifteen minutes had gone. A restless murmur rose from the ranks of younger kids. He barely noticed the sculptured brunette in a French cut on the other side who tried to lock eyes. What the hell was the matter with him, anyway? Babes like her were the only reason he risked sunstroke at the pool lifeguarding. It sure wasn't for the pay.

The whistles blew, his own adding its piercing note to the chorus, and the pool's glassy stillness was shattered as swimmers tumbled in like lemmings.

That night he dreamed of Pamela Hartman and awoke in his bedroom smelling chlorine and something rotted. He'd tried to scream before waking, but his mouth had been full of cold blue water.

He shivered, disoriented, huddled miserably in the sweaty sheets. Already the images were blurring, melting away. Weren't you supposed to recall dreams (okay, nightmares) best after one woke you?

But he remembered enough. He'd driven to the pool to swim laps, but in the illogic of dreams the sun had long since disappeared; it was well past midnight, in fact. The

pool was deserted and ominous in the moonlight—a black
living mirror waiting to swallow him. He peeled off his
clothes and dived in, no trunks, stroking to the far side of
the deep end as if it was the morning warmup with the
other lifeguards.

Darren swam back and forth, smoothly. Back and forth.
And as an almost delicious fatigue began to creep into his
shoulders, arms, and legs, he had felt something brush his
left foot. Something cold and sharp, like a finger stripped of
its flesh. A bony hand closed around his ankle like a vise.

He had looked down into the shadowy water in surprise
and seen what was left of Pamela's gray, bloated face grin-
ning up, pulling him down for one last kiss—

Darren rolled out of bed and staggered to the bathroom
beyond his work desk. His parents liked to keep the air con-
ditioning set on Arctic, and he felt gooseflesh crawl down
his back and legs.

He ran the sink faucet, cupped his hands, and drank. The
water tasted tangy, like pool water. A chemical taste, mask-
ing any impurities. But at least it replaced the dry, stale
taste of fear.

Crossing his dark bedroom, Darren plopped back into
bed. The nightmares had started a week after he'd earned a
berth as summer lifeguard at the pool. They were growing
steadily worse. And today, he had been hallucinating.
Look, Ma, no LSD!

It was this heat wave, and too much partying. His parents
were ragging him to quit the pool and get a job that netted
some major paychecks for his college account. Yeah, well,
he had no intention of spending the final summer dressed in
a baggy polyester tunic flipping Big Macs. Or searing his
wrists on smoky pizza ovens.

No, sitting all day beneath the blazing sun-god and scop-
ing chicks was the only way to go, even if four twenty-five
an hour wasn't exactly swelling the college coffers.

Darren wiped the sheen of perspiration from his face.
Why start dreaming about Pamela Hartman now, and why
associate her with the deep end? The accident had been
four years ago, when he was fourteen, charming the girls as
if he were seventeen with his blue eyes and broad shoul-

ders. It had been an awful thing, but he had put it behind him. His folks never mentioned it, at least never in front of him. He shouldn't dwell on it now. He should enjoy his last summer before his four-year sentence commenced. Kick up his heels and dip his wick as often as possible.

But it was a long time before he drifted back to sleep, still smelling rotted fish and chlorine.

Darren was manning the middle chair when it happened, so he had a front row seat for the whole nasty affair—Marc rescuing the unconscious little boy, the nearly failed resuscitation by the paramedics . . . and the redhaired girl who couldn't have been watching from the high dive board, leering at him.

He was daydreaming again, this time about how he might best get into Mindy Clark's skintight pants, when Marc's whistle abruptly sliced the air. Darren's heart tripped like a blind man at a two-foot curb.

Marc was already diving toward the water, the muscles in his legs and shoulders standing out in sharp relief. He disappeared under the surface like a torpedo.

On the far bank, Steph was hurrying down from her chair, towel in hand, pale pale underneath her caramel tan. She shouted something at Darren and gestured wildly. The sound of her voice, clearly scared spitless, broke his paralysis, and he scrambled down from his tower.

Marc surfaced a moment later, coughing and gasping, the limp body of a boy under his meaty left arm. Steph hurriedly spread her towel on the wet concrete, then ran to call 911. Darren helped hoist the unconscious kid, later identified as Jimmy Donnely, out of the water. His spindly, eleven-year-old body couldn't have weighed more than eighty pounds sopping wet but it felt like two hundred. Jimmy was still wearing a cheap black rubber diving mask (an apprentice of Kyle Berryman?) and goofy, kid-sized flippers. Darren quickly stripped them off. Jimmy's eyes were closed, and his skinny chest wasn't rising and falling. Limp as a dishrag, too.

Marc began trying to force the life back into Jimmy's body before a spellbound ringlet of onlookers. His trembling hands compressed the kid's chest, and a fountain of water magically erupted from his mouth and nose. Tilting the head back to clear the windpipe, as per their Red Cross training, Marc started CPR.

He was still propelling air into Jimmy's lungs and pumping his chest when two paramedics arrived. Ten minutes later Jimmy still wasn't breathing, and his pulse was flagging. Darren stood rooted to the spot, fighting a feeling of faintness and nausea.

The thirty-something paramedics were starting to eye one another when Jimmy convulsed, sputtered, and resumed living. There were enough claps, cheers, and sighs to fill a game show laughtrack. Darren felt the tension flow out of his body like warm recycled beer.

Everyone was watching the paramedics carry Jimmy away on a gurney, so no one saw the redhaired girl in the jet one-piece standing on the end of the high dive board. No one except Darren.

She waved at him, blew him a kiss, and dived. Her slender body made no sound when it arrowed through the surface. No concussion . . . no spreading, circular wave. She didn't surface, and Darren could only stare at the tiny, distorted drain vent in disbelief.

He'd seen her out of the water this time. Even from the height of the diving board there could be no mistaking who it was. Pamela.

That night the horror show inside his head didn't replay the midnight scene at the pool. Instead, he was fourteen again, visiting Nassau with his parents. Summer vacation, 1988. He met Pamela Hartman on the white powder beach, knew by her eyes immediately that she was interested. Barely sixteen, Pamela was a knockout; gorgeous red hair and a firm, freckle-skinned body to kill for. He'd often passed for seventeen and didn't think it wise to admit he was only in junior high.

Or that he couldn't swim very well.

Pamela couldn't swim at all, so he offered to teach her. Mainly so he could play with her . . . lay his hands on some of that foxy flesh. Maybe even slide some fingers under that suit, if she was willing.

He hadn't counted on the undercurrent, or that she would panic so quickly when they both lost hold of his air mattress. In over his head with waves spinning him and water rushing into his mouth, he had . . . simply freaked out. Lost his cool. He heard Pamela's choking pleas for help, behind him. But he'd paddled the other way, toward shore. Every sailor for himself, right? He'd read that a drowning person's first reaction is to grab something in a death-grip and pull it down with them. All Darren wanted was air to breathe and solid land under his feet. And he made it . . . barely.

Pamela didn't.

The Coast Guard dragged the water, and the beach patrol scoured the pristine shores for her body. But the Caribbean tides had swallowed her, sucked her down and away. It had been an accident, and though devastated, the Hartmans had not tried to cause any trouble. Darren was hysterical—had cried until his eyes burned and sticky snot ran from his nose, like a little kid—yet a tiny, terrible voice deep in his head reminded him, better her than you, cowboy.

A year later, with the approval of his parents, Darren had enrolled in Red Cross training to become a certified lifeguard.

It happened again a week later, when the water was awash with flotillas of swimmers, cannonballing boys and copper women drifting on silver airmats. The unending heat wave was killing lawns, flowerbeds, and the town's elderly shut-ins, but it was great for pool attendance.

This time it was Steph who rescued the teenage girl, Patti Cox, from the deep end. Her pallid, pimple-spotted face was vaguely familiar, as if she'd sat next to Darren in a homeroom class. Steph had rotated to the third chair, having traded places with Darren for the day, when Patti's head erupted from the water like a goggle-eyed bass, her mouth gasping. She cried out, and the water-choked words sounded like *GABBEDME!* Then her head popped under like a cork on a fishing line.

Unlike little Jimmy, she started breathing again after less than a minute of CPR, briskly applied by a white-faced

Steph. Patty's eyes snapped open like window shades and she spit up a cup of clear pool water. She was definitely getting air, screaming and flailing, something about her leg. There *was* a thin bruise above her right ankle, probably from being hauled over the concrete lip of the pool.

Darren began cutting practices and kept far away from the water during breaks. A few times he gazed down at a girl in a nearly nonexistent two-piece and saw something else below her, out near the center. A pale hand waving from the drain vent, beckoning to him.

Come on in, the water's fine. Christ!

Was it possible to develop a phobia at eighteen? He was the *lifeguard*. Decorated ex-member of the high school swim team! And who the hell had ever heard of a haunted swimming pool?

Darren didn't see Pamela again until the last blistering Saturday of July.

The dreams had intensified, become exponentially more horrifying each night. In these airless night terrors she told him that she had been searching for him, that it wasn't so bad below the waves. He could only imagine her green eyes and sylphlike form swimming through miles of briny ocean depths, inlets, rivers, streams, city water pipes . . . until she had finally poured herself into the pool.

He'd managed to scream last night, waking his parents as well.

The pool was clogged with swimmers by two, the water transformed into a rippling, flawed diamond. Darren was manning the third chair; none of the other lifeguards had been willing to trade. The two chairs above the deep end were bad luck. Marc sat on the other bank, looking smaller somehow.

Immediately after the three o'clock break, Darren saw a fortyish woman duck beneath the surface, kick off the side wall, and begin gliding to the far side. Her hair was going gray, but she had a fine, shapely body. Darren followed her progress, admiring her graceful form.

The water seemed to shiver. Pamela was suddenly below her, hovering above the drain vent like an evil aquatic genie, reaching up with pale starfish hands.

Darren's breath clogged in his throat. He squeezed his eyes shut behind his polarized sunglasses. Then opened them.

Pamela was choking the woman, who thrashed and kicked and bubbled furiously.

Rearing up, his body numb despite the heat, Darren delivered the glittering whistle to his lips and made it shriek. Without a glance at the other stations he tore off his sunglasses and dived far out above the pool, feeling for a second that weightless, dreamy terror. He nearly forgot to gulp some air before the blood-warm water closed over his head.

Darren stroked downward through the topaz water, chlorine biting his staring eyes, down and away from the sun and surface. The rough bottom scraped his toes and elbows as he skimmed above it. He saw black, fuzzy dots that might be coins or the curled bodies of waterlogged insects. From the height of the chair the pool assumed a tidy, familiar geometry, but deep beneath its surface the sunken plain of the bottom seemed to stretch indefinitely. The surface looked fathoms above him, a glowing concave lens.

He moved in to grasp the woman, who was beginning to sink, her face a picture of shock and pain. Pamela had disappeared, presumably back down the drain vent. Darren circled an arm around the unconscious woman's torso and prepared to kick up to the surface—

—and would have, except that something clamped around his right ankle. Darren kicked in panic and lost his purchase on the gritty bottom. It was Pamela. She quickly trapped his other ankle in a crushing grip. Darren twisted, released the dying woman he'd been about to rescue, and found himself face to face with Pamela.

She looked the same as in his dreams. The sleek black tank suit was stained a seaweed green and stretched too tightly across her bloated body. There were lots of tiny holes in the suit, as if nibbling fish had been at it, perhaps the same ones who had fed on Pamela's eyes. Moss covered her swollen face like a rotting beard.

They sank together. Darren grappled with her desperately, but it was like battling empty air . . . or slippery water. *Let go of me, you bitch!*

Pamela gurgled something from her grotesque white lips and pulled him closer.

Darren felt his panic spike, peak, and overload some integral circuit breaker of reason. He opened his mouth and screamed a cloud of silver bubbles that raced upward to the light. Water immediately tried to snake up his nose, and he swallowed some, gagging reflexively. His temples pounded a frantic warning. Black spots swam in his vision like playful amoebae.

The last thing Darren saw was his own dislocated body settling gently on the bottom, blue eyes wide below a floating corona of sand-colored hair. He saw this clearly, though he wasn't wearing a mask.

Pamela held only his hand now . . . or an appendage of whatever fluid thing he had become. She was taking him down the drain vent, down to wherever she lived. To whatever cold darkness waited.

DRACULA'S GUEST

BRAM STOKER

When we started for our drive the sun was shining brightly on Munich, and the air was full of the joyousness of early summer. Just as we were about to depart, Herr Delbrück (the maître d'hôtel of the Quatre Saisons, where I was staying) came down, bareheaded, to the carriage and, after wishing me a pleasant drive, said to the coachman, still holding his hand on the handle of the carriage door:

"Remember you are back by nightfall. The sky looks bright but there is a shiver in the north wind that says there may be a sudden storm. But I am sure you will not be late." Here he smiled, and added, "For you know what night it is."

Johann answered with an emphatic, "Ja, mein Herr," and, touching his hat, drove off quickly. When we had cleared the town, I said, after signalling to him to stop:

"Tell me, Johann, what is to-night?"

He crossed himself, as he answered laconically: "Walpurgis nacht." Then he took out his watch, a great, old-fashioned German silver thing as big as a turnip, and looked at it, with his eyebrows gathered together and a little impatient shrug of his shoulders. I realised that this was his way of respectfully protesting against the unnecessary delay, and sank back in the carriage, merely motioning him to proceed. He started off rapidly, as if to make up for lost time. Every now and then the horses seemed to throw up their heads and sniff the air suspiciously. On such occasions I often looked round in alarm. The road was pretty bleak, for we were traversing a sort of high, wind-swept plateau. As we drove, I saw a road that looked but little used, and which seemed to dip through a little, winding valley. It looked so inviting that, even at the risk of offending him, I called Johann to stop—and when he had pulled up, I told him I would like to drive down that road. He made all sorts of excuses, and frequently crossed himself as he spoke. This somewhat piqued my curiosity, so I asked him various questions. He answered fencingly, and repeatedly looked at his watch in protest. Finally I said:

"Well, Johann, I want to go down this road. I shall not ask you to come unless you like; but tell me why you do not like to go, that is all I ask." For answer he seemed to throw himself off the box, so quickly did he reach the ground. Then he stretched out his hands appealingly to me, and implored me not to go. There was just enough of English mixed with the German for me to understand the drift of his talk. He seemed always just about to tell me something—the very idea of which evidently frightened him; but each time he pulled himself up, saying, as he crossed himself: "Walpurgis nacht!"

I tried to argue with him, but it was difficult to argue with a man when I did not know his language. The advantage certainly rested with him, for although he began to speak in English, of a very crude and broken kind, he always got excited and broke into his native tongue—and every time he did so, he looked at his watch. Then the horses became restless and sniffed the air. At this he grew very pale, and, looking around in a frightened way, he suddenly jumped forward, took them by the bridles and led them on some twenty feet. I followed, and asked why he had done this. For answer he crossed himself, pointed to the spot we had left and drew his carriage in the direction of the other road, indicating a cross, and said, first in German, then in English: "Buried him—him what killed themselves."

I remembered the old custom of burying suicides at cross-roads: "Ah! I see, a suicide. How interesting!" But for the life of me I could not make out why the horses were frightened.

Whilst we were talking, we heard a sort of sound between a yelp and a bark. It was far away; but the horses got very restless, and it took Johann all his time to quiet them. He was pale, and said: "It sounds like a wolf—but yet there are no wolves here now."

"No?" I said, questioning him. "Isn't it long since the wolves were so near the city?"

"Long, long," he answered, "in the spring and summer; but with the snow the wolves have been here not so long."

Whilst he was petting the horses and trying to quiet them, dark clouds drifted rapidly across the sky. The sunshine passed away, and a breath of cold wind seemed to drift past us. It was only a breath, however, and more in the nature of a warning than a fact, for the sun came out brightly again. Johann looked under his lifted hand at his horizon and said:

"The storm of snow, he comes before long time." Then he looked at his watch again, and, straightway holding his reins firmly—for the horses were still pawing the ground restlessly and shaking their heads—he climbed to his box as though the time had come for proceeding on our journey.

I felt a little obstinate and did not at once get into the carriage.

"Tell me," I said, "about this place where the road leads," and I pointed down.

Again he crossed himself and mumbled a prayer, before he answered: "It is unholy."

"What is unholy?" I enquired.

"The village.

"Then there is a village?"

"No, no. No one lives there hundreds of years." My curiosity was piqued: "But you said there was a village."

"There was."

"Where is it now?"

Whereupon he burst out into a long story in German and English, so mixed up that I could not quite understand exactly what he said, but roughly I gathered that long ago, hundreds of years, men had died there and been buried in their graves; and sounds were heard under the clay, and when the graves were opened, men and women were found rosy with life, and their mouths red with blood. And so, in haste to save their lives (aye, and their souls!—and here he crossed himself) those who were left fled away to other places, where the living lived, and the dead were dead and not—not something. He was evidently afraid to speak the last words. As he proceeded with his narration, he grew more and more excited. It seemed as if his imagination had got hold of him, and he ended in a perfect paroxysm of fear—white-faced, perspiring, trembling and looking round him, as if expecting that some dreadful presence would manifest itself there in the bright sunshine on the open plain. Finally, in an agony of desperation, he cried:

"Walpurgis nacht!" and pointed to the carriage for me to get in. All my English blood rose at this, and, standing back, I said:

"You are afraid, Johann—you are afraid. Go home; I shall return alone; the walk will do me good." The carriage door was open. I took from the seat my oak walking-stick—which I always carry on my holiday excursions—and closed the door, pointing back to Munich, and said, "Go home, Johann—Walpurgis nacht doesn't concern Englishmen."

The horses were now more restive than ever, and Johann was trying to hold them in, while excitedly imploring me not to do anything so foolish. I pitied the poor fellow, he was so deeply in earnest; but all the same I could not help laughing. His English was quite gone now. In his anxiety he had forgotten that his only means of making me understand was to talk my language, so he jabbered away in his native German. It began to be a little tedious. After giving the direction, "Home!" I turned to go down the cross road into the valley.

With a despairing gesture, Johann turned his horses towards Munich. I leaned on my stick and looked after him. He went slowly along the road for a while: then there came over the crest of the hill a man tall and thin. I could see so much in the distance. When he drew near the horses, they began to jump and kick about, then to scream with terror. Johann could not hold them in; they bolted down the road, running away madly. I watched them out of sight, then looked for the stranger, but I found that he, too, was gone.

With a light heart I turned down the side road through the deepening valley to which Johann had objected. There was not the slightest reason, that I could see, for his objection; and I daresay I tramped for a couple of hours without thinking of time or distance, and certainly without seeing a person or a house. So far as the place was concerned, it was desolation itself. But I did not notice this particularly till, on turning a bend in the road, I came upon a scattered fringe of wood; then I recognised that I had been impressed unconsciously by the desolation of the region through which I had passed.

I sat down to rest myself, and began to look around. It struck me that it was considerably colder than it had been at the commencement of my walk—a sort of sighing sound seemed to be around me, with, now and then, high over-head, a sort of muffled roar. Looking upwards I noticed that great thick clouds were drifting rapidly across the sky from north to south at a great height. There were signs of a coming storm in some lofty stratum of the air. I was a little chilly, and, thinking that it was the sitting still after the ex-ercise of walking, I resumed my journey.

The ground I passed over was now much more pic-turesque. There were no striking objects that the eye might single out; but in all there was a charm of beauty. I took lit-tle heed of time and it was only when the deepening twi-light forced itself upon me that I began to think of how I should find my way home. The brightness of the day had gone. The air was cold, and the drifting of clouds high overhead was more marked. They were accompanied by a sort of far-away rushing sound, through which seemed to come at intervals that mysterious cry which the driver had said came from a wolf. For a while I hesitated. I had said I would see the deserted village, so on I went, and presently came on a wide stretch of open country, shut in by hills all around. Their sides were covered with trees which spread down to the plain, dotting, in clumps, the gentler slopes and hollows which showed here and there. I followed with my eye the winding of the road, and saw that it curved close to one of the densest of these clumps and was lost behind it.

As I looked there came a cold shiver in the air, and the

snow began to fall. I thought of the miles and miles of bleak country I had passed, and then hurried on to seek the shelter of the wood in front. Darker and darker grew the sky, and faster and heavier fell the snow, till the earth before and around me was a glistening white carpet the further edge of which was lost in misty vagueness. The road was here but crude, and when on the level its boundaries were not so marked, as when it passed through the cuttings; and in a little while I found that I must have strayed from it, for I missed underfoot the hard surface, and my feet sank deeper in the grass and moss. Then the wind grew stronger and blew with ever increasing force, till I was fain to run before it. The air became icy-cold, and in spite of my exercise I began to suffer. The snow was now falling so thickly and whirling around me in such rapid eddies that I could hardly keep my eyes open. Every now and then the heavens were torn asunder by vivid lightning, and in the flashes I could see ahead of me a great mass of trees, chiefly yew and cypress all heavily coated with snow.

I was soon amongst the shelter of the trees, and there, in comparative silence, I could hear the rush of the wind high overhead. Presently the blackness of the storm had become merged in the darkness of the night. By-and-by the storm seemed to be passing away: it now only came in fierce puffs or blasts. At such moments the weird sound of the wolf appeared to be echoed by many similar sounds around me.

Now and again, through the black mass of drifting cloud, came a straggling ray of moonlight, which lit up the expanse, and showed me that I was at the edge of a dense mass of cypress and yew trees. As the snow had ceased to fall, I walked out from the shelter and began to investigate more closely. It appeared to me that, amongst so many old foundations as I had passed, there might be still standing a house in which, though in ruins, I could find some sort of shelter for a while. As I skirted the edge of the copse, I found that a low wall encircled it, and following this I presently found an opening. Here the cypresses formed an alley leading up to a square mass of some kind of building. Just as I caught sight of this, however, the drifting clouds obscured the moon, and I passed up the path in darkness. The wind must have grown colder, for I felt myself shiver as I walked; but there was hope of shelter, and I groped my way blindly on.

I stopped, for there was a sudden stillness. The storm had passed; and, perhaps in sympathy with nature's silence, my heart seemed to cease to beat. But this was only momentarily; for suddenly the moonlight broke through the clouds, showing me that I was in a graveyard, and that the square object before me was a great massive tomb of marble, as white as the snow that lay on and all around it. With the moonlight there came a fierce sigh of the storm, which appeared to resume its course with a long, low howl, as of many dogs or wolves. I was awed and shocked, and felt the cold perceptibly grow upon me till it seemed to grip me by the heart. Then while the flood of moonlight still fell on the marble tomb, the storm gave further evidence of renewing, as though it was returning on its track. Impelled by some sort of fascination, I approached the sepulchre to see what it was, and why such a thing stood alone in such a place. I walked around it, and read, over the Doric door, in German—

COUNTESS DOLINGEN OF GRATZ
IN STYRIA
SOUGHT AND FOUND DEATH.
1801.

On the top of the tomb, seemingly driven through the solid marble—for the structure was composed of a few vast blocks of stone—was a great iron spike or stake. On going to the back I saw, graven in great Russian letters:

"The dead travel fast."

There was something so weird and uncanny about the whole thing that it gave me a turn and made me feel quite faint. I began to wish, for the first time, that I had taken Johann's advice. Here a thought struck me, which came under almost mysterious circumstances and with a terrible shock. This was Walpurgis Night!

Walpurgis Night, when, according to the belief of millions of people, the devil was abroad—when the graves were opened and the dead came forth and walked. When all evil things of earth and air and water held revel. This very place the driver had specially shunned. This was the depopulated village of centuries ago. This was where the suicide lay; and this was the place where I was alone—unmanned, shivering with cold in a shroud of snow with a wild storm gathering again upon me! It took all my philosophy, all the religion I had been taught, all my courage, not to collapse in a paroxysm of fright.

And now a perfect tornado burst upon me. The ground shook as though thousands of horses thundered across it; and this time the storm bore on its icy wings, not snow, but great hailstones which drove with such violence that they might have come from the thongs of Balearic slingers— hailstones that beat down leaf and branch and made the shelter of the cypresses of no more avail than though their stems were standing-corn. At the first I had rushed to the nearest tree; but I was soon fain to leave it and seek the only spot that seemed to afford refuge, the deep Doric doorway of the marble tomb. There, crouching against the massive bronze door, I gained a certain amount of protection from the beating of the hailstones, for now they only drove against me as they ricocheted from the ground and the side of the marble.

As I leaned against the door, it moved slightly and opened inwards. The shelter of even a tomb was welcome in that pitiless tempest, and I was about to enter it when there came a flash of forked-lightning that lit up the whole expanse of the heavens. In the instant, as I am a living man, I saw, as my eyes were turned into the darkness of the tomb, a beautiful woman, with rounded cheeks and red lips, seemingly sleeping on a bier. As the thunder broke overhead, I was grasped as by the hand of a giant and hurled out into the storm. The whole thing was so sudden that, before I could realise the shock, moral as well as physical, I found the hailstones beating me down. At the same time I had a strange, dominating feeling that I was not alone. I looked towards the tomb. Just then there came another blinding flash, which seemed to strike the iron stake that surmounted the tomb and to pour through to the earth, blasting and crumbling the marble, as in a burst of flame. The dead woman rose for a moment of agony, while she was lapped in the flame, and her bitter scream of pain was drowned in the thundercrash. The last thing I heard was this mingling of dreadful sound, as again I was seized in the giant-grasp and dragged away, while the hailstones beat on me, and the air around seemed reverberant with the howling of wolves. The last sight that I remembered was a vague, white, moving mass, as if all the graves around me had sent out the phantoms of their sheeted-dead, and that they were closing in on me through the white cloudiness of the driving hail.

Gradually there came a sort of vague beginning of consciousness; then a sense of weariness that was dreadful. For a time I remembered nothing; but slowly my senses returned. My feet seemed positively racked with pain, yet I could not move them. They seemed to be numbed. There was an icy feeling at the back of my neck and all down my spine, and my ears, like my feet, were dead, yet in torment; but there was in my breast a sense of warmth which was, by comparison, delicious. It was as a nightmare—a physical nightmare, if one may use such an expression; for some heavy weight on my chest made it difficult for me to breathe.

This period of semi-lethargy seemed to remain a long time, and as it faded away I must have slept or swooned. Then came a sort of loathing, like the first stage of sea-sickness, and a wild desire to be free from something—I knew not what. A vast stillness enveloped me, as though all the world were asleep or dead—only broken by the low panting as of some animal close to me. I felt a warm rasping at my throat, then came a consciousness of the awful truth, which chilled me to the heart and sent the blood surging up through my brain. Some great animal was lying on me and now licking my throat. I feared to stir, for some instinct of prudence bade me lie still; but the brute seemed to realize that there was now some change in me, for it raised its head. Through my eyelashes I saw above me the two great flaming eyes of a gigantic wolf. Its sharp white teeth gleamed in the gaping red mouth, and I could feel its hot breath fierce and acrid upon me.

For another spell of time I remembered no more. Then I became conscious of a low growl, followed by a yelp, renewed again and again. Then, seemingly very far away, I heard a "Holloa! Holloa!" as of many voices calling in unison. Cautiously I raised my head and looked in the direction whence the sound came; but the cemetery blocked my view. The wolf still continued to yelp in a strange way, and a red glare began to move round the grove of cypresses, as though following the sound. As the voices drew closer, the wolf yelped faster and louder. I feared to make either sound or motion. Nearer came the red glow, over the white pall which stretched into the darkness around me. Then all at once from beyond the trees there came at a trot a troop of horsemen bearing torches. The wolf rose from my breast and made for the cemetery. I saw one of the horsemen (soldiers by their caps and their long military cloaks) raise his carbine and take aim. A companion knocked up his arm, and I heard the ball whizz over my head. He had evidently taken my body for that of the wolf. Another sighted the animal as it slunk away, and a shot followed. Then, at a gallop, the troop rode forward—some towards me, others following the wolf as it disappeared amongst the snow-clad cypresses.

As they drew nearer I tried to move, but was powerless, although I could see and hear all that went on around me. Two or three of the soldiers jumped from their horses and knelt beside me. One of them raised my head, and placed his hand over my heart.

"Good news, comrades!" he cried. "His heart still beats!"

Then some brandy was poured down my throat; it put vigour into me, and I was able to open my eyes fully and look around. Lights and shadows were moving amongst the trees, and I heard men call to one another. They drew together, uttering frightened exclamations; and the lights flashed as the others came pouring out of the cemetery pell-mell, like men possessed. When the further ones came close to us, those who were around me asked them eagerly:

"Well, have you found him?"

The reply rang out hurriedly:

"No! No! Come away quick—quick! This is no place to stay, and on this of all nights!"

"What was it?" was the question, asked in all manner of keys. The answer came variously and all indefinitely as though the men were moved by some common impulse to speak, yet were restrained by some common fear from giving their thoughts.

"It—it—indeed!" gibbered one, whose wits had plainly given out for the moment.

"A wolf—and yet not a wolf!" another put in shudderingly.

"No use trying for him without the sacred bullet," a third remarked in a more ordinary manner.

"Serve us right for coming out on this night! Truly we have earned our thousand marks!" were the ejaculations of a fourth.

"There was blood on the broken marble," another said after a pause—"the lightning never brought that there. And for him—is he safe? Look at his throat! See, comrades, the wolf has been lying on him and keeping his blood warm."

The officer looked at my throat and replied:

"He is all right; the skin is not pierced. What does it all mean? We should never have found him but for the yelping of the wolf."

"What became of it?" asked the man who was holding up my head, and who seemed the least panic-stricken of the party, for his hands were steady and without tremor. On his sleeve was the chevron of a petty officer.

"It went to its home," answered the man, whose long face was pallid, and who actually shook with terror as he glanced around him fearfully. "There are graves enough there in which it may lie. Come, comrades—come quickly! Let us leave this cursed spot."

The officer raised me to a sitting posture, as he uttered a word of command; then several men placed me upon a horse. He sprang to the saddle behind me, took me in his arms, gave the word to advance; and, turning our faces away from the cypresses, we rode away in swift, military order.

As yet my tongue refused its office, and I was perforce silent. I must have fallen asleep; for the next thing I remembered was finding myself standing up, supported by a soldier on each side of me. It was almost broad daylight, and to the north a red streak of sunlight was reflected, like a path of blood, over the waste of snow. The officer was telling the men to say nothing of what they had seen, except that they found an English stranger, guarded by a large dog.

"Dog! That was no dog," cut in the man who had exhibited such fear. "I think I know a wolf when I see one."

The young officer answered calmly: "I said a dog."

"Dog!" reiterated the other ironically. It was evident that his courage was rising with the sun; and, pointing to me, he said, "Look at his throat. Is that the work of a dog, master?"

Instinctively I raised my hand to my throat, and as I touched it I cried out in pain. The men crowded round to look, some stooping down from their saddles; and again there came the calm voice of the young officer:

"A dog, as I said. If aught else were said we should only be laughed at."

I was then mounted behind a trooper, and we rode on into the suburbs of Munich. Here we came across a stray carriage, into which I was lifted, and it was driven off to the Quatre Saisons—the young officer accompanying me, whilst a trooper followed with his horse, and the others rode off to their barracks.

When we arrived, Herr Delbrück rushed so quickly down the steps to meet me, that it was apparent he had been watching within. Taking me by both hands he solicitously led me in. The officer saluted me and was turning to withdraw, when I recognized his purpose, and insisted that he should come to my rooms. Over a glass of wine I warmly thanked him and his brave comrades for saving me. He replied simply that he was more than glad, and that Herr Delbrück had at the first taken steps to make all the searching party pleased; at which ambiguous utterance the maître d'hôtel smiled, while the officer pleaded duty and withdrew.

"But Herr Delbrück," I enquired, "how and why was it that the soldiers searched for me?"

He shrugged his shoulders, as if in depreciation of his own deed, as he replied:

"I was so fortunate as to obtain leave from the commander of the regiment in which I served, to ask for volunteers."

"But how did you know I was lost?" I asked.

"The driver came hither with the remains of his carriage, which had been upset when the horses ran away."

"But surely you would not send a search party of soldiers merely on this account?"

"Oh, no!" he answered; "but even before the coachman arrived, I had this telegram from the Boyar whose guest you are," and he took from his pocket a telegram which he handed to me, and I read:

BISTRITZ.

"Be careful of my guest—his safety is most precious to me. Should aught happen to him, or if he be missed, spare nothing to find him and ensure his safety. He is English and therefore adventurous. There are often dangers from snow and wolves and night. Lost not a moment if you suspect harm to him. I answer your zeal with my fortune.—Dracula."

As I held the telegram in my hand, the room seemed to whirl around me; and, if the attentive maître d'hôtel had not caught me, I think I should have fallen. There was something so strange in all this, something so weird and impossible to imagine, that there grew on me a sense of my being in some way the sport of opposite forces—the mere vague idea of which seemed in a way to paralyse me. I was certainly under some form of mysterious protection. From a distant country had come, in the very nick of time, a message that took me out of the danger of the snow-sleep and the jaws of the wolf.

A SALESMAN'S TALE

DAVID DEAN

They're back. The woman and the girl. I keep pretending I haven't noticed them, but I have. I certainly have.

They don't seem to be looking for me, though I must be the reason they've returned. Why else do the dead come back but to haunt their killers?

So far, they appear dazed and lethargic. They just sit very still, facing the altar, as if gathering strength. They remind me of moths that have just crawled from their cocoons, weak and quivering, not quite recognizable until they've dried and spread their wings. Maybe that's how they've gotten so close without me noticing, and more importantly, remembering. They've been taking shape and mass for so long that it's been almost imperceptible.

To think that it was only a few weeks ago that I first noticed the woman at all! Even then I didn't recognize her. She crept in unannounced.

Now, I can hardly keep my eyes off them. Each Sunday, as Barb and the kids and I enter the church, I look for them. They're never there when we arrive. I always spot them later, already sitting amongst the other parishioners, as if they'd never left the church. I never see them enter. That wouldn't be their way. This is far more unnerving. The woman knows I have to show up each Sunday. What excuse would I give Barb or the Monsignor? After all, I'm a family man. I'm not about to let the two of them disrupt my life just by occupying a pew! They tried once before and look where it got them! I admit, I'm a little curious, too.

She was always demanding . . . in more ways than one, if you know what I mean. She wanted me to be part of her, and the girl's, life. And I was . . . for a while. I was still in the sales department and spent a lot of time on the road and away from home. Naturally, I was not averse to a little feminine companionship. In fact, the city she lived in was one that my company did a lot of business in, so it was convenient. For both of us.

She was one of those recently divorced young mothers whose husband's whereabouts are unknown. No child support, no family, no skills, and no future. I was a godsend. She was appreciative. The girl was quiet. I never made any promises!

I did not, however, tell her that I had a wife and kids two states away. She didn't even know my real name. Each time I'd roll into town I'd make sure I tossed my wallet and wedding ring into my briefcase, which I'd leave in the car. I knew I was being eyed for promotion and I couldn't afford a scandal. I had my sights on the main office.

I always made a point of showing up after dark and leaving before light. The neighbors never really saw me or my car. It was a different company car each week, in any case.

Everything was just fine. I liked the woman. The woman was crazy about me. The little girl was a problem. She was too quiet. She reminded me of her father, whom I never met. I seemed to find her around every corner. Never smiling, never speaking. She watched me a lot. I knew she didn't like me. I even mentioned it to her mother a few times. She would always find a way to take my mind off the girl though, at least for a while. I took to thumping her when her mother wasn't around. Not hard, just enough to make her stay clear. I knew the woman would find out, but what could she do?

Then I got the promotion. I would not be returning to that town on any regular basis. I decided to tell them. Why? I'm not sure. If I had just walked out, like any other time, and not come back, that would have been the end of it. They could never have traced me. They didn't even know my name. The woman believed I worked for my company's biggest rival! That was one of my little jokes.

Maybe I wanted to see how much I meant to the woman. A few tears shed on my behalf seemed appropriate. I also wanted a shot at the little girl. I had decided to make her the reason for my leaving. Something for her mother to mull over in my absence. It would have made for a neat wrap-up except for one thing. My timing was bad.

Instead of waiting till the next morning, when I was preparing to leave, to break the news, I told them the night before. I had looked forward to an evening of tearful pleas and enticing promises and that's exactly what I got. I fell asleep, with a good meal in my belly, to the pleasing sounds of the woman lashing out at the daughter.

When I woke the next morning I found mother and daughter waiting for me at the kitchen table. They had my briefcase open and my driver's license and company cards spread out before them. They sat side by side and looked at me. They had closed ranks. I knew this was the girl's doing. She had been suspicious of me all along and after last night had decided to do something about it.

They both sat there without saying a word. They looked pale and dark around the eyes. They looked as if they had sat there all night waiting for me. Just like they do in church now. They never looked more like mother and daughter. I was afraid. They had power over me.

Looking into their eyes, I only took a moment to decide. Along with my papers and ID, they had brought in my samples. My samples are surgical instruments and a neatly wrapped package of them lay right inside the briefcase. I reached in, unwrapped them, and went to work.

That was many long years ago and I haven't given it much thought since. They were dead. Now they're back. But they're weak. Just like before. Laughably weak. I'm not easily frightened.

The woman and child are sitting four rows directly in front of my family and me when suddenly the priest raises his voice and points at them. I don't know what he's saying as I'm a little distracted, understandably. I glance up just in time to see him single them out as if they're an example or proof of his sermon. A number of people in the congrega-

tion turn to look at them. I'm not sure, but I think one or
two glance in my direction also.

As if animated by the priest's gesture, the woman begins
to slowly, almost mechanically turn her head to the left. I
know instantly that she is scanning the church for me. The
effort seems to cost her dearly. Her skin is pale and has a
sickly, feverish glow. Her head stops turning just short of
looking over her shoulder. She gazes for a few moments
into the pews on her left. Then, without turning her head or
body any further, her eyes, or should I say eye, as I can
only see the one, begins to shift further yet to the left. It re-
minds me of an animal that is too sick or wounded to move,
trying to see its executioner walking up behind it. The eye
travels with painstaking slowness to the outer corner of the
socket and stops, straining. On her full lips is just the
slightest smile. I shift a few inches to my right, nudging
Austin over. He kicks me. At this moment I'm glad to be
behind her.

She holds that pose for just a few moments longer and
then turns slowly forward. She didn't see me but she knows
I'm here. The girl never moves. She's like a large doll
propped up front as a good example to other children.

I've decided against taking communion today. The idea
of walking into her field of vision makes my palms sweat.
Not that I'm afraid, but she may call out something. They
are gathering strength.

It's next Sunday already, and here we are back at Mass
again. All of us. I didn't really want to come. Not because
of them, they can't hurt me, I know that, but because I
haven't been sleeping well. It's not unusual for a man who
carries a lot of responsibility.

Barbara nudges me to stand for prayer, as I've been daydreaming. I notice as I do that the woman and girl are
standing also. I hadn't seen them do that before now. They
usually remain seated. I also notice they're only three rows
in front of us now. They've crept up!

As I watch, the little girl snakes her spindly arm around
the woman's waist. The arm seems grubby or bruised. I
imagine my fingerprints etched in purple on her pale flesh.

The woman raises her head, squares her shoulders and begins slowly to turn in my direction. I cannot look away.

Her face is vacant and unanimated as her gaze sweeps across the worshipers. When she reaches about three-quarters profile, she stops. I realize that I'm holding my breath. With what I imagine as an almost audible click the head swivels an inch more to the right and stops again. I am in her line of vision. She sees me.

The eyes quicken and focus. They are large and almond-shaped, the blue so brilliant that they seem lit from within. The skin is like milk, with high spots of color at the cheeks. The lips are full and moist and slightly parted. The woman's face is framed by dark, humid tendrils of hair, giving the impression that she has just risen from a warm and active bed. She looks exactly as she did the last night I saw her. I'm suddenly weak with longing. I feel tears welling up. She smiles. As if acknowledging the distress she has caused, the corners of her mouth turn up. Just the hint of a smile. A smirk, really. She's letting me know that she's not so weak anymore. I hear myself speak her name and then bite down hard on my lip, wishing I could call it back. I taste my blood, warm and salty in my mouth.

Barbara has me by the arm and is whispering something urgent in my ear. A number of people are staring at me. I turn away with an effort and begin up the aisle. I feel her eyes burning into my back and the only thing that keeps me from running is the weakness in my knees.

I step out into a brilliant, cold day and think of her parted lips revealing small, yellowing teeth. As I bring my handkerchief to my mouth, I picture those same teeth crushing my bones and faint.

It's Sunday morning again and I'm lying here wondering what they want and what I'm going to do. I can guess what they want. I think I know. What do all ghosts want? They want their murderer known. A sordid disclosure of his hidden past! Isn't that the way these stories go? The killer exposed like something poisonous found under a rock, pleading for forgiveness from a horrified world?

They won't find me that easily. I was always smarter

than the woman; she knows that. She even told me so on
occasion. I wouldn't be where I am today if I weren't. And
they wouldn't be where they are if they hadn't tried to out-
smart me! They must have felt pretty smug sitting there
with my future spread out over their kitchen table. I wonder
how smug they felt when I unwrapped my little present?

That's it, isn't it? Initiative. I must take action. It's no
good lying about the house, pretending to be ill and waiting
for God only knows what! Barbara knows something isn't
right. We haven't had sex for a week! Since last Sunday, I
just can't do it! And the children. Every time they're
around I start to get weepy. And I can't explain it, and they
just stare at me as if I were a stranger. So I must do something . . . and I think I know what. I'm going to beat them
to the punch!

Probably, in cases like this, it's the remorse and regret
that eventually wear a person down and make him do
something stupid. But what if that person were to rid himself of the so-called guilt by confession, and I don't mean
to the authorities? They suggested the answer themselves
by appearing at Mass. I'll be first in line for the confessional! The church has to forgive, and after that, what
power could they have over me?

The church is almost empty upon our arrival, which is no
surprise as we're nearly thirty minutes early. I've convinced Barb that I must attend confession prior to Mass.
She wants to ask questions but is afraid, I think. I scan the
interior quickly as we enter, just to make sure. They're not
here. I would have been very surprised if they were. Everything is going as I'd hoped.

I get Barb and the children situated in our usual spot,
which is on the opposite side of the church and somewhat
forward of the confessional. I genuflect, turn, and cross the
aisles to the booth. I can see that there's no one ahead of
me by virtue of a small light fixture attached to the side of
the booth. A red light is illuminated when the confessional
is in use, and a green when it is vacant and a priest is on
duty within. The green lamp is on. I kneel at the nearest
pew to say a quick prayer before entering, in case a priest is

watching, and glance underneath the half-curtain shrouding the entrance as I do so.

In the dimly lit interior I see small, white legs ending in a scruffy pair of Mary Janes. The feet are on the floor pointing in my direction and I see, even in this dim light, that the legs are lacerated in many places, forming a crisscross pattern. The wounds are not bleeding, having dried without healing. The child on the other side of this curtain is clearly not kneeling for confession. Suddenly I'm aware of the priest at the front of the church, attending the altar. I realize now that there is no one to hear her confession. That's not why she's there. She is waiting for me to pull back that curtain and join her there in the darkness.

I stand up, swaying, and begin walking away. My legs will barely support me and I grab at several people on my way, who must think I'm drunk. I can't stop looking over my shoulder for fear that she'll come out of that box behind me. I don't want to see her face! Barb is clutching a child in each arm and staring at me white-faced as I stumble towards the door. She doesn't see the woman kneeling not ten feet from them stand and slowly begin that awful turn. I shout a warning as I rush out through the doorway.

It's Sunday again! No matter. I'm not going to Mass today. A simple solution to a complex problem. They can have the church. I'll stay right here at home. Not that it makes much difference.

Barbara took the kids and left last Sunday, right after my little episode at confession. She's frightened. Austin and Vivian, picking up on their mother's mood, just stared at me while Barb packed. That made me very uncomfortable. They ran when I tried to hold them. I was in no condition to make them stay.

Barb's suspicious, too, I think. She says I shouted out the word "murder" as I fled church last week. I know I didn't say that, I was trying to warn her of the woman. It's funny under the circumstances that she should hear that, though I can't recall what I did say.

I haven't been in to work all this week, either. The office has phoned several times and left messages on my answer-

ing machine, but with Barb gone I just can't seen to find
the energy to lie about being ill. Barb used to do that for me
sometimes. In fact, I can't seem to summon up any energy
at all. Perhaps they're draining me. Maybe that's how
they've grown in strength. By sucking out my strength and
resolve, they leave behind a vacuum that draws in all the
weaker emotions, like guilt and remorse. I can almost feel
them forming a lump in my chest. Something hard yet brit-
tle. If I press down on my rib cage I can feel it crack and
slide from underneath the pressure of my palm. Tears
spring to my eyes, and my muscles become weak and flac-
cid, unable to support me. It's a sickening feeling. Mostly, I
just lie here and pretend not to notice.

It's a bright, sunny day out, though it rained most of last
night. The rain made me wakeful as I kept thinking that I
could hear voices just beneath my bedroom window. The
gurgling of water through the gutters was the cause. Still, I
was expectant. Several times the sound of the rain blowing
through the shrubbery put me in mind of women in long
dresses strolling through the yard. Dresses that would trail
across the grass as they walked, rustling slightly. It was a
peculiar thought and I guess that's why I dreamt so
strangely afterwards.

I must have fallen asleep close to dawn. In my dream,
the sun was rising above the drenched earth. My house had
that clean, windswept but slightly drowned look that it
probably has this very moment. I was lying in my bed,
dreaming, when there was just the slightest of sounds. The
soft scrape of a tiny shoe on the walkway leading to my
front door. Barely audible, yet instantly recognized.

I felt myself trying desperately to wake up, but I couldn't
seem to open my eyes! Even though I was dreaming, I
couldn't see! Somehow, I managed to sit up in bed and
I began to force my eyelids apart with my fingers. Then I
could see again.

My room was flooded with the morning sun and I could
see that I was alone, but as sometimes happens with
dreams, I could see outside my house as well. As if I were
floating, disembodied, above my home looking down at the
vacant scene. There was no one there, only an empty, con-

crete pathway leading to my front door, which was standing wide open!

I wanted desperately to rejoin my body, which was hidden beneath the roof now, and warn myself! There was someone in the house with me! Then, as is the nature of dreams, I was there. Sitting up in bed, staring at my bedroom doorway. Waiting for them to step into my vision. There was a loud bang in the hallway, followed by silence. I choked off a scream. Then the whispering began. Just outside of my line of vision. Hushed, conspiratorial tones, as if a course of action was being discussed. Finally, the conversation ended and I could hear small female laughter drifting away.

I awoke sitting up in bed, staring at my bedroom doorway. I could feel a cool, fresh breeze blowing into my room. I slept with all windows and doors closed and locked.

When I went into the hall, I could see small patches of damp leading to my room and returning to the front door, which stood open. I noticed the hall closet was also open and a shambles. An old briefcase lay on the bare floor in front of it. I recognized it. This was what had made the loud bang in my dream. It had been flung from its shelf. It would contain my samples.

I picked it up, carried it into the kitchen, and set it on the table. I didn't need to look inside. They were still there. I had never bothered to remove them. The police would never connect me with the scene and even if they did, I had thoroughly cleaned the instruments. Even so, I don't know why I've kept them. Easier than getting rid of them, I suppose.

I walked into the living room and closed the front door. Oddly enough, I didn't feel so much frightened as disappointed. I was weak, after all. They could now come and go in my life as they pleased and I was powerless to stop them. I knew what they were waiting for. My wife and children were gone, my career as good as finished. Only one thing was left and they were waiting for it. Confession. Humiliation. But I think I know something that they don't want me to.

Confession only occurs if there's guilt and conscience and they are drawing mine out and nurturing it. It's become a cancer that I can't ignore or trust, yet it's mine! That's the key! Ultimately, I can remove it. They may have underestimated me, after all.

I have a few shots to steady my nerves and take the parcel from the briefcase. Originally, I was studying to be a doctor, but financial hardships diverted me to business. Even so, I remained on the fringes and still take great pride in the instruments we manufacture. As I unwrap them, I can see they gleam as if new.

Something strikes the windowpane in the kitchen door, startling me, and I drop a surgical knife with a clatter. The door is locked and I'm not foolish enough to open it. Standing off to one side, I tease back the curtain and put my eye to the glass. A cardinal, bright as a splash of blood, lies broken on my rear stoop. My eyes are drawn in the direction it came from. That's what they've been waiting for.

The two of them are standing close together under a barren maple tree, facing the door. The woman's eyes are riveted on mine. The child's face remains an accusing shadow. As if on cue, the woman begins moving across the lawn towards me, her face a mask of rage, flecked with spittle. Somehow, she knows what I intend to do. I can see her mouth working grotesquely, grinding without sound. Her stride is impossibly long and she covers the distance with a nightmarish speed. I can't take my eyes from her and it's only an involuntary reaction that makes me fall back, releasing the curtain just as she reaches the door. I see her silhouette on the other side of the material. I expect her face to thrust through the glass! But the glass does not break and the door does not burst open. She remains as she is, a frozen outline on the fabric, radiating hatred. I watch, unable to move, and understand how strong they have become. By the end of the day they will not have to wait for me to sleep to enter this house. No barrier will stop them. Now is my only chance to act! Knowing this, I can turn my back on my guardian and begin to work. I reach for a scalpel.

* * *

Suicide is never a pretty sight and this one was particularly gruesome. The detective-lieutenant surveyed the carnage and grimaced. How, he asked himself, could a person open himself from sternum to pelvis? Surely there were easier, less agonizing ways to kill oneself? He would have to wait for the medical examiner's report, but he felt certain that this old boy had done some digging around while he was at it. What in the world for?

As the wrecked body was being carried out and the scene-of-crime officers began their exhaustive cataloguing, the lieutenant held a scrap of paper up to his eyes. He clasped it with a pair of tweezers and reread its contents. It should have pleased him but it didn't. On this piece of paper was both the explanation for the suicide and quite probably the solution to a ten-year-old double slaying. In other words, a confession. It must have been written by the eviscerated man, as all the doors were dead-bolted from the inside, but his experience told him that it was in a distinctly feminine hand.

THE WONDERFUL DEATH OF DUDLEY STONE

RAY BRADBURY

"Alive!"

"Dead!"

"Alive in New England, damn it."

"Died twenty years ago!"

"Pass the hat, I'll go myself and bring back his head!"

That's how the talk went that night. A stranger set it off with his mouthings about Dudley Stone dead. Alive! we cried. And shouldn't we know? Weren't we the last frail remnants of those who had burnt incense and read his books by the light of blazing intellectual votives in the Twenties?

The Dudley Stone. That magnificent stylist, that proudest of literary lions. Surely you recall the head-pounding, the cliff-jumping, the whistlings of doom that followed on his writing his publishers this note:

Sirs: Today, aged 30, I retire from the field, renounce writing, burn all my effects, toss my latest manuscript on the dump, cry hail and fare thee well. Yrs., affect.

Dudley Stone

Earthquakes and avalanches, in that order.

"Why?" we ask ourselves, meeting down the years.

In fine soap-opera fashion we debated if it was women who caused him to hurl his literary future away. Was it the Bottle? Or Horses that outran him and stopped a fine pacer in his prime?

We freely admitted to one and all that were Stone writing now, Faulkner, Hemingway, and Steinbeck would be buried in his lava. All this sadder that Stone, on the brink of his greatest work, turned one day and went off to live in a town we shall call Obscurity by the sea best named The Past.

"Why?"

That question forever lived with those of us who had seen the glints of genius in his piebald works.

One night a few weeks ago, musing off the erosion of the years, finding each other's faces somewhat more pouched and our hairs more conspicuously in absence, we became enraged over the typical citizen's ignorance of Dudley Stone.

At least, we mutter, Thomas Wolfe had had a full measure of success before he seized his nose and jumped off the rim of Eternity. At least the critics gathered to stare after his plunge into darkness as after a meteor that made much fire in its passing. But who now remembered Dudley Stone, his coteries, his frenzied followers of the Twenties?

"Pass the hat," I said. "I'll travel three hundred miles, grab Dudley Stone by the pants, and say: 'Look here, Mr. Stone, why did you let us down so badly? Why haven't you written a book in twenty-five years?' "

The hat was lined with cash; I sent a telegram and took a train.

I do not know what I expected. Perhaps to find a doddering and frail praying mantis, whisping about the station, blown by seawinds, a chalk-white ghost who would husk at me with the voices of grass and reeds blown in the night. I clenched my knees in agony as my train chuffed into the station. I let myself down into a lonely countryside a mile from the sea, like a man foolishly insane, wondering why I had come so far.

On a bulletin board in front of the boarded-up ticket office I found a cluster of announcements, inches thick, pasted and nailed one upon another for uncountable years. Leafing under, peeling away anthropological layers of printed tissue I found what I wanted. Dudley Stone for alderman, Dudley Stone for sheriff, Dudley Stone for mayor!

On up through the years, his photograph, bleached by sun and rain, faintly recognizable, asked for ever more responsible positions in the life of this world near the sea. I stood reading them.

"Hey!"

And Dudley Stone plunged across the station platform behind me suddenly. "Is that you, Mr. Douglas!" I whirled to confront this great architecture of a man, big but not in the least fat, his legs huge pistons thrusting him on, a bright flower in his lapel, a bright tie at his neck. He crushed my hand, looked down upon me like Michelangelo's God creating Adam with a mighty touch. His face was the face of those illustrated North Winds and South Winds that blow hot and cold in ancient mariners' charts. It was the face that symbolizes the sun in Egyptian carvings, ablaze with life!

My God! I thought. And this is the man who hasn't written in twenty-odd years. Impossible. He's so alive it's sinful. I can hear his *heartbeat!*

I must have stood with my eyes very wide to let the look of him cram in upon my startled senses.

"You thought you'd find Marley's Ghost," he laughed. "Admit it."

"I—"

"My wife's waiting with a New England boiled dinner, we've plenty of ale and stout. I like the ring of those words. To *ale* is not to sicken, but to revive the flagging spirit. A tricky word, that. And *stout*? There's a nice ruddy sound to it. Stout!" A great golden watch bounced on his vest-front, hung in bright chains. He vised my elbow and charmed me along, a magician well on his way back to his cave with a luckless rabbit. "Glad to see you! I suppose you've come, as the others came, to ask the same question, eh? Well, this time I'll tell everything!"

My heart jumped. "Wonderful!"

Behind the empty station sat an open-top 1927-vintage Model-T Ford. "Fresh air. Drive at twilight like this, you get all the fields, the grass, the flowers coming at you in the wind. I hope you're not one of those who tiptoe around shutting windows! Our house is like the top of a mesa. We let the weather do our broom-work. Hop in!"

*   *   *

Ten minutes later we swung off the highway onto a drive
that had not been leveled or filled in years. Stone drove
straight on over the pits and bumps, smiling steadily. Bang!
We shuddered the last few yards to a wild, unpainted two-
story house. The car was allowed to gasp itself away into
mortal silence.

"Do you want the truth?" Stone turned to look me in the
face and hold my shoulder with an earnest hand. "I was
murdered by a man with a gun twenty-five years ago almost to this very day."

I sat staring after him as he leapt from the car. He was
solid as a ton of rock, no ghost to him, but yet I knew that
somehow the truth was in what he had told me before firing
himself like a cannon at the house.

"This is my wife, and this is the house, and that is our
supper waiting for us! Look at our view. Windows on three
sides of the living room, a view of the sea, the shore, the
meadows. We nail the windows open three out of four sea-
sons. I swear you get a smell of limes here midsummer, and
something from Antarctica, ammonia and ice cream, come
December. Sit down! Lena, isn't it *nice* having him here?"

"I hope you like New England boiled dinner," said Lena,
now here, now there, a tall, firmly built woman, the sun in
the East, Father Christmas's daughter, a bright lamp of a
face that lit our table as she dealt out the heavy useful
dishes made to stand the pound of giants' fists. The cutlery
was solid enough to take a lion's teeth. A great whiff of
steam rose up, through which we gladly descended, sinners
into Hell. I saw the seconds-plate skim by three times and
felt the ballast gather in my chest, my throat, and at last my
ears. Dudley Stone poured me a brew he had made from
wild Concords that had cried for mercy, he said. The wine
bottle, empty, had its green glass mouth blown softly by
Stone, who summoned out a rhythmic one-note tune that
was quickly done.

"Well, I've kept you waiting long enough," he said, peering at me from that distance which drinking adds between
people and which, at odd turns in the evening, seems close-

ness itself. "I'll tell you about my murder. I've never told anyone before; believe me. Do you know John Oatis Kendall?"

"A minor writer in the Twenties, wasn't he?" I said. "A few books. Burnt out by '31. Died last week."

"God rest him." Mr. Stone lapsed into a special brief melancholy from which he revived as he began to speak again.

"Yes. John Oatis Kendall, burnt out by the year 1931, a writer of great potentialities."

"Not as great as yours," I said quickly.

"Well, just wait. We were boys together, John Oatis and I, born where the shade of an oak tree touched my house in the morning and his house at night, swam every creek in the world together, got sick on sour apples and cigarettes together, saw the same lights in the same blond hair of the same young girl together, and in our late teens went out to kick Fate in the stomach and get beat on the head together.

"We both did fair, and then *I* better and still better as the years ran. If his first book got one good notice, mine got six; if I got one bad notice, he got a dozen. We were like two friends on a train the public has uncoupled. There went John Oatis on the caboose, left behind, crying out, 'Save me! You're leaving me in Tank Town, Ohio! We're on the same track!' And the conductor saying, 'Yes, but not the same *train*!' And myself yelling '*I* believe in you, John, be of good heart, I'll come back for you!' And the caboose dwindling behind with its red and green lamps like cherry and lime pops shining in the dark and we yelling our friendship to each other. 'John, old man!' 'Dudley, old pal!' while John Oatis went out on a dark siding behind a tin baling-shed at midnight and my engine, with all the flag-wavers and brass bands, boiled on toward dawn."

Dudley Stone paused and noticed my look of general confusion.

"All this to lead up to my murder," he said. "For it was John Oatis Kendall who, in 1930, traded a few old clothes and some remaindered copies of his books for a gun and came out to this house and this room."

"He really meant to kill you?"

"Meant to, hell! He did! Bang! Have some more wine?
That's better."

A strawberry shortcake was set upon the table by Mrs.
Stone, while he enjoyed my gibbering suspense. Stone
sliced it into three huge chunks and served it around, fixing
me with his kindly approximation of the Wedding Guest's
eye.

"There he sat, John Oatis, in that chair where you sit
now. Behind him, outside in the smokehouse, seventeen
hams; in our wine cellars five hundred bottles of the best;
beyond the window open country, the elegant sea in full
lace; overhead a moon like a dish of cool cream, everywhere the full panoply of spring; and Lena across the table,
too, a willow tree in the wind, laughing at everything I said
or did not choose to say, both of us thirty, mind you—thirty
years old, life our magnificent carousel, our fingers playing
full chords, my books selling well, fan mail pouring upon
us in crisp white founts, horses in the stables for moonlight
rides to coves where either we or the sea might whisper all
we wished in the night. And John Oatis seated there where
you sit now, quietly taking the little blue gun from his
pocket."

"I laughed, thinking it was a cigar lighter of some sort,"
said his wife.

"But John Oatis said quite seriously: 'I'm going to kill
you, Stone.' "

"What did you do?"

"Do? I sat there, stunned, riven; I heard a terrible slam!
the coffin lid in my face! I heard coal down a black chute;
dirt on my buried door. They say all your *past* hurtles by at
such times. Nonsense. The *future* does. You see your face a
bloody porridge. You sit there until your fumbling mouth
can say, 'But why, John, what have I *done* to you?'

" 'Done!' he cried.

"And his eye skimmed along the vast bookshelf and the
handsome brigade of books drawn stiffly to attention there
with my name on each blazing like a panther's eye in the
Moroccan blackness. 'Done!' he cried, mortally. And his
hand itched the revolver in a sweat.

" 'Now, John,' I cautioned. 'What do you want?'

" 'One thing more than anything else in the world,' he said. 'To kill you and be famous. Get my name in head-lines. Be famous as you are famous. Be known for a life-time and beyond as the man who killed Dudley Stone!'

" 'You can't mean that!'

" 'I do. I'll be very famous. Far more famous than I am today, in your shadow. Oh, listen here, no one in the world knows how to hate like a writer does. God, how I love your work and, God, how I hate you because you write so well. Amazing ambivalence. But I can't take it any more, not being able to write as you do, so I'll take my fame the easy way. I'll cut you off before you reach your prime. They say your next book will be your very finest, your most brilliant!'

" 'They exaggerate.'

" 'My guess is they're right,' he said.

"I looked beyond him to Lena, who sat in her chair, frightened, but not frightened enough to scream or run and spoil the scene so it might end inadvertently.

" 'Calm,' I said. 'Calmness. Sit there, John. I ask only one minute. Then pull the trigger.'

" 'No!' Lena whispered.

" 'Calmness,' I said to her, to myself, to John Oatis.

"I gazed out the open windows, I felt the wind, I thought of the wine in the cellar, the coves at the beach, the sea, the night moon like a disc of menthol cooling the summer heavens, drawing clouds of flaming salt, the stars, after it in a wheel toward morning. I thought of myself only thirty, Lena thirty, our whole lives ahead. I thought of all the flesh of life hung high and waiting for me to really *start* banqueting! I had never climbed a mountain, I had never sailed an ocean, I had never run for mayor, I had never dived for pearls, I had never owned a telescope, I had never acted on a stage or built a house or read all the classics I had so *wished* to read. All the *actions* to be done!

"So in that almost instantaneous sixty seconds, I thought at last of my career. The books I had written, the books I *was* writing, the books I intended to write. The reviews, the sales, our huge balance in the bank. And, believe or disbe-lieve me, for the first time in my life I got free of it all. I be-

came, in one moment, a critic. I cleared the scales. On one
hand I put all the boats I hadn't taken, the flowers I hadn't
planted, the children I hadn't raised, all the hills I hadn't
looked at, with Lena there, goddess of the harvest. In the
middle I put John Oatis Kendall with his gun—the upright
that held the balances. And on the empty scale opposite I
laid my pen, my ink, my empty paper, my dozen books. I
made some minor adjustments. The sixty seconds were
ticking by. The sweet night wind blew across the table. It
touched a curl of hair on Lena's neck. Oh Lord, how softly,
softly it touched . . .

"The gun pointed at me. I have seen the moon craters in
photographs, and that hole in space called the Great Coal
Sack Nebula, but neither was as big, take my word, as the
mouth of that gun across the room from me.

" 'John,' I said at last, 'do you hate me *that* much? Because I've been lucky and you not?'

" 'Yes, damn it!' he cried.

"It was almost funny he should envy me. I was not that
much better a writer than he. A flick of the wrist made the
difference.

" 'John,' I said quietly to him, 'if you want me dead, I'll
be dead. Would you like for me to never write again?'

" 'I'd like nothing better!' he cried. 'Get ready!' He
aimed at my heart!

" 'All right,' I said, 'I'll never write again.'

" 'What!' he said.

" 'We're old friends, we've never lied to each other,
have we? Then take my word, from this night on I'll never
put pen to paper.'

" 'Oh *God*,' he said, and laughed with contempt and disbelief.

" 'There,' I said, nodding my head at the desk near him,
'are the only original copies of the two books I've been
working on for the last three years. I'll burn one in front of
you now. The other you yourself may throw in the sea.
Clean out the house, take everything faintly resembling lit-
erature, burn my published books, too. Here.' I got up. He
could have shot me then, but I had him fascinated. I tossed
one manuscript on the hearth and touched a match to it.

" 'No!' Lena said. I turned. 'I know what I'm doing,' I said. She began to cry. John Oatis Kendall simply stared at me, bewitched. I brought him the other unpublished manuscript. 'Here,' I said, tucking it under his right shoe so his foot was a paperweight. I went back and sat down. The wind was blowing and the night was warm and Lena was white as apple-blossoms there across the table.

"I said, 'From this day forward I will not write ever again.'

"At last John Oatis managed to say, 'How can you do this?'

" 'To make everyone happy,' I said. 'To make you happy because we'll be friends again, eventually. To make Lena happy because I'll be just her husband again and no agent's performing seal. And myself happy because I'd rather be a live man than a dead author. A dying man will do anything, John. Now take my last novel and get along with you.'

"We sat there, the three of us, just as we three are sitting tonight. There was a smell of lemons and limes and camellias. The ocean roared on the stony coastland below—God, what a lovely moonlit sound. And at last, picking up the manuscripts, John Oatis took them, like my body, out of the room. He paused at the door and said, 'I believe you.' And then he was gone. I heard him drive away. I put Lena to bed. That was one of the few nights in my life I ever walked down by the shore, but walk I did, taking deep breaths and feeling my arms and legs and my face with my hands, crying like a child, walking and wading in the surf to feel the cold salt water foaming about me in a million suds."

Dudley Stone paused. Time had made a stop in the room. Time was in another year, the three of us sitting there, enchanted with his telling of the murder.

"And did he destroy your last novel?" I asked.

Dudley Stone nodded. "A week later one of the pages drifted up on the shore. He must have thrown them over the cliff, a thousand pages—I see it in my mind's eye, a flock of white sea-gulls it might seem, flying down to the water and going out with the tide at four in the black morning. Lena ran up the beach with that single page in her hand, crying, 'Look, look!' And when I saw what she handed me, I tossed it back in the ocean."

"Don't tell me you honored your promise!"

Dudley Stone looked at me steadily. "What would *you* have done in a similar position? Look at it this way: John Oatis did me a favor. He didn't kill me. He didn't shoot me. He took my word. He honored my word. He let me live. He let me go on eating and sleeping and breathing. Quite suddenly he had broadened my horizons. I was so grateful that standing on the beach hip-deep in water that night, I cried. I was grateful. Do you really understand that word? Grateful he had let me live when he had had it in his hand to annihilate me forever."

Mrs. Stone rose up; the dinner was ended. She cleared the dishes, we lit cigars, and Dudley Stone strolled me over to his office-at-home, a rolltop desk, its jaws propped wide with parcels and papers and ink bottles, a typewriter, documents, ledgers, indexes.

"It was all rolling to a boil in me. John Oatis simply spooned the froth off the top so I could see the brew. It was very clear," said Dudley Stone. "Writing was always so much mustard and gallweed to me; fidgeting words on paper, experiencing vast depressions of heart and soul. Watching the greedy critics graph me up, chart me down, slice me like sausage, eat me at midnight breakfasts. Work of the worst sort. I was *ready* to fling the pack. My trigger was set. Boom! There was John Oatis! Look here."

He rummaged in the desk and brought forth handbills and posters. "I had been *writing* about living. Now I wanted to live. *Do* things instead of tell about things. I ran for the board of education. I won. I ran for alderman. I won. I ran for mayor. I won! Sheriff! Town librarian! Sewage disposal official. I shook a lot of hands, saw a lot of life, did a lot of things. We've lived every way there is to live, with our eyes and noses and mouths, with our ears and hands. We've climbed hills and painted pictures, there are some on the wall! We've been three times around the world! I even delivered our baby son, unexpectedly. He's grown and married now—lives in New York! We've done and done again." Stone paused and smiled. "Come on out in the yard; we've set up a telescope. Would you like to see the rings of Saturn?"

We stood in the yard, and the wind blew from a thousand miles at sea and while we were standing there, looking at the stars through the telescope, Mrs. Stone went down into the midnight cellar after a rare Spanish wine.

It was noon the next day when we reached the lonely station after a hurricane trip across the jouncing meadows from the sea. Mr. Dudley Stone let the car have its head, while he talked to me, laughing, smiling, pointing to this or that outcrop of Neolithic stone, this or that wild flower, falling silent again only as we parked and waited for the train to come and take me away.

"I suppose," he said, looking at the sky, "you think I'm quite insane."

"No, I'd never say that."

"Well," said Dudley Stone, "John Oatis Kendall did me one other favor."

"What was that?"

Stone hitched around conversationally in the patched leather seat.

"He helped me get out when the going was good. Deep down inside I must have guessed that my literary success was something that would melt when they turned off the cooling system. My subconscious had a pretty fair picture of my future. I knew what none of my critics knew, that I was headed nowhere but down. The two books John Oatis destroyed were very bad. They would have killed me deader than Oatis possibly could. So he helped me decide, unwittingly, what I might not have had the courage to decide myself, to bow gracefully out while the cotillion was still on, while the Chinese lanterns still cast flattering pink lights on my Harvard complexion. I had seen too many writers up, down, and out, hurt, unhappy, suicidal. The combination of circumstances, coincidence, subconscious knowledge, relief, and gratitude to John Oatis Kendall to just *be alive* were fortuitous, to say the least."

We sat in the warm sunlight another minute.

"And then I had the pleasure of seeing myself compared to all the greats when I announced my departure from the literary scene. Few authors in recent history have bowed out to such publicity. It was a lovely funeral. I looked, as they say, natural. And the echoes lingered. 'His *next* book,' the critics cried, 'would have been *it*! A masterpiece!' I had them panting, waiting. Little did they know.

"Even now, a quarter century later, my readers who were college boys then make sooty excursions on drafty kerosene-stinking short-line trains to solve the mystery of why I've made them wait so long for my 'masterpiece.' And thanks to John Oatis Kendall I still have a little reputation; it has receded slowly, painlessly. The next year I might have died by my own writing hand. How much better to cut your own caboose off the train, before others do it for you.

"My friendship with John Oatis Kendall? It came back. It took time, of course. But he was out here to see me in 1947—it was a nice day, all around, like old times. And now he's dead and at last I've told someone everything. What will you tell your friends in the city? They won't believe a word of this. But it *is* true, I swear it, as I sit here and breathe God's good air and look at the calluses on my hands and begin to resemble the faded handbills I used when I ran for county treasurer."

We stood on the station platform.

"Goodbye, and thanks for coming and opening your ears and letting my world crash in on you. God bless to all your curious friends. Here comes the train. I've got to run—Lena and I are going to a Red Cross drive down the coast this afternoon! Goodbye!"

I watched the dead man stomp and leap across the platform, felt the plankings shudder, saw him jump into his Model-T, heard it lurch under his bulk, saw him bang the floorboards with a big foot, idle the motor, roar it, turn, smile, wave to me, and then roar off and away toward that suddenly brilliant town called Obscurity by a dazzling seashore called The Past.

HOWLER

JO BANNISTER

It didn't look like a haunted house. It looked like a 1950s seaside bungalow, with bow windows and pebble-dash walls. Before the garden ran riot it would have been indistinguishable from all the other seaside bungalows in the area: prim, square, gazing out over the Channel with an air of cosy smugness.

But something happened at Mon Repose which, having no echo at Sans Souci up the lane or Dun Roamin on the corner, lifted it forever out of the seaside bungalow main sequence—for seaside bungalows, like stars, have their natural paths and life spans. The only difference is that stars grow to greatness while bungalows are at their brightest soon after construction and slip slowly down the scale of magnitude until they become weekend cottages for art teachers from Birmingham, the seaside bungalow equivalent of white dwarfdom.

What happened at Mon Repose was, in truth, a common enough little tragedy. A man discovered that his wife loved someone else. His reaction was swift and extreme. When it was learned that Arthur Smith had murdered his wife Amanda, dismembered her, buried her in a series of small holes along the garden perimeter and planted a fast-growing cypress hedge on top of her, a quiver of delicious shock ran through the bungalow community; coupled with relief that they had not after all asked him to be chairman of the Residents' Association.

He might have got away with it, except for the dog.

Everyone in Channel Vista knew about Amanda. Arthur
may have been the last person on the south coast to learn
about her and Reginald Spink, and when he put it about that
she had left him there was much pensive nodding, exchang-
ing of significant glances, and offers of tea.

But the dog kept digging up the cypresses. There was divided opinion afterwards as to whether it was looking for
Amanda, accusing her murderer, or just digging for bones.
Whatever, its persistence seemed finally to drive Arthur
mad. When he pursued it at a dead run down Channel Vista
one Sunday morning, swinging a shovel and shouting, "I
can dig another hole for you, you bastard!" suspicions were
aroused.

The police talked to Arthur, dug in the garden and took
away what they found there in plastic bags. They took
Arthur as well. But there was no trial. Arthur Smith hanged
himself from the bars of his remand cell, using the dog's
lead which he had somehow secreted about his person.

That should have been the end of the matter. There was a
brief flurry of publicity in the newspapers, then a member
of the government was caught in a bed he should not have
been in and Mon Repose dropped out of the news as if it
had never been.

The bungalow was sold to a retired grocer and his wife.
After one summer they put it on the market again, saying
they missed the city. The music teacher who came next
found it too remote for his pupils, and the cat fancier said
her cats didn't like it. For a few years it was rented out on
weekly lets for the season, then even that small demand
dried up. For a decade the bungalow stood empty and the
cypresses grew tall around it, hiding it from the road.

Miss Coghlan came upon Channel Vista while on a cycling holiday, discovered Mon Repose, fell in love with it
and bought it all in the course of one week in April.

Miss Frank, who taught with her companion at Four
Winds Junior School near Slough, thought Miss Coghlan
had taken leave of her senses. "But my dear, look at the
state of it! It'll be years before you can move in."

"Nonsense," Miss Coghlan said briskly. (No one had
ever told her that adults don't usually address each other

quite so dismissively. Of course children don't like it either, but they can't do much about it. Adults avoid people who are rude to them, which is why many teachers' only friends are other teachers.) "It's Easter now. I'll get men in right away to do any structural work, they should be through before we break up for the summer. Then I'll give up my flat and move in here. I'll put in my notice when we get back, work till July, then hang up my mortarboard. Then I'll have all the time in the world to decorate and do the garden."

Miss Frank was almost lost for words. "But—it's so sudden!"

"It's nothing of the sort. I've been thinking of retiring for a couple of years. If I don't jump soon I'll be pushed. A project to sink my teeth into is just the incentive I need."

"But Joan," wailed Miss Frank, almost in tears, "to give up your job, and your flat, and move away from the area you know, and your friends . . . it's so—"

The word she was looking for was rash, or possibly foolhardy. But Joan Coghlan let a great beam spread across her strong face, sandwiched between the short iron-grey hair and the several chins, and nodded enthusiastically. "Isn't it?" she agreed. "Absolutely splendid."

In the event, there was little structural work to be done. Seaside bungalows were built well in the 1950s and Mon Repose remained basically sound despite the years of neglect. Which was just as well, because Miss Coghlan had unexpected difficulties getting men to work there.

The local contractor said he had work coming out of his ears and couldn't touch Mon Repose before September. She informed him that there's no such word as "can't." Mr. Stone explained that his workmen were already promised to other clients and Miss Coghlan suggested that where there's a will there's a way. He lost patience then, told her she could complain to his mother if she wanted but he still couldn't do anything for her until September. Cycling back to the guesthouse where she and Miss Frank were staying, she pondered—not for the first time—on how unhelpful grown-ups were.

Just before she had to return to Slough for the new term,

Miss Coghlan found a contractor five miles down the coast
who could start the repairs immediately. When the solicitor
gave her the key to Mon Repose she passed it on to Mr.
Wiggins. It did not at that time occur to her to wonder why
Mr. Wiggins had so much less work on his books than Mr.
Stone.

But later she concluded it was because Mr. Wiggins was
an incompetent and his staff were work-shy layabouts.
Every time she phoned to check on progress there was
none. She accepted the first excuse he gave—that flu had
been playing havoc with his schedule. She did not query
the second, that the men had downed tools to search for a
child lost on the Downs. But when he tried to tell her that
he had three men off work attending the funerals of elderly
female relatives, she told him tersely that he would attend
her at "Mon Repose" at noon on Saturday to show her what
had been done and explain the continuing delays.

Mr. Wiggins was waiting when she arrived, an uneasy
figure in dungarees and a flat hat framed by the towering
cypresses.

The tour of inspection did not take long. Very little work
had been done in the weeks since Miss Coghlan gave him
the keys. A path had been cleared through the jungle to the
front door. A broken window had been removed and a ply-
wood square tacked in its place. Two men could have done
it in one not-very-energetic afternoon. The rotten window
frame, the rewiring, and the plastering were untouched, and
the lease on Miss Coghlan's flat ran out in three weeks'
time.

"Mr. Wiggins, I don't know what to say." She had been a
teacher for forty years, had never been lost for words before. "My bags are packed. We agreed I could move in at
the end of the month."

Mr. Wiggins squirmed. "We've had—problems."

"You told me. Flu. Missing children. A surfeit of funerals."

He had the grace to blush. "Not that. The men—"

"Yes?"

"Don't like—"

"Don't like what?"

He finally got it out. "They don't like being here, Miss Coghlan. They say it's—weird. Spooky. Because of what happened here."

Miss Coghlan's eyebrows climbed like a couple of grey squirrels. "What did happen here?"

So he told her.

She didn't know whether to laugh or smack his wrist. "Mr. Wiggins! You mean to tell me that a gang of brawny builders are scared to work in a seaside bungalow, in broad daylight, because of something that happened twenty years ago?"

"They say there's—something here," he muttered.

"Something?"

"A presence."

"A presence!" she scoffed. "What, Amanda Smith hopping through the living room with her left leg tucked under her right armpit?"

Mr. Wiggins was embarrassed but dogged. "They say they've heard things. Heavy breathing. Groans."

"They've probably been listening to one another!"

"You ask in the village," he retorted, stung by her attitude. "They know. They know how many people have come here and couldn't get away quick enough. Ask them about the Howler. They know."

"Howler?"

He wished he hadn't said it. His eyes dropped from hers and settled on his reinforced toe-caps. "Well, none of my lads has heard it. You wouldn't catch them here after dark, which is when it howls. But them as have heard it says it sounds like a soul in torment. They say it's enough to turn your hair white."

He looked at her again, apologetic but determined. "Miss Coghlan, I'm sorry, but you'll have to find someone else to do your work. We can't finish. I know we're letting you down. I won't charge for what we've done already. But I'd be lying to you if I said my lads would set foot here again." He would not be argued with but left her standing alone outside her bungalow, astonished and alarmed. Not by the Howler but by the difficulties of renovating Mon Repose when builders' labourers were afraid to work there.

In despair she returned to Mr. Stone. She rather wished that she had not told him, when they parted, that the devil finds work for idle hands. But if he remembered he did not refer to it. He was a younger man than Mr. Wiggins; she hoped that might incline him to be less impressionable.

He received her courteously enough but held out no false hopes. "I can't improve on September. In fact, it'll likely be October now."

She had already considered her options. She could camp in the bungalow as it stood, waiting meekly for him to come and hoping that word of her dealings with Mr. Wiggins would not reach him. Or she could put her cards on the table.

Miss Coghlan had many faults but cowardice was not one of them. She told him that Mr. Wiggins had been to "Mon Repose," and why he had left. Her steely gaze challenged him to make the same excuse.

Instead a slow smile broke across his rather craggy face, weathered like the materials he worked with. "You're kidding!"

Miss Coghlan did not approve of slang. She said sternly, "No, Mr. Stone, I am not joking. That was the reason Mr. Wiggins gave for withdrawing his services. It's only fair to give you the opportunity to do the same. I should not wish to be responsible for an outbreak of the screaming hab-dabs among your employees."

Matthew Stone had left school at sixteen, mainly because of teachers like Miss Coghlan, and learnt the building trade at the elbows of successive bricklayers, carpenters, plasterers, and electricians. He was competent in every branch of house repair. At the age of twenty-seven he took a night-school course in bookkeeping, then he rented a yard and hung up a sign with his name on it. Five years on he employed bricklayers, carpenters, plasterers, and electricians, so his own input was mainly managerial. It was probably inevitable but it didn't altogether please him. He liked to feel mortar under his fingernails.

He regarded the teacher levelly. "Listen, Miss Coghlan. What I told you was the honest truth. I can't give you men without taking them away from people who've been wait-

ing longer than you have and more patiently. But nobody's
waiting for me. If it's any use, I'll come up to the Channel
Vista with you and see if we can work something out."

Relief swept over her. "Good boy," she beamed, making
him wince. He would never know how close he came to
having his head patted as well.

He put Miss Coghlan's bicycle in the back of his pickup.
When he parked in Channel Vista they sat a moment, look-
ing at Mon Repose through the new gap in the vegetation.
"It doesn't look like a haunted house," said Matt Stone.

"Did you know about the Smiths?"

"Oh yes—they were celebrities round here. Small com-
munities like nothing better than a good grisly murder. And
when the grocer left there was talk of unquiet spirits and
stuff. I was at school then. A few of us sneaked up here to
keep watch, but either we were too rowdy for even an unquiet spirit or there was nothing to see. I haven't heard
mention of it for years. I didn't know anyone still took it
seriously."

"Perhaps only Mr. Wiggins's workmen do. Perhaps it really was only an excuse to get out of doing the work."

"Let's go inside."

Mon Repose was a box divided down the middle by the
hall. On the right were the living room, the bathroom, and
the kitchen. On the left were the main bedroom, the second
bedroom, and a box room. Above the front door there was a
stained-glass fanlight. The fireplace in the living room was
framed in imitation Dutch tiles. It wasn't a grand house.
Some of Miss Coghlan's university-educated colleagues
would have said it was a rather common, vulgar little
house.

But she liked it, despite all the trouble. Perhaps because
it was rather like her: full-bosomed, down-to-earth, practi-
cal rather than aesthetic, enduring. It didn't feel like a
house that would allow an unquiet spirit to take advantage
of it.

"Which of them is it supposed to be?" She found herself whispering and deliberately spoke up. "Amanda or
Arthur?"

Stone shrugged. "Amanda, I suppose. She's the one who died here."

"But Arthur killed himself. It could be him."

Stone grinned at her. "Miss Coghlan, surely you don't believe there's a ghost at Mon Repose?"

She frowned. "Of course not, Mr. Stone, I was merely asking, since as a local man I presumed you would know which of the unfortunate Smiths was held responsible for the phenomenon known as the Howler."

The way she spoke threatened to reduce him to hysterics. He cleared his throat. "I'll take a look around. See what needs doing first." After he closed the door Miss Coghlan thought she heard laughter.

She stayed in the living room. It was a tip now, but in a few weeks or months she'd turn it into the kind of home she'd always wanted. The china cabinet would go there, the floral-chintz settee there, and she would look out from her bow window across a dozen Downland acres to the pewter glitter of the Channel. And she thought she would have a pet. The lease of her flat had made it impossible, and anyway she didn't approve of leaving animals alone all day. But now she could have a cat—better still a dog, that she could walk along the edge of the cliffs when the wind beat in from France.

At first when she heard the noise she assumed Matt Stone was playing silly devils. The little boys in her class were inveterate trick-players, and nothing she had seen of men persuaded her that they matured much as they grew older. She presumed he was breathing heavily at her through the crack of the door, and that his reason for doing so was that he thought it witty. She breathed rather heavily herself and said, "Mr. Stone, have you nothing better to do?"

"Than what?" He was in the front garden and turned at her voice, leaning his elbows on the window sill.

The front door was only a few steps away, the garden a few steps beyond that, but still . . . Nonplussed, Miss Coghlan shook her head. "Oh—nothing."

He came back inside, joined her in the living room. He poked at the window frame with a blunt spike. "That'll have to go. What do you want instead, wood or aluminum?"

While he was looking at her, and her lips were pursed to say "wood," they both felt it: a quiver in the air, a shock of cold travelling between them, as if Mon Repose had had a close encounter with an iceberg. That was all. Only from the surprise in Miss Coghlan's face did Stone know that he hadn't imagined it. "What the hell—?"

She didn't approve of swearing either. "How odd," she murmured pointedly.

Stone shrugged off the chill that had stroked him under his shirt. "Er—OK, so that's the first thing to do. Get a decent window in to keep out the draughts."

Miss Coghlan said faintly, "Mr. Stone—"

He followed her eyes to the corner of the room. Ten years of dirt and flaking wallpaper had gathered there, and on top—as if set there by a Japanese flower-arranger—was a bone.

"Mr. Stone—you don't think—?"

He barked a hoarse laugh. "No way. The police took her away, didn't they, in plastic bags. This house has been empty for years. I expect a fox found its way in."

The idea appealed to her. Foxes made some very odd sounds, mostly after dark. Perhaps the Howler was only a vixen which had set up home in Mon Repose. "Yes—yes, of course," she murmured, feeling foolish. "A fox."

But he could see it was disturbing her, so Stone bent to move the bone. "Christ!" He straightened up abruptly, snatching his hand back, alarm in his eyes and a cold sweat breaking on his skin. Forming on top of his hand was a pattern of four red dots that grew quickly to black bruises. Stone and Miss Coghlan stared at it together.

Then the sensations began in earnest. A cold touch behind the knee of Miss Coghlan's stocking. A dampness trailed across the back of Stone's hand. The air in the room moved lightly as if something was passing unseen between them.

And a feeling of deep, unsupportable sorrow clutched each of them by the heart. Sorrow, and grief, and incomprehension. And guilt. The guilt welled like a fountain through all the other sensations, vast and bottomless, mind-sapping, soul-crushing, intolerable. A little moan that was more pity than fear crept from Stone's lips.

And then it was gone. Miss Coghlan staggered as if a great weight she was holding was suddenly removed. White-faced, their eyes stretched with shock, they stared round the room. But nothing had changed. They were alone, in every sense of the word. The bone atop its mound of rubbish had not moved.

By wordless agreement they moved outside. Dry twigs snapped under their feet as they passed through the hall.

The breeze on the cliffs restored a little of Miss Coghlan's colour. "Well, Mr. Stone," she managed at length, "you wanted to see my haunted house. Is there anything you want to go back and see again?"

He gave a gruff chuckle. She might be rude, overbearing, and self-important, but her nerve was steadier than his. "What are you going to do?"

"Do?" she echoed. "I thought we'd agreed. First the window frame, then—"

"You still mean to live here?" His voice cracked.

"I have nowhere else to go. All my savings are in this house. I thought it was a bargain: now I doubt if I could sell it at any price. Either I move in here in three weeks or I try the YWCA."

If it had been Stone's choice he'd have thought about it longer. But it wasn't. The only choice he had was staying or leaving. "We could try the vicar."

"We?"

He shrugged. "We have an arrangement about making your house habitable. It sure as hell isn't habitable like this."

She appreciated his support if not his language. Her eyes thanked him. "I didn't feel it was—inimical. Did you?"

He combed his memory for what inimical meant, then shook his head. It had felt neither hostile nor evil, just very very unhappy—a soul that quite literally didn't know where to put itself. Even though it had hurt and frightened him, he had not felt it meant to threaten them. "All the same, you can't live with that much—misery. We have to try and—"

"Lay it?" she suggested, a faint returning humour lifting one corner of her wide mouth. "Exorcise it?"

"Set it at peace," he countered, refusing to be baited.

She smiled. "You're right. Let's see the vicar."

As soon as they explained the problem, the vicar warned them that he wouldn't be able to help. Attempts had been made to exorcise Mon Repose ten years before, as a last resort before it was abandoned. An expert had been summoned, a cleric who evicted unquiet spirits with the practised ease of a bouncer removing rowdy guests from a nightclub. But the presence at Mon Repose defeated his best efforts, slinking back as soon as he had gone on three separate occasions.

"Was he able to explain his failure?" asked Miss Coghlan.

The vicar's brow creased with remembering. "Not really. The thing didn't fight him, it just got out of the way while he was there and came back when he left. Like you, he thought it wasn't an evil thing. No nasty smells at the mention of the Lord's name or anything like that. It just—" He shrugged. "It didn't seem interested in what he had to say."

As they went to leave, Miss Coghlan paused in the doorway. "Which of them is it? Arthur or Amanda?"

The vicar shook his head sadly. "We failed to establish even that. My colleague called it in the names both of the victim and the perpetrator but it wouldn't answer." He recalled another detail. "It tried to bar his way with sticks. Wherever he went in the house he found sticks lying in his way. He threw them away but somehow they always found their way back."

Glancing at her, Matt Stone thought he saw a glimmer of understanding in Miss Coghlan's eye.

Outside he challenged her. "You've got a line on this, haven't you?"

"Well—perhaps," she allowed. "I'm not sure. There's something I can try. If I'm right, we can solve this problem."

"Where now?"

"I've some shopping to do. Then back to the bungalow."

"It'll be going dark in an hour."

"I know. That's when we can talk to him."

"Who?" Stone was afraid he already knew.

Miss Coghlan nodded. "The Howler."

The last of the day was dying out of the sky when Stone parked his pickup in front of Mon Repose. Oyster-coloured streaks on the high clouds pointed westward. But no light fell on the still house, for the moon was not yet risen. A few stars, frosty with distance, watched through breaks in the clouds. When Stone turned off the engine they could hear the wind. They could not be sure if that was all they could hear.

Miss Coghlan led the way, a broad-beamed Amazon in lisle stockings. Stone followed with her shopping bag.

He flashed a torch round the dark rooms. The scene was as they had left it: the dirt, the dry twigs, the bone. The only footprints in the dust were theirs.

From the bag Miss Coghlan drew out two cushions, one of which she passed to Stone. "We may as well be comfortable."

She sat down like a collapsing marquee. "Oh, Mr. Stone—if it's all right with you, I think we should have the light out."

What could he say?—"Certainly not, I'm a bundle of nerves already, if you put the light out I may well cry?" If he had any function here at all it was to protect her: he couldn't say he was afraid of the dark. Nor was he, normally; but this wasn't a normal sort of darkness. He turned off the torch.

Softly, in the blackness, Miss Coghlan said, "We may have quite a wait."

"I'm in no hurry," muttered Stone.

Half an hour passed, then an hour. Still there was no moon, no light of any kind. Miss Coghlan got a cramp. Shifting her position on the cushion on the bare boards, she made enough noise to frighten away any number of Howlers. Stone wondered how long she would wait if it declined to make an appearance.

Then, between one moment and the next, it was with them. There was nothing to see. They didn't even hear it at first. But the temperature dropped abruptly as it had that af-

ternoon, the air moved fractionally against their cheeks as if
something had passed close by them, and Stone felt something like breath and something like a kiss on his sore hand.
"Miss Coghlan . . ."

"Yes, Mr. Stone," she said quietly. "I know." He mar-
velled at the massive calm in her voice. He was rigid with
tension, the hairs standing up on his neck and his arms, his
skin suddenly cool with sweat. "It's all right." Something
in her tone made him think she wasn't talking only to him.

Then in the darkness the sounds began. Heavy breathing
that rose quickly to a rapid pant. A clicking on the floorboards. A soft plaintive whine like a child crying. And
through it all came pouring the grief and the terrible guilt,
the timeless damnation of blame, the overarching wretched-
ness. Miss Coghlan had not known that such profound, ex-
coriating misery could exist even for a moment. The idea of
it persisting eternally in a single lost soul appalled her. She
whispered, "Please—it's all right—"

But the soft whine grew first to a plangent keening, so
close beside them that it set their skin crawling and their
teeth on edge, and then to the howling which had given the
thing its name. The disembodied voice in the darkness
soared in a crescendo of almost tangible despair, incon-
solable arpeggios of remorse and regret playing over the
dominant theme of grief. The sound filled the room, filled
the house, battered down on the crouched listeners in a Nia-
gara of torment.

Gradually then the sounds of despair began to abate, the
terrible wailing to break as if for breath. Miss Coghlan
began to punctuate the gaps with her own voice, her firm-
but-kind schoolmarm's voice, reassuring, confident,
promising order.

"It's all right," she said again, somehow keeping her tone
low, even, and rhythmical. "It wasn't your fault. You're not
to blame for what happened. None of it was your fault.

"Mummy and Daddy fell out. Mummy was a bad girl
and Daddy got cross. Sometimes cross people do things
they don't mean to. I know you loved them both, and they
both loved you. Even when Daddy was cross with you, it

was more because of what he'd done than what you'd done. He was very unhappy.

"He blamed you for giving him away, didn't he? But you didn't mean to. It was your nature to dig in the garden. If he'd thought, he'd have known that. Anyway, he couldn't have lived with what he'd done even if no one ever found out. He chose to die for what he did to Mummy. He'd have done the same thing at home if he hadn't been taken to prison. You couldn't have stopped him. If he hadn't used the lead he'd have used something else."

Stone, listening to the rhythmical sing-song of the teacher's voice, his flesh alive with the soft keen that the unearthly howling had sunk to, finally understood. The Howler was—of course. That was why Miss Coghlan had bought what she had, which at the time had made him doubt her sanity.

As if she read his mind, her broad hands moved to the shopping bag. "I've brought some things for you." Unseen in the dark, she laid them out on the floor. "There's a nice bit of steak. There's a tennis ball, and an old slipper of mine—it's not the same as one of Mummy's, I know, but you're very welcome to it. And there's this." Chain jangled in the dark. "Daddy took yours, didn't he? Never mind, you'll like this one. I thought we could bury them in the garden, so you'll know where they are and you can come for them any time you're lonely.

"It's bedtime now. You haven't had much rest these last twenty years, have you? Never mind, it's all over. You're a good boy, you mustn't blame yourself for what happened anymore. Go to sleep; and if you're still feeling bad tomorrow come back and we'll talk some more. I'm going to be here from now on and you're always welcome. I'd like to have a dog about the place."

Stone dug a hole in the garden and Miss Coghlan carefully put the contents of the bag in the bottom. She said softly, "If I knew where your body was I could bring it here too. But I don't know where you died. I hope these will serve."

"It's—quieter, isn't it?" murmered Stone, feeling the difference like fading electricity.

The moon had risen while he was digging. He saw Miss Coghlan smile. "Yes, I think he's at peace now."

They walked back to the pickup. The Channel moved below them like a sleeper under silk.

"How did you know it was the dog?"

"I didn't know," she said, "but I began to suspect. It didn't answer to either Arthur or Amanda, and it wasn't interested in the exorcist's homilies. The Church can't have it both ways: if animals have no souls they can't be expected to acknowledge the Lord's name.

"That poor dog had the whole burden of what happened here dumped on him. The master he loved murdered the mistress he loved in the house he loved. When instinct drove him to dig her up, his master tried to kill him. Then he used the dog's lead to end his own life. The poor creature has spent the last twenty years not understanding why his world fell apart but firmly believing it was his fault. Of course he howled."

"If you'd been wrong—if you'd found yourself trying to appease something evil with half a pound of steak and an old slipper—!"

"Oh, I was pretty sure by then," said Miss Coghlan, growing smug now that the drama was over and everything was going to be all right. "These things we felt and heard— the heavy breathing was a dog panting, the cold touch was his nose—and he bit you when you went to take his bone. Then he licked you to say sorry."

"And dogs howl when they're unhappy." Stone frowned. "What was that clicking sound?"

"Toenails on the floorboards. But it was the sticks that clinched it."

He stared at her. "Sticks?"

"You remember what the vicar said: that the exorcist couldn't move for the sticks the Howler put in front of him. Then he threw them away but they kept reappearing." She laughed, a deep ringing tone like a bell. "The poor dog wanted someone to play with him. The exorcist threw the sticks away and the dog brought them back."

A MOST UNUSUAL MURDER

ROBERT BLOCH

Only the dead know Brooklyn.

Thomas Wolfe said that, and he's dead now, so he ought to know.

London, of course, is a different story.

At least that's the way Hilary Kane thought of it. Not as a story, perhaps, but rather as an old-fashioned, outsize picaresque novel in which every street was a chapter crammed with characters and incidents of its own. Each block a page, each structure a separate paragraph unto itself within the sprawling, tangled plot—such was Hilary Kane's concept of the city, and he knew it well.

Over the years he strolled the pavements, reading the city sentence by sentence until every line was familiar; he'd learned London by heart.

And that's why he was so startled when, one bleak afternoon late in November, he discovered the shop in Saxe-Coburg Square.

"I'll be damned!" he said.

"Probably." Lester Woods, his companion, took the edge off the affirmation with an indulgent smile. "What's the problem?"

"This." Kane gestured toward the tiny window of the establishment nestled inconspicuously between two residential relics of Victoria's day.

"An antique place." Woods nodded. "At the rate they're springing up there must be at least one for every tourist in London."

"But not here." Kane frowned. "I happen to have come by this way less than a week ago, and I'd swear there was no shop in the Square."

"Then it must have opened since." The two men moved up to the entrance, glancing through the display window in passing.

Kane's frown deepened. "You call this new? Look at the dust on those goblets."

"Playing detective again, eh?" Woods shook his head. "Trouble with you, Hilary, is that you have too many hobbies." He glanced across the Square as a chill wind heralded the coming of twilight. "Getting late—we'd better move along."

"Not until I find out about this."

Kane was already opening the door and Woods sighed. "The game is afoot, I suppose. All right, let's get it over with."

The shop bell tinkled and the two men stepped inside. The door closed, the tinkling stopped, and they stood in the shadows and the silence.

But one of the shadows was not silent. It rose from behind the single counter in the small space before the rear wall.

"Good afternoon, gentlemen," said the shadow. And switched on an overhead light. It cast a dim nimbus over the countertop and gave dimension to the shadow, revealing the substance of a diminutive figure with an unremarkable face beneath a balding brow.

Kane addressed the proprietor. "Mind if we have a look?"

"Is there any special area of interest?" The proprietor gestured toward the shelves lining the wall behind him. "Books, maps, china, crystal?"

"Not really," Kane said. "It's just that I'm always curious about a new shop of this sort—"

The proprietor shook his head. "Begging your pardon, but it's hardly new."

Woods glanced at his friend with a barely suppressed smile, but Kane ignored him.

"Odd," Kane said. "I've never noticed this place before."

"Quite so. I've been in business a good many years, but this *is* a new location."

Now it was Kane's turn to glance quickly at Woods, and his smile was not suppressed. But Woods was already eyeing the artifacts on display, and after a moment Kane began his own inspection.

Peering at the shelving beneath the glass counter, he made a rapid inventory. He noted a boudoir lamp with a beaded fringe, a lavaliere, a tray of pearly buttons, a durbar souvenir programme, and a framed and inscribed photograph of Matilda Alice Victoria Wood *aka* Bella Delmare *aka* Marie Lloyd. There was a miscellany of old jewelry, hunting-watches, pewter mugs, napkin rings, a toy bank in the shape of a miniature Crystal Palace, and a display poster of a formidably mustached Lord Kitchener with his gloved finger extended in a gesture of imperious command.

It was, he decided, the mixture as before. Nothing unusual, and most of it—like the Kitchener poster—not even properly antique but merely outmoded. Those fans on the bottom shelf, for example, and the silk toppers, the opera glasses, the black bag in the far corner covered with what was once called "American cloth."

Something about the phrase caused Kane to stoop and make a closer inspection. *American cloth.* Dusty now, but once shiny, like the tarnished silver nameplate identifying its owner. He read the inscription.

J. Ridley, M.D.

Kane looked up, striving to conceal his sudden surge of excitement.

Impossible! It couldn't be—and yet it was. Keeping his voice and gesture carefully casual, he indicated the bag to the proprietor.

"A medical kit?"

"Yes, I imagine so."

"Might I ask where you acquired it?"

The little man shrugged. "Hard to remember. In this line one picks up the odd item here and there over the years."

"Might I have a look at it, please?"

The elderly proprietor lifted the bag to the countertop. Woods stared at it, puzzled, but Kane ignored him, his gaze intent on the nameplate below the lock. "Would you mind opening it?" he said.

"I'm afraid I don't have a key."

Kane reached out and pressed the lock; it was rusted, but firmly fixed. Frowning, he lifted the bag and shook it gently.

Something jiggled inside, and as he heard the click of metal against metal his elation peaked. Somehow he suppressed it as he spoke.

"How much are you asking?"

The proprietor was equally emotionless. "Not for sale."

"But—"

"Sorry, sir. It's against my policy to dispose of blind items. And since there's no telling what's inside—"

"Look, it's only an old medical bag. I hardly imagine it contains the Crown jewels."

In the background Woods snickered, but the proprietor ignored him. "Granted," he said. "But one can't be certain of the contents." Now the little man lifted the bag and once again there was a clicking sound. "Coins, perhaps."

"Probably just surgical instruments," Kane said impatiently. "Why don't you force the lock and settle the matter?"

"Oh, I couldn't do that. It would destroy its value."

"What value?" Kane's guard was down now; he knew he'd made a tactical error but he couldn't help himself.

The proprietor smiled. "I told you the bag is not for sale."

"Everything has its price."

Kane's statement was a challenge, and the proprietor's smile broadened as he met it. "One hundred pounds."

"A hundred pounds for *that*?" Woods grinned—then gaped at Kane's response.

"Done and done."

"But, sir—"

For answer Kane drew out his wallet and extracted five twenty-pound notes. Placing them on the countertop, he lifted the bag and moved toward the door. Woods followed hastily, turning to close the door behind him.

The proprietor gestured. "Wait—come back—"

But Kane was already hurrying down the street, clutching the black bag under his arm.

He was still clutching it half an hour later as Woods moved with him into the spacious study of Kane's flat overlooking the verdant vista of Cadogan Square. Dappled splotches of sunlight reflected from the gleaming oilcloth as Kane set the bag on the table and carefully wiped away the film of dust with a dampened rag. He smiled triumphantly at Woods.

"Looks a bit better now, don't you think?"

"I don't think anything." Woods shook his head. "A hundred pounds for an old medical kit—"

"A *very* old medical kit," said Kane. "Dates back to the Eighties, if I'm not mistaken."

"Even so, I hardly see—"

"Of course you wouldn't! I doubt if anyone besides myself would attach much significance to the name of J. Ridley, M.D."

"Never heard of him."

"That's understandable." Kane smiled. "He preferred to call himself Jack the Ripper."

"Jack the Ripper?"

"Surely you know the case. Whitechapel, 1888—the savage slaying and mutilation of prostitutes by a cunning mass-murderer who taunted the police—a shadow, stalking his prey in the streets."

Woods frowned. "But he was never caught, was he? Not even identified."

"In that you're mistaken. No murderer has been identified quite as frequently as Red Jack. At the time of the crimes and over the years since, a score of suspects were named. A prime candidate was the Pole, Klosowski, alias George Chapman, who killed several wives—but poison was his method and gain his motive whereas the Ripper's victims were all penniless prostitutes who died under the knife. Another convicted murderer, Neil Cream, even openly proclaimed he was the Ripper—"

"Wouldn't that be the answer, then?"

Kane shrugged. "Unfortunately, Cream happened to be

in America at the time of the Ripper murders. Egomania prompted his false confession." He shook his head. "Then there was John Pizer, a bookbinder known by the nickname of 'Leather Apron'—he was actually arrested, but quickly cleared and released. Some think the killings were the work of a Russian called Konovalov who also went by the name of Pedachenko and worked as a barber's surgeon; supposedly he was a Tsarist secret agent who perpetrated the slayings to discredit the British police."

"Sounds pretty far-fetched if you ask me."

"Exactly." Kane smiled. "But there are other candidates, equally improbable. Montague John Druitt for one, a barrister of unsound mind who drowned himself in the Thames shortly after the last Ripper murder. Unfortunately, it has been established that he was living in Bournemouth, and on the days before and after the final slaying he was there, playing cricket. Then there was the Duke of Clarence—"

"Who?"

"Queen Victoria's grandson in direct line of succession to the throne."

"Surely you're not serious?"

"No, but others are. It has been asserted that Clarence was a known deviate who suffered from insanity as the result of venereal infection, and that his death in 1892 was actually due to the ravages of his disease."

"But that doesn't prove him to be the Ripper."

"Quite so. It hardly seems possible that he could write the letters filled with Americana slang and crude errors in grammar and spelling which the Ripper sent to the authorities; letters containing information which could be known only by the murderer and the police. More to the point, Clarence was in Scotland at the time of one of the killings and at Sandringham when others took place. And there are equally firm reasons for exonerating suggested suspects close to him—his friend James Stephen and his physician, Sir William Gull."

"You've really studied up on this," Woods murmured. "I'd no idea you were so keen on it."

"And for good reason. I wasn't about to make a fool of myself by advancing an untenable notion. I don't believe the Ripper was a seaman, as some surmise, for there's not a scintilla of evidence to back the theory. Nor do I think the Ripper was a slaughterhouse worker, a midwife, a man disguised as a woman, or a London bobby. And I doubt the very existence of a mysterious physician named Dr. Stanley, out to avenge himself against the woman who had infected him, or his son."

"But there do seem to be a great number of medical men amongst the suspects," Woods said.

"Right you are, and for good reason. Consider the nature of the crimes—the swift and skillful removal of vital organs, accomplished in the darkness of the streets under constant danger of imminent discovery. All this implies the discipline of someone versed in anatomy, someone with the cool nerves of a practising surgeon. Then too there's the matter of escaping detection. The Ripper obviously knew the alleys and byways of the East End so thoroughly that he could slip through police cordons and patrols without discovery. But if seen, who would have a better alibi than a respectable physician, carrying a medical bag on an emergency call late at night?

"With that in mind, I set about my search, examining the rolls of London Hospital in Whitechapel Road. I went over the names of physicians and surgeons listed in the Medical Registry for that period."

"All of them?"

"It wasn't necessary. I knew what I was looking for—a surgeon who lived and practised in the immediate Whitechapel area. Whenever possible, I followed up with a further investigation of my suspects' histories—researching hospital and clinic affiliations, even hobbies and background activities from medical journals, press reports, and family records. Of course, all this takes a great deal of time and patience. I must have been tilting at this windmill for a good five years before I found my man."

Woods glanced at the nameplate on the bag. "J. Ridley, M.D.?"

"John Ridley. *Jack,* to his friends—if he had any." Kane paused, thoughtful. "But that's just the point. Ridley appears to have had no friends, and no family. An orphan, he

received his degree from Edinburgh in 1878, ten years before the date of the murders. He set up private practise here
in London, but there is no office address listed. Nor is there
any further information to be found concerning him; it's as
though he took particular care to suppress every detail of
his personal and private life. This, of course, is what roused
my suspicions. For an entire decade J. Ridley lived and
practised in the East End without a single mention of his
name anywhere in print, except for his Registry listing.
And after 1888, even *that* disappeared."

"Suppose he died?"

"There's no obituary on record."

Woods shrugged. "Perhaps he moved, emigrated, took
sick, abandoned practise?"

"Then why the secrecy? Why conceal his whereabouts?
Don't you see—it's the very lack of such ordinary details
which leads me to suspect the extraordinary."

"But that's not evidence. There's no proof that your Dr.
Ridley was the Ripper."

"That's why this is so important." Kane indicated the bag
on the tabletop. "If we knew its history, where it came
from—"

As he spoke, Kane reached down and picked up a brass
letter-opener from the table, then moved to the bag.

"Wait." Woods put a restraining hand on Kane's shoulder. "That may not be necessary."

"What do you mean?"

"I think the shopkeeper was lying. He knew what the bag
contains—he had to, or else why did he fix such a ridiculous price? He never dreamed you'd take him up on it, of
course. But there's no need for you to force the lock any
more than there was for him to do so. My guess is that he
has a key."

"You're right." Kane set the letter-opener down. "I
should have realized, if I'd taken the time to consider his re-
luctance. He must have the key." He lifted the shiny bag and
turned. "Come along—let's get back to him before the shop
closes. And this time we won't be put off by any excuses."

Dusk had descended as Kane and his companion has-
tened through the streets, and darkness was creeping across

the deserted silence of Saxe-Coburg Square when they arrived.

They halted then, staring into the shadows, seeking the spot where the shop nestled between the residences looming on either side. The shadows were deeper here and they moved closer, only to stare again at the empty gap between the two buildings.

The shop was gone.

Woods blinked, then turned and gestured to Kane. "But we were here—we saw it—"

Kane didn't reply. He was staring at the dusty, rubble-strewn surface of the space between the structures; at the weeds which sprouted from the bare ground beneath. A chill night wind echoed through the emptiness. Kane stooped and sifted a pinch of dust between his fingers. The dust was cold, like the wind that whirled the fine grains from his hand and blew them away into the darkness.

"What happened?" Woods was murmuring. "Could we both have dreamed—"

Kane stood erect, facing his friend. "This isn't a dream," he said, gripping the black bag.

"Then what's the answer?"

"I don't know." Kane frowned thoughtfully. "But there's only one place where we can possibly find it."

"Where?"

"The 1888 Medical Registry lists the address of John Ridley as Number 17 Dorcas Lane."

The cab which brought them to Dorcas Lane could not enter its narrow accessway. The dim alley beyond was silent and empty, but Kane plunged into it without hesitation, moving along the dark passage between solid rows of grimy brick. Treading over the cobblestones, it seemed to Woods that he was being led into another era, yet Kane's progress was swift and unfaltering.

"You've been here before?" Woods said.

"Of course." Kane halted before the unlighted entrance to Number 17, then knocked.

The door opened—not fully, but just enough to permit

the figure behind it to peer out at them. Both glance and greeting were guarded.

"Whatcher want?"

Kane stepped into the fan of light from the partial opening. "Good evening. Remember me?"

"Yes." The door opened wider and Woods could see the squat shadow of the middle-aged woman who nodded up at his companion. "Yer the one what rented the back vacancy last Bank 'oliday, ain'tcher?"

"Right. I was wondering if I might have it again."

"I dunno." The woman glanced at Woods.

"Only for a few hours." Kane reached for his wallet. "My friend and I have a business matter to discuss."

"Business, eh?" Woods felt the unflattering appraisal of the landlady's beady eyes. "Cost you a fiver."

"Here you are."

A hand extended to grasp the note. Then the door opened fully, revealing the dingy hall and the stairs beyond.

"Mind the steps now," the landlady said.

The stairs were steep and the woman was puffing as they reached the upper landing. She led them along the creaking corridor to the door at the rear, fumbling for the keys in her apron.

" 'Ere we are."

The door opened on musty darkness, scarcely dispelled by the faint illumination of the overhead fixture as she switched it on. The landlady nodded at Kane. "I don't rent this for lodgings no more—it ain't properly made up."

"Quite all right." Kane smiled, his hand on the door.

"If there's anything you'll be needing, best tell me now. I've got to run over to the neighbor for a bit—she's been took ill."

"I'm sure we'll manage." Kane closed the door, then listened for a moment as the landlady's footsteps receded down the hall.

"Well," he said. "What do you think?"

Woods surveyed the shabby room with its single window framed by yellowing curtains. He noted the faded carpet with its pattern wellnigh worn away, the marred and chipped surfaces of the massive old bureau and heavy morris-chair, the brass bed covered with a much-mended spread, the ancient gas-log in the fireplace framed by a cracked marble mantelpiece, and the equally cracked washstand fixture in the corner.

"I think you're out of your mind," Woods said. "Did I understand correctly that you've been here before?"

"Exactly. I came several months ago, as soon as I found the address in the Registry. I wanted a look around."

Woods wrinkled his nose. "More to smell than there is to see."

"Use your imagination, man! Doesn't it mean anything to you that you're standing in the very room once occupied by Jack the Ripper?"

Woods shook his head. "There must be a dozen rooms to let in this old barn. What makes you think this is the right one?"

"The Registry entry specified 'rear.' And there are no rear accommodations downstairs—that's where the kitchen is located. So this has to be the place."

Kane gestured. "Think of it—you may be looking at the very sink where the Ripper washed away the traces of his butchery, the bed in which he slept after his dark deeds were performed! Who knows what sights this room has seen and heard—the voice crying out in a tormented nightmare—"

"Come off it, Hilary!" Woods grimaced impatiently. "It's one thing to use your imagination, but quite another to let your imagination use you."

"Look." Kane pointed to the far corner of the room. "Do you see those indentations in the carpet? I noticed them when I examined this room on my previous visit. What do they suggest to you?"

Woods peered dutifully at the worn surface of the carpet, noting the four round, evenly spaced marks. "Must have been another piece of furniture in that corner. Something heavy, I'd say."

"But what sort of furniture?"

"Well—" Woods considered. "Judging from the space, it wasn't a sofa or chair. Could have been a cabinet, perhaps a large desk—"

"Exactly. A rolltop desk. Every doctor had one in those days." Kane sighed. "I'd give a pretty penny to know what became of that item. It might have held the answer to all our questions."

"After all these years? Not bloody likely." Woods glanced away. "Didn't find anything else, did you?"

"I'm afraid not. As you say, it's been a long time since the Ripper stayed here."

"I didn't say that." Woods shook his head. "You may be right about the desk. And no doubt the Medical Registry gives a correct address. But all it means is that this room may once have been rented by a Dr. John Ridley. You've already inspected it once—why bother to come back?"

"Because now I have this." Kane placed the black bag on the bed. "And this." He produced a pocketknife.

"You intend to force the lock after all?"

"In the absence of a key I have no alternative." Kane wedged the blade under the metal guard and began to pry upwards. "It's important that the bag be opened here. Something it contains may very well be associated with this room. If we recognize the connection we might have an additional clue, a conclusive link—"

The lock snapped.

As the bag sprang open, the two men stared down at its contents—the jumble of vials and pillboxes, the clumsy old-style stethoscope, the probes and tweezers, the roll of gauze. And, resting atop it, the scalpel with the steel-tipped surface encrusted with brownish stains.

They were still staring as the door opened quietly behind them and the balding, elderly little man entered the room.

"I see my guess was correct, gentlemen. You too have read the Medical Registry." He nodded. "I was hoping I'd find you here."

Kane frowned. "What do you want?"

"I'm afraid I must trouble you for my bag."

"But it's my property now—I bought it."

The little man sighed. "Yes, and I was a fool to permit it. I thought putting on that price would dissuade you. How was I to know you were a collector like myself?"

"Collector?"

"Of curiosa pertaining to murder." The little man smiled. "A pity you cannot see some of the memorabilia I've acquired. Not the commonplace items associated with your so-called Black Museum in Scotland Yard, but true rarities with historical significance." He gestured. "The silver jar in which the notorious French sorceress, La Voisin, kept her poisonous ointments, the actual dirks which dispatched the unfortunate nephews of Richard III in the Tower—yes, even the poker responsible for the atrocious demise of Edward II at Berkeley Castle on the night of September 21st, 1327. I had quite a bit of trouble locating it until I realized the date was reckoned according to the old Julian calendar."

Kane frowned impatiently. "Who are you? What happened to that shop of yours?"

"My name would mean nothing to you. As for the shop, let us say that it exists spatially and temporally as I do—when and where necessary for my purposes. By your current and limited understanding, you might call it a sort of time machine."

Woods shook his head. "You're not making sense."

"Ah, but I am, and very good sense too. How else do you think I could pursue my interests so successfully unless I were free to travel in time? It is my particular pleasure to return to certain eras in this primitive past of yours, visiting the scenes of famous and infamous crimes and locating trophies for my collection.

"The shop, of course, is just something I used as a blind for this particular mission. It's gone now, and I shall be going too, just as soon as I retrieve my property. It happens to be the souvenir of a most unusual murder."

"You see?" Kane nodded at Woods. "I told you this bag belonged to the Ripper!"

"Not so," said the little man. "I already have the Ripper's murder weapon, which I retrieved directly after the slaying of his final victim on November 9th, 1888. And I can assure you that your Dr. Ridley was not Jack the Ripper but merely and simply an eccentric surgeon—" As he spoke, he edged toward the bed.

"No you don't!" Kane turned to intercept him, but he was already reaching for the bag.

"Let go of that!" Kane shouted.

The little man tried to pull away, but Kane's hand swooped down frantically into the open bag and clawed. Then it rose, gripping the scalpel.

The little man yanked the bag away. Clutching it, he retreated as Kane bore down upon him furiously.

"Stop!" Woods cried. Hurling himself forward, he stepped between the two men, directly into the orbit of the descending blade.

There was a gurgle, then a thud, as he fell.

The scalpel clattered to the floor, slipping from Kane's nerveless fingers and coming to rest amidst the crimson stain that seeped and spread.

The little man stooped and picked up the scalpel. "Thank you," he said softly. "You have given me what I came for." He dropped the weapon into the bag.

Then he shimmered.

Shimmered—and disappeared.

But Woods's body didn't disappear. Kane stared down at it—at the throat ripped open from ear to ear.

He was still staring when they came and took him away.

The trial, of course, was a sensation. It wasn't so much the crazy story Kane told as the fact that nobody could ever find the fatal weapon.

It was a most unusual murder . . .

THE HAUNTED CHAIR

STEPHEN F. WILCOX

The Ternicks first approached me about their haunted chair one Sunday morning in April, buttonholing me in the gravel parking lot next to the church. It was the first truly warm spring day of the year after four months of long and bitter winter in upstate New York, and I wasn't eager to spend any of it listening to a superstitious yarn. I had a yard to mow and a garden plot that needed turning; but conscience—and the morning's sermon—held me.

I already knew something of the Ternicks' dilemma, thanks to our church pastor, the Reverend James. He had spoken to me about it the previous Thursday, following our weekly youth counseling session with a few of the congregation's teenagers. "It seems Mr. and Mrs. Ternick are suffering under the delusion that old Mr. Brecht, Mrs. Ternick's late father, has been paying noctural visits," Reverend James told me. "They've obviously been under a great deal of strain since the old gentleman passed on in February, and frankly, I'm worried about the both of them. They're quiet, almost stoic people by nature, so I know it took a great deal of soul-searching for them to ask for help. I've done what I can to encourage them to deal with their problem rationally; I even suggested psychiatric evaluation, but they won't hear of it. Then I brought up your name and suggested you might be of help. They took to the idea immediately. I hope you don't mind."

"It's not that I mind exactly, Reverend," I hedged, "but what good could I possibly do?"

"You studied psychology in college. And your volunteer work with the church's youth counseling program has been exemplary."

"Still, I'm hardly qualified for something like this. I'm a newspaperman, not Sigmund Freud."

"Ah, but there's the beauty of it." The good pastor smiled devilishly. "You see, I believe you may be able to provide the Ternicks with sage counsel. I knew, however, that they would be reluctant to open up to you in such a role, so I sold them the idea on the basis of your experience as a newsman. Investigative journalism and all that."

"Reverend James, I publish and edit a small-town weekly, not the Washington *Post*."

He patted my arm reassuringly. "Totally irrelevant for our purposes. The important thing is your willingness to lend your counseling skills to a neighbor in need, yes? Say, that might make for a good sermon this Sunday: 'Help Thy Neighbor.' "

And so it was that I found myself in the church parking lot on a sunny Sunday morning, listening to a tale that would have been ludicrous if not for the utterly sincere look of pain etched into the face of Ruth Ternick.

"My father hadn't a sick day in his life until the last couple years," Mrs. Ternick began. She was a tall, heavy-boned woman in her late forties, her mouse-brown hair strewn with gray. "He kept the farm up nice, did the chores with Arno here," she nodded toward her husband, "even pitched in with the hayin' every summer right up to the age of seventy-five. That's when he started havin' the problems with his lungs. Caught pneumonia two years ago last October and went downhill from there. The doctors found somethin' bad with his heart, too, a weak valve, they said.

"Anyway, he was in the hospital from last Christmas to the middle of January. Bills were beginnin' to eat us alive, so the doctors let us take him home to look after him ourselves. That was my job, only I don't guess I did too good."

"Now, woman, don't start that again," Mr. Ternick cut in. He was an angular man in his mid-fifties, with a wind-burned face and a freckled scalp where hair used to grow.

He wore thick glasses that made his eyes appear unnaturally small and sunken. "She goes on thataway sometimes," the farmer said to me, "even though ol' Da—that's what we called Ruth's dad—had one foot in the grave the minute he set foot in the hospital. Blames herself 'cause she was off to do the grocery shoppin' when ol' Da had his last fit and died. Figures she coulda done somethin' if she'd been home, but that don't make sense. It was God's will is all."

I made the appropriate noises of sympathy and then, in spite of my misgivings, asked them to tell their story.

"Well, it started about a month after Da passed on," Mrs. Ternick said. "I come downstairs one mornin' and smell Da's old burley pipe tobacco. Arno here, he's a chewer, don't smoke at all, so I figured I must be dreamin'. But when I go into the livin' room, I find old Da's pipe sittin' in the ashtray and his easy chair up next to the fireplace, just like he always had it."

I interrupted. "You mean, the chair had been moved?"

She nodded. "After he passed on, you see, I put his chair and smokestand off in the corner, so's we could watch the television better. Only there it was, right back by the fireplace. Well, I asked Arno here if he did it, though I couldn't imagine why he'd be movin' stuff and smokin' Da's old pipe and everythin'."

" 'Course not," Mr. Ternick growled.

"Anyhow," his wife continued, "we couldn't figure it out at all, except maybe someone got in the house some way in the night and did it, who knows why? So, after a while, we just stopped thinkin' about it and went on about our chores. What else could we do?" I nodded my agreement, and she went on. "Well, next mornin' when Arno comes down to head out to the milk barn, he takes a look and darned if that old chair isn't right back in front of the fireplace again, pipe lyin' out and ashes in the ashtray. And it kept on like that for a week; I'd move the chair and smokestand back in the corner, next mornin' it's back in front of the fireplace.

"Like I say, this goes on for a week, and finally Arno here says he's had enough. He don't believe in ghosts and he's gonna get to the bottom of this thing, even if it costs him a night's sleep. So he decides to sit up and watch the chair."

I was still reluctant to get involved, but I'll admit I was warming to the tale. "What happened that night?" I asked.

Ternick shrugged. "I fell asleep. Ain't used to them late hours. Farm people, we gotta get up early. I remember I was watchin' that Carson fella on the TV and I just dozed off. Didn't wake up till near five o'clock. When I did, the TV had nothin' but snow on it—and that old chair was right back in front of the fireplace."

"Hmmm" was all I had a chance to say before Mrs. Ternick resumed the strange story.

"I guessed I'd try stayin' up the next night and see if I could do better. Arno went up to bed around nine-thirty and I set there on the sofa with my crewel work, watchin' the television with one eye and that old chair with the other. Along about midnight—I remember I was watchin' some news show with some fella looked a little like Howdy Doody—I all of a sudden smell pipe tobacco, so I sorta blink my eyes and quick look over at the chair, and Da had it moved again. Happened so fast, I never really saw it. It was just there."

"You're sure you didn't fall asleep?"

"I don't think so. I was sleepy, I remember. I coulda closed my eyes for a few seconds, I suppose. You know how it is when you get so relaxed you get kinda drowsy? Anyway, I sure stayed awake the rest of the night. I mean, I even tried talkin' to him . . . you know, to the chair. Kept askin', 'Da, why're you doin' this?' I told him how sorry I was . . . but nothin' came of it. He didn't answer me back."

With that Mrs. Ternick lowered her head and tried to suppress a deep sob. She failed. Her husband began to raise a hand to comfort her, then dropped it to his side. Instead, he squinted at me through his thick glass lenses and implored, "Can't you just see what this . . . this hauntin' is doin' to us? We gotta do somethin'. Somebody's gotta help us . . . make him go away."

I had them go over their story again, point by point, inserting a question here and there, all the while hoping to latch onto a plausible explanation that might satisfy them and get me out of it. I dredged up what psycho-babble I could recall from college lectures, tried reasoning with them as I would with one of the troubled teens in my youth counseling group, and, as a last resort, I badly posited that grief and guilt over old Mr. Brecht's death had somehow created a hysteria that was causing them to hallucinate. But they weren't having any of it. Ironically, they found it easier to believe that ol' Da was haunting their living room than to accept the possibility of mental aberration within themselves.

I then decided on the obvious tack and suggested they remove from the house the chair, the smokestand, and pipe, anything that had belonged to Mr. Brecht. Unfortunately, they weren't having any of that, either.

"The missus here, she don't want to let go of none of ol' Da's stuff," Ternick said, sounding equal parts frustrated and disgusted. "Claims it's all she's got left of the old man."

"Wouldn't do any good anyhow, gettin' rid of those few things," his wife defended herself. "Sakes alive, everythin' in the house used to be Da's, almost, includin' the house. It was him that first owned the farm, y'see. Arno came on as a partner like, after we married. So we'd have to get rid of the whole house, and then he'd probably start turnin' up in the milk barn."

It was a peculiar piece of logic, admittedly, but at the time I could think of nothing to refute it. There was a long silence, the Ternicks staring at me expectantly while I ground the toe of my best black shoe into the gravel of the parking lot. It seemed I had no choice, so I offered to go out to the farm and spend a night on the Ternicks' sofa. There was an explanation, I knew; one that didn't include the ghost of old Mr. Brecht haunting his favorite chair. Perhaps I, unburdened with the baggage of guilt and superstition that weighed down these simple people, could expose the truth behind their torment. Whatever it might be.

What with the demands of putting out the weekly paper, I was unable to make it out to the Ternick farm until the following Thursday. In the interim—when I wasn't busy rewriting the Kiwanis Club's monthly news bulletin or covering the Four-H Fair at the high school or any of a dozen other duties associated with a small-town newspaper—I managed to stop by the library and peruse everything I could find on parapsychology and unexplained phenomena. What sparse and inconclusive information I was able to dig up merely served to convince me that I was a fool to let the Reverend involve me in the affair in the first place.

Nevertheless, I drove out to the farm around seven o'clock that Thursday evening, as agreed. The Ternicks, looking even more drawn and subdued than they had on Sunday, stood waiting for me on the porch of the house. It was a large, vaguely Victorian place of gabled roof lines and intricate latticework which, on the whole, could have been handsome with a fresh coat of paint. After a somber, perfunctory greeting, my hosts ushered me into a long rectangular living room with a huge brick fireplace at one end, several pieces of overstuffed furniture hugging the walls and a flowery carpet stretched across the floor. The chair and smoking stand that had prompted my visit were tucked off into a corner several feet removed from the fireplace.

"Up till this mornin', we been leavin' the chair in Da's spot, over by the fireplace," Mrs. Ternick explained matter-of-factly. "Figurin', why keep movin' it back to the corner, since it don't stay put anyhow. I had Arno here move it back this mornin', though, so you could see for yourself what we mean. In the mornin', I mean."

"Did anything happen while the chair was left in its old spot by the fire?" I asked.

Mrs. Ternick nodded. "He still come by every night to smoke that old briar pipe. I know, 'cause every mornin' I have to dump out the ashtray."

The first half of the evening was uneventful in every sense. We each staked out a seat in the living room—leaving the late Mr. Brecht's favorite chair unoccupied, of course—and watched a procession of television shows; a moronic game show, a half-decent detective serial, a couple of improbable sitcoms, each stuffed with enough corn to fill the Ternicks' silo. I tried several times to engage my hosts in a discussion of the possible psychological reasons behind their "haunted chair," employing every buzz word and catch phrase I could remember from my research, but my attempts were rebuffed with skeptical mumblings and knowing glances from husband to wife and back again.

At nine thirty precisely, as the schoolhouse clock on the mantel chimed once for the half hour, Ruth Ternick brought from the kitchen a steaming pot of tea and a dish of home-made oatmeal cookies. Arno Ternick stood, yawned as only a farmer can yawn at the end of a hard day, and shuffled off to bed.

"You keep awake, now," Mrs. Ternick admonished me as she followed her husband up the stairs. "You'll see how it is."

I waited a few pregnant minutes until I heard a toilet flush, a closet door slam, and a set of bedsprings moan. Then, satisfied that my hosts had retired, I began a thorough examination of the living room—although I couldn't say what I expected to find. I looked behind the sofa, I drew back the drapes, I got on hands and knees and rolled back a corner of the carpet, I flicked lamps on and off and on again, I even stirred the ashes in the grate. Last, and I admit not without some irrational but heartfelt trepidation, I inspected the inside of the old man's smokestand—nothing unusual there—and gently eased myself into the mysterious chair.

As expected, nothing happened. No tingling sensations, no sudden chills along the spine, no groaning protests from disembodied voices in the night. I was simply sitting in a tattered Morris chair, all alone in a dowdy living room. Satisfied with my own sanity at least, I got up and returned to the sofa where I set to work on the tea and cookies.

The schoolhouse clock on the mantel chimed twelve times. The fabled witching hour, I reminded myself with a somewhat self-conscious chuckle. The cookies were gone, as was most of the tea in the heavy pewter pot that rested on the end table beside me. Perhaps Mr. Brecht's ghost was gone, too, for it surely hadn't disturbed the furniture this night. I had spent the previous two hours staring into the corner at the chair and smokestand, almost daring them to move while, at the same time, I tried to think of a way to get through to the Ternicks, when they came down for breakfast in the morning, something that might jar them back to reality.

It was then that I heard footsteps above me, quiet and slow, making their way from the second floor bedroom to the top of the stairway. I twisted around on the sofa and watched as a pair of pink fuzzy feet descended behind the balustrade. As they reached the bottom of the stairs, I realized that the slippered feet belonged to Mrs. Ternick. I started to stand and to speak, but the vacuous look in her eyes held me in place. Her long flannel nightgown billowing out from her sides, she walked past me as if I didn't exist and strode to the corner where her father's chair and smokestand sat waiting. Noiselessly on the heavy carpet she slid the smokestand across the room to a spot next to the fireplace.

"Mrs. Ternick?" I called to her softly. She didn't reply but instead pushed the cumbersome Morris chair until it joined the smokestand beside the fireplace. And then she sat down.

"Mrs. Ternick?" I tried again, more forcefully. Again, no acknowledgment. Standing, I positioned myself halfway between the sofa and the fireplace and watched, fascinated, as she took her father's briar from the stand, slowly filled it with fibrous burley tobacco, and lit the bowl with a wooden kitchen match.

"Of course," I mumbled to myself as she puffed away contentedly, still oblivious to my presence. "You just couldn't shake loose the guilt of your father dying when you weren't there to help him. So you bring him back to his favorite spot every night, a contented old man nursing his pipe in front of the fire."

I knew there had to be a logical explanation, I thought, giving myself a mental pat on the back as I turned and headed toward the stairs. Simple enough now to fetch Mr. Ternick and let him witness the scene for himself, after which we could gently awaken his troubled wife and go from there.

"Nooooooo!" I was halfway across the room when I heard it, a deep guttural cry that arrested me in midstride. I turned back to Mrs. Ternick, who was now staring up at me from the chair, her eyes burning like the pipe she held in her hand. I had nearly convinced myself that I had imagined the cry—it had been an old man's ragged voice I had heard—when her mouth opened again and another incongruous rumbling roared from her lips. "Murrrr-derrr."

Startled out of my paralysis, I jumped backward into the end table. The clatter of the heavy pewter tea service as it hit the floor resounded through the house, but Ruth Ternick's smoldering gaze remained steady. Now came heavy footsteps hurrying across the ceiling and down the stairs. I lost all equilibrium and fell back onto the sofa just as Arno Ternick came through the living room archway, his bathrobe hanging on him like a shroud, his eyes without the heavy spectacles blinking furiously against the lamplight, his hands gripping a shotgun.

"Youuuuu . . . mur-der-errrr!" came again the old man's voice from the woman in the chair.

"No, Da," Arno Ternick cried, his eyes squinting, terror and confusion amplifying his words. "You were already dyin' . . . there was no use . . . the doctor bills . . . eatin' away our savin's . . ."

"Youuuuu," the terrible, alien voice screamed as Ruth Ternick, her arm outstretched, finger pointing at her husband, began to rise from the Morris chair.

I remember seeing her body lift up suddenly and slam against the fireplace while, in the same frozen instant, a deafening gun blast voided all else. Then time began again, and Mrs. Ternick lay in a heap upon the hearth, her flannel nightgown dotted everywhere crimson, her mouth bleeding like an open sore.

And Arno Ternick, shotgun lying at his feet, standing still as death in the archway, eyes fixed on the empty chair, softly saying over and over again, "Had to, Da . . . Had to, Da . . . Had to, Da . . ."

It wasn't until Arno Ternick's trial for manslaughter that the whole story came out. The medical bills piling up, the second mortgage due on the farm in March, the old man lying up in his room and dying a day at a time, but somehow hanging on. Until the morning Ruth went off to shop and Arno came in from the milk barn and heard the dreadful wheezing. There was old Mr. Brecht on the bedroom floor, gasping for the pills that sat on the bureau not ten feet away. Arno stood in the doorway and looked at the old man, and the old man looked at him, and both men knew the pills would never leave the bureau.

The trial was over by early June, just as the strawberries in my garden came ready. Arno was put away in a hospital with barred windows and steel doors. Ruth already rested beside her father in the little cemetery next to our church. How she knew what Arno had done . . . well, that was just one of many questions that none of us could answer.

Of course the newspapers in the city wrote the story up big. But I never wrote it up at all. It just wasn't the kind of thing that belonged in a small-town weekly. At least, not in mine.

THIS CHURCH IS OPEN

ROBERT CAMPBELL

Artemidorus had been a professor of comparative religion for more than thirty years and how held the chair in Humanities at a small college in New England. He was considered an authority on the origins of Satan. Not the Satan of popular horror films and novels, but the Satan of many and varied names who was central to the ancient religions, the basic magic and superstitions of which come to us nearly whole, from Paleolithic and Neolithic times. Several scholarly books were among his credits, one of which had some financial success when an imaginative publisher marketed the paperback version of it with a lurid cover showing some devil with horns and tail having his way with a swooning maiden.

He did not believe in devils except as the abstract embodiment of evil, just as he did not believe in saints except as the symbolic embodiment of good.

He was nominally a Christian but had left the raising of their children in the Episcopalian faith to his wife, his own church attendance being limited to obligatory weddings, christenings, and funerals, with the occasional midnight mass attended for the sake of tradition at Christmas.

For years he had given faith a sidelong glance and had he been questioned sharply about his trust in God, he would have said that he had none and scarcely any belief at all in more than the mere idea of God, some intention—before the forming of the universe—to be God.

His wife was dead these five years and the children

grown, making lives elsewhere, one in California, one in Florida, and one in Texas.

He lived alone, but not lonely, in the house to which he'd taken his bride twenty-eight years before, when he was just a poverty-stricken associate and immortality was possible, surrounded by his books and a collection of vinyl records become collector's pieces, twice made obsolete, once by tape cassettes and again by CDs.

He often thought that he himself had been twice made obsolete, once by the *Time* cover that asked the question, "Is God Dead?" and again when the born-again Christian Fundamentalists seemed about to convert all of America.

It was at that time that he'd narrowed his field of study and gathered his reputation for knowing the origins and nature of Satan better than any but a very few of his fellow scholars.

What they did not know—what no one but his acolytes, witches and warlocks recruited from students given to curiosity and rebellion and certain women of the college town given to hysteria and repressed sexuality knew—was that he had made himself a magus, the leader of an original cult of his own design and manufacture.

It had started harmlessly enough with walks and gatherings in the woods beside the campus, the telling of stories and the breathing of certain herbs, the occasional naked mass and innocent orgy, but as all leaders discover sooner or later, he'd found it necessary to spike the emotional cocktail he offered his congregation with darker stuff, black masses, the ritual kissing of his buttocks, more shameful perversions—willingly committed but needing the legitimacy of ritual, the sacrifice of dogs and cats, and finally the sacrifice of one of their number who threatened to betray them.

Having escaped discovery once—the murder going unsolved and himself undiscovered—he tested his power to rule and take the lives of others again . . . and again . . . and again . . . choosing the time and place with great care, making certain that the murders took place far from the college where he taught, his sense of omnipotence growing, disdainful of every belief and faith except his belief and faith in his own masquerade, no longer needing or wanting any ceremony or excuse when the desire to kill took hold.

Through the years, he'd developed a devilish skill at identifying his half-willing victims at practically a single glance, knowing almost without fail that young man or woman, that thin-lipped housewife or balding clerk, whose midnight fantasies would urge them to strike up a conversation with him and go willingly into some dark copse of trees beside a river, or glade within a wood, which would become their grave.

He'd been asked to Oxford to give the Merlin Sylvester Lecture at Christ's College, the seminar named for that magus who prophesied to Edward the Confessor, the last Anglo-Saxon king of the English.

Rather than accept the offer of accommodations at the college, which he feared might afford him little privacy but, instead, an endless round of meals with well-meaning graduate students and dons anxious that he should not lack for any gesture of hospitality, he'd arranged for a per diem with which he might secure his own rooms at the hotel or bed and breakfast of his choice.

A man of frugal habits, he'd chosen a modest establishment two miles from the city center along the Bodley Road, at the bottom of a quiet lane, where a clean bed and private toilet, a pleasant lounge with a television, and what proved to be a better than merely decent breakfast cost him a third as much as a plain room in a city hotel would have done.

It had the added advantage of giving him a morning and evening constitutional during each of the five days of his stay, and hours of unobserved privacy which no one would ever question or intrude upon.

Each day, going into town, he noted a small wooden church, set well back from the road, its entry apparently secured with a lattice gate of wood painted green, a piece of paper fixed to it which, he idly surmised, must be the announcement of Sunday worship. There was nothing distinguished about it. In a country where great antiquity was commonplace and in a city where significant architecture was everywhere to be seen, he felt no compulsion to explore its interior or surrounds, but found every reason to

simply hurry by on his way to the paths along the canal and
river, the bustling streets of the commercial city, or the
quiet greenswards and broad playing fields of the colleges
assembled.

Yet each time, after the first time, that he walked past the
little church, morning or evening, he found himself wondering what exactly was written on the sign.

One evening, during a lull in the television program-
ming, he asked the owner of the bed and breakfast if he
ever attended the church along the Bodley Road and did he
know its denomination. His host, a Mr. Fluelis, seemed to
find it difficult to identify the building to which he referred,
in the end calling upon his wife to refresh his memory,
which she was unable to do, laughingly admitting that she
had no interest in churches along the Bodley Road, scarcely
ever walking there herself since they'd acquired their first
automobile ten years before.

It was of no consequence. Things seen every day of
one's life often made no impression. It was like asking di-
rections of someone in the neighborhood in which they
lived; they could easily lead you to your destination on
foot, but to describe the turns and street names was often
beyond their ability.

The lecture was a great success, his delivery wry and
funny, his material crisp and full of meat, his theme just
challenging enough to warrant some debate over a glass in
a local pub right after.

So it was well after dark when he was ready to go back
to his rented bed.

He might have taken a taxi; it was an inexpensive journey. Or he might have taken a bus; there were more than
enough going along the Bodley Road even at that hour. But
there was a full moon, the bite in the air was invigorating,
and he was warmed by the three glasses of port he'd drunk.
The prospect of a long walk home appealed to him.

He'd not gone a hundred yards along the Bodley Road
when he became acutely aware that he was being followed
by one of his companions in the pub, a young man, delicate
and feminine of face and figure, who'd had little to say and
equally little to drink, but had merely stared at him as he'd

informally expanded upon his lecture with anecdotes about Satan and Satanism which would not have been appropriate in a lecture hall setting.

At the railroad station, he hesitated, turned aside and then faced the student, remarking upon the fact that they seemed to be walking in the same direction and asking if the student was taking the last train to some neighboring town.

The young man replied that he had been overstimulated by the lecture and the ensuing conversation in the public house, and was walking to restore a measure of calm before returning to his rooms at Christ's Church College.

Artemidorus suggested that he walk with him and gave the student his promise that they would not talk of stimulating matters, intellectual or otherwise. It was enough to set the hook, and of course they did talk of the old religions and of faith expressed through carnality, of Druidic ritual and witchcraft, and of *la vecchia religione,* that primitive religion that had survived through the ages in Catholic Europe.

When they passed the bridge that arched over the canal, Artemidorus suggested they walk along the path for a distance before returning, at which time they would part ways, he going on the mile to his room in the bed and breakfast and the student returning to Oxford and his bed in the school dormitory.

Fifty yards along the canal, with the moon lying like a silver coin on a sea of molten lead, at a place where a foot-bridge sheltered a thick stand of water reeds and climbing vines, Artemidorus first kissed, then undressed, and finally murdered the young student, never having even asked his name.

After concealing the clothes and body in the vegetation, he washed his hands and returned to the Bodley Road, coming up from the towpath in sight of the church.

Somehow, it no longer looked so commonplace and undistinguished. Even though it was clearly modern, no more than fifty or sixty years old, the thought came to him that the fabric of the building might well incorporate a stone altar-screen or a window, a tomb or even an entire wall, from some early church that had once stood upon the spot. With the intention of walking around the perimeter, inspecting the windows and foundation as best he could, he walked down the path of the latticework gate with the sign upon it.

Instead of the schedule of masses, it bore the words, "This Church Is Open. Please Secure the Gate and Door Behind You When You Enter or Leave."

A little thrill went through him. He felt as though an opportunity for a small adventure had been thrust upon him very unexpectedly. He'd thought he'd just have a stroll around the exterior of a commonplace little church building but, instead, here he was, given the opportunity to explore its modest secrets and mysteries on toward midnight in the full of the moon after having committed a terrible act.

The latch gave easily to his hand. It swung open without a sound. He closed it behind him as he'd been admonished to do and went into the archway, where the moonlight was prohibited by the overhanging eaves. The iron-hinged oak door gave to his hand as easily as had the gate. He stepped inside, closed it behind him, turned for the first full view of the interior and was nearly overcome with wonder at the extraordinary grandeur that presented itself to him.

This was no common wooden church fifty or sixty years old. The outer structure was no more than a skin, a concealment of and protection for the ancient temple of stone within.

He could not date it precisely, there were a dozen architectural epochs jumbled there, centuries lying cheek to jowl, a sixteenth-century wall burrowing into a wall from the tenth, a stained-glass Gothic window, filled with the light of the moon, illuminating a Norman memorial stone set into the floor. The pews were carved with a hand that had been alive during the historical Arthur's time. The christening font was so ancient that he believed it might well be pre-Christian. It was a treasure filled with pieces worthy of the greatest museums in the world.

It was all quite dumbfounding.

But nothing was so overwhelming as the painting on the wall behind the altar. The power and magnificence of it burst upon him like a revelation, the moonlight suddenly striking through a clerestory set high beneath the roof, bringing it to blazing life, as though the thousand writhing figures in the painted hell below and the ascending souls on their way to heaven above moved before his gaze.

He had seen most of the world's great altarpieces in his scholarly travels, even the one by Michaelangelo in the Sistine Chapel, which was said by many to be the greatest of them all. But none, he would swear, matched the one before him now.

He glanced at the lucky few on their way to heaven and union with Christ, but his eyes were inexorably drawn to the tortured men and women burning in the lake of fire. Never had he seen such graphic descriptions of human torment and despair. Never had he felt such horror.

All at once, it was as though he could hear the cries and laments of the damned, so vivid was the impression made upon him, and then he became aware that someone besides himself had come into the church and admitted the sounds of the sighing trees and what traffic there might be along the Bodley Road.

Artemidorus turned to face whoever it might be.

A very tall man wearing a black suit and dickey, a ribbon of white collar gleaming at his neck, pale face, pale, pale hands, black hair, and pointed beard, stood there smiling at him. "Good morning," he said.

"Is it morning?"

"Well, it's past one o'clock."

"I've been here more than an hour?"

"Time plays tricks in here, I've been told."

"Are you a Roman priest?"

The cleric—if that was what he was—didn't answer, but merely made a gesture with his hand that might have been a blessing or might have been merely dismissive, telling Artemidorus that what he might be was of no matter.

The great altarpiece drew Artemidorus back and he turned away from the man in black, astonished anew at the brilliant verisimilitude of the work. He felt that, were he to reach out his hand, his fingers would be singed by the flame.

"A remarkable representation of the fate that awaits all sinners, is it not?" the cleric said.

"I've never seen the like."

"Do you believe in hell?"

Artemidorus turned around again, the altarpiece at his back, and smiled in his gentle, dismissive way. "I believe in the power of the superstition that presents such a notion to the human race."

"But not in the actuality of it?"

"Well, of course I don't believe in hellfire and brimstone," Artemidorus said.

There was a great rush of hot wind. Artemidorus turned around another time.

The painting seemed to burst apart and collapse upon itself in a blaze of flame and fire. The damned souls twisted and turned in their agony, reaching out their hands, trying to grasp Artemidorus by the sleeve. There was a path that opened that descended into darkness.

The pale vicar smiled. "Oh, you will," he said. "I assure you that you will."

Outside, the sign on the green lattice gate red, "This Church Is Closed. Mass on Sunday at 8:00, 9:00, and 10:00."

WEEPER

DAVID BRALY

Perhaps no man on the whole of Washington's Olympic Peninsula was less trusted than James Palmer Cooke. He had never actually been accused of doing anything illegal or immoral and a few people trusted him more than they did anyone else in the world, but the vast majority of the population felt that his physical appearance and his gloomy personality were a reflection of something evil inside him. The fact that some people did trust him so completely was a catalyst for, and not a mitigation of, the suspicions of the others, who felt that if he were trusted without reason, and indeed when there was every reason for distrust, surely he had gained that trust by means sinister and evil.

Cooke had arrived in Port Townsend aboard a two-masted schooner from San Francisco in 1889, bringing with him a carpetbag filled with clothes and a heavy and quite large trunk stuffed with books. He also brought a letter of recommendation from a San Francisco school where he had taught mathematics and science for six years. Neither the letter nor Mr. Cooke volunteered the reason why he had left San Francisco, but the Port Townsend school board were not suspicious and, had they been, probably wouldn't have inquired too closely anyway, there being at that time an acute shortage of qualified teachers on the peninsula. The letter, and a glance at Cooke's diploma from the California State Normal School, dated 1881 and signed by its presti-gious president Charles H. Allen, were all the recommendations they required, and James Palmer Cooke was hired the day of his arrival to teach mathematics at the high school.

Only later did members of the board as well as other people in the community become aware of Cooke's strange behavior. He wasn't guilty of anything outlandish, merely of a gloominess and surliness that did not fit the general conception of how a schoolmaster should act. His appearance added to this impression, for he was a thin, stooped man who stood almost six four at a time when people generally were much shorter than they are today. He had enormous, bushy black eyebrows, restless and forever shifting green eyes, a large nose that had been broken at some time and in consequence was long, hooked, and bent slightly to the left, a drooping black mustache above enormous lips and crooked yellow teeth, and a jutting jaw cleft down the middle. His ears were big and long; his neck skinny, host to a huge Adam's apple; his hair shoulder-length, black, and stringy; his skin deeply brown and sun-aged; and he wore always a faded old black suit with patches on its elbows and knees, visible despite the near perfect match with the rest of the material. Even so, Cooke would have been accepted had it not been for the odd behavior he exhibited, for the citizens of Port Townsend thought it only normal that a man of books be unconventional in dress and manners. What people would not tolerate was his refusal to return greetings, his apparent inability to smile, and his absorption in his books to the exclusion of all people and all other things. Nor were they pleased when word got around town that Cooke had told his class that Port Townsend was doomed and would soon become a ghost town.

They were even less pleased when it appeared that his terrible prediction would come true. All through the 1880's and into the early 1890's Port Townsend had been one of the nation's leading ports. The ships traveling up the Strait of Juan de Fuca to drop anchor there rivaled in number those that visited New York, New Orleans, and San Francisco. Port Townsend was a booming, bustling seaman's city, a shipping point for timber and iron, its prosperity evident by the multistoried brick buildings along Water Street and by the three- and four-story Victorian houses that occupied the hills above the town. But in the mid-1890's the ships began to go elsewhere, and Port Townsend began to die. Activity on the docks was slow, many stores on Water Street closed, and deposits declined at the First National and other banks. Optimism drained out of the community's lifeblood, replaced by doubt, worry, and suspicion. Port Townsend began to lose population. Enrollment at the schools declined. The first teacher whose services the school board decided they could dispense with was James Palmer Cooke.

Everyone expected that Cooke would leave town after he lost his job. Even hoped he would. But he fooled them. He rented the building where Magennis's Chandler Store had been located and opened a "dealer in everything" shop, buying, selling, and trading. He must have had a knack for commerce because despite his unpopularity he managed to survive. All he did was survive, not prosper, but that was doing well in Port Townsend at the turn of the century. He lived in a room at the back of the store and was open for business fourteen hours a day, six days a week. On Sundays and holidays Cooke went for long walks through the wooded hills above town. He never showed the slightest interest in society, religion, or politics, which was thought to be rather peculiar, nor in women, which was thought to be most peculiar and more than a little suspicious. Indeed, there was no evidence that Cooke had ever had a girlfriend during his entire forty years of life, but most people attributed this oddity to his physical appearance rather than to any personal preference. And there were a few people in the area, as mentioned previously, who looked to Cooke for all manner of advice concerning not only when to plant their crops or what the weather might be like next year, but also sought him out to provide remedies for their ailments and solutions for their legal problems. Cooke, although looked upon as being stingy and even miserly with money, was generous with advice. It was said that no one ever took any sort of problem to him that he could not offer some opinion about.

Probably it came as no great surprise to Cooke that on the cold, foggy afternoon of October 27, 1901, a man who had traveled over from Port Angeles arrived in his shop to deliver a message from John Adair, who had stopped him on his way. The message was oral, to the effect that the presence of Mr. Cooke was much desired at the Adair farm as soon as Mr. Cooke could manage. This said, the traveler bade him good day and departed. Cooke wasted no time. The Adairs were one of those families who had respect for his opinions on all matters, and he closed his shop immediately. He went to Brown's Livery and rented a buggy and horse, then rode north out of town. The Adair farm was on the other side of the National Guard fort.

There were only three Adairs living on the farm now. Originally there had been five: John Adair, the head of the family; Molly, his wife, who, at forty-six, was ten years his junior; James, the eldest son; Cullen, the next eldest; and Thomas, the youngest. But James and Cullen had left the depressed Port Townsend area and gone to Oregon, where they were partners in a boat that trolled for salmon at the mouth of the Columbia. Tom remained. He was sixteen, handsome and strong like his father. Cooke had never taught Tom. But he had been a teacher to the older boys, and it was then that the Adairs had come to know and respect him. They were among the families who continually asked him for medical advice. He always gave it freely. Local physicians once hauled him into court for practicing medicine without a license, but they lost their case because they could not prove that the gifts he took from the families he advised were fees and there was no evidence that he ever took money in payment. Generally the medical advice he gave was correct. He even advised farmers on the sicknesses of their animals. Once, a mule on the Adair farm became sick and Cooke was called out. He examined the mule, pronounced that the malady was cholera, and ordered the Adairs to slaughter all their animals that had been in contact with the mule during the past two weeks. The Adairs did this, wiping out a third of their livestock, and the cholera—or rather the disease he had declared to be cholera—did not spread further. After that the Adairs and Cooke's other admirers regarded him as a hero.

If Cooke had not loved the respect he held from people

like the Adairs, he would never have made the journey that day. His threadbare coat, old suit, and faded derby were no protection from the piercing cold. The heavy fog made the air itself wet, and Cooke was damp and uncomfortable sitting on the buggy seat. He hated fogs. They reminded him of the frightening stories the grown-ups used to tell when he was a child in Louisiana. He had become accustomed to fogs when he lived in San Francisco, but had never learned to like them. It was bad enough indoors on a foggy day when the dampness penetrated the walls, but it was much worse being out in it, especially on the seat of a buggy with a journey of several miles ahead. The fog, which disappeared over the strait on one side of him and into the wooded hills of spruce and hemlock on the other, imposed an eerie, cold silence upon everything around him that was broken only by the pounding hooves of his horse and the creaking of the buggy wheels. Although Cooke was a man of science and as such not frightened by elements of nature, the grey silence put him on edge. He would have been glad to hear even the hollow moan of a foghorn, just to know that there were other people out there, but although that sound was familiar in San Francisco and not uncommon on the strait, today he did not hear it.

During the long journey to the Adair farm he failed to meet any other human being. His horse continued to trot into the endless grey, more sure than Cooke of the road, while Cooke himself shifted positions on the seat minute after minute, trying to find more warmth or comfort than he had thus far discovered. Dark spots would appear in the fog, which, as the buggy drew nearer, gradually hardened in outline and shade, becoming at last spruce or hemlock trees. For a while they were beside a rail fence, each splinter clear at ten feet but the rails beyond vanishing into the universal grey. The posts became visible in the grey as the buggy approached them, gradually strengthened in form until it had passed them. Each post did that in turn, and Cooke played a mental game of guessing when the last post would appear. Eventually it did. Afterward there were only the spruces and hemlocks and pines, until they reached and passed the great gate of the fort, at which time Cooke realized that despite all the bumpy travel and damp discomfort he was only halfway to his destination. He settled into the left corner of the seat, pulled the collar of his coat tighter around his neck, and waited for the buggy to reach the Adair farm. He continued to stare at the appearing and vanishing forms of trees, fence posts, and, occasionally, cows, but did so without interest. It would have interested him greatly had he met another human being on that road, if only to prove that he was not the only man insane enough to be there, but he met no one. He would have closed his eyes and tried to sleep despite his discomfort, but if he did he would miss seeing the weathered rail gate that opened into the Adair farm.

Eventually he reached that gate. It appeared slowly out of the fog, fuzzy at first and then clearer, until there was no doubt that it was a gate nor which gate among all the gates of the world it was. Cooke reined in the horse, got down, and opened it. He led the horse through, then closed the gate, and remounted the buggy. He could not see the Adair house and barn, but he knew where they were. Cooke had been in both. The house was a two-story, white clapboard structure with a red shingle roof and red-framed bay windows. It was about fifteen years old, having been built over the ruins of an older log house, and was solid and warm. Cooke liked it. He also liked the Adair barn, larger than the house, sturdy and red. The house and barn were only fifty feet from each other, and both two hundred feet from the gate, so Cooke wondered whether he would see the white house first or the red barn. He saw the barn first.

When Cooke stopped the buggy, the front door of the house opened and John Adair stepped out onto the porch. Standing five nine, he was a big barrel-chested and muscular man. His hair was brown and moderately long, and like Abraham Lincoln, who had spent most of his life in the Adairs' hometown of Springfield, Illinois, he wore a beard but no mustache. He had a round, handsome face, and lively if somewhat nervous brown eyes. John Adair had been a farmer all his life. While not an educated man, he was better read than most and had managed to acquire a complete set of Ridpath's *History of the World,* bound in leather, around the bookcase of which the sofa and chairs of the living room had been arranged.

John Adair stepped off the porch and approached Cooke. "Why Mr. Cooke, I didn't expect you out here this afternoon—especially in this fog."

"You sent word that you needed me. I always try to go where I'm needed."

"Well, yes, but we didn't look for you today. Hoped you might come out tomorrow, but . . ."

Cooke got down from the buggy and shook hands with Adair. "What's the problem, John? Another sick animal?"

"Wish it was."

"Oh?"

"It's my son. Tom, that is. He's been acting crazy."

When they entered the house, Cooke was struck by the sharpness in detail of everything in the living room. He couldn't remember ever before seeing colors as bright nor lines as sharp. Being in the fog for so long had done that, had made his eyesight sharper at least for a while, or maybe just made it seem sharper. Several small logs were crackling in the fireplace. The Adairs had nice furniture, most of it aimed at the oak bookcase beside the fireplace, and the room reflected their mild prosperity. Most important to Cooke at the moment was that the room was warm and dry.

"We weren't expecting you today," Molly Adair repeated, standing at the kitchen door. She was a short woman with sparkling hazel eyes. Although she was a decade younger than her husband, the tough and hard life of the farm had aged her more. Her face was deeply wrinkled and her hair showed only a few streaks of auburn amid the grey. "Can I get you a cup of coffee or something?"

"A cup of hot chocolate, if you have it."

"Certainly." She disappeared into the kitchen.

Cooke sat on the sofa. It was long and green and protected by a red cloth cover. John Adair sat opposite Cooke in the room's only armchair, also green. The sofa's right side was near the left side of the chair, and they were at a forty-five-degree angle to one another, with the bookcase and fireplace forming the base of the triangle. In this way Adair and Cooke were able to face each other by looking to their sides. A coffee table was in front of both the chair and the sofa, with flowers, an ashtray, and the latest newspaper from Seattle resting on it.

"Now," said Cooke, "what's this problem with Tom?"

"Do you remember the Greer girl?"

"Greer," said Cooke thoughtfully.

"Samantha Greer."

"Yes, of course. Fifteen years old, blonde, pretty, but mentally unbalanced. She realized it and . . . That was the year I arrived in Port Townsend. It happened near here, didn't it?"

"At the Tankard Cave, about half a mile behind this house, on the strait."

"Yes, I remember now. Tragic. But what's that got to do with young Tom?"

"He . . . uh . . ." Adair cleared his throat. "He's been . . . He *says* he's been seeing her. That they're in love with each other."

"In love? But, John, the Greer girl is—"

"I know. Dead."

"I didn't know she was dead when I first saw her," said Tom. He'd been called down from his bedroom and was seated on the sofa next to Cooke. He was a broad-shouldered boy with long brown hair and a classical face only slightly marred by large ears. His eyes were brown, like his father's, and nervous. He fingered the lowest button on his plaid shirt while he talked. "I just thought she was a girl like any other when she appeared in the barn."

"I see," said Cooke. "And where did she come from, Tom?"

"I don't know, sir. I was cleaning out a stall and suddenly felt I was being watched. I turned around, and she was standing there looking at me, and smiling. She was all there. I mean, solid, not a cloud or anything like that."

"Then what?"

"She said hello, and I said hello, and first thing you know we were talking. She was very nice."

"Go on."

"Well, I saw her after that almost every day. Almost every day for more than a week now."

"Always in the barn?" asked Cooke.

"Yes." Tom's eyes were wide and piercing. They looked to Cooke like the eyes of a madman he'd seen once in San Francisco. "Until yesterday."

"What happened yesterday?" asked Cooke.

"We met in the barn again. We were talking and I asked her where she lived."

"And what did she say?"

"She said that she didn't live anywhere, but she would show me where she stayed. I asked her what she meant, and she said to follow her. So I did. She took me out across the fields toward the strait. She went down the bluff on an old trail, and then over to Tankard Cave. She said that was where she stayed. I looked around and didn't see any personal belongings. I had figured she was a gypsy or something, but by then I was thinking she was pulling a joke. I asked her about there not being any personal belongings there. She said she didn't need anything, that she had everything she needed except someone to be with her."

"When he returned home," said John Adair, "he told me about this girl and described her. She fit the description of the Greer girl who committed suicide at Tankard Cave twelve years ago."

"And you sent for me," concluded Cooke.

"Not then," said John Adair. "I thought it might be some girl pulling a joke on Tom. I didn't know who it could be. The area is thinly populated enough that a boy ought to know every girl around here who's his age. I figured it had to be a joke, though. Until this morning."

"What happened this morning?"

Molly Adair entered the room carrying a small white tray with two white cups on it. She placed the tray on the coffee table, then returned to the kitchen. John Adair lifted one of the cups, Cooke the other. Cooke sipped gingerly of the hot chocolate. It was delicious. Warming.

"I went out to the barn," said Tom. "She was there. Pa had told me about Samantha Greer after I told him about the girl. I'd heard about her before, of course, but never what she looked like. Anyway, she and I talked. Eventually I said as how I didn't know her name and she said she'd rather not say what it was. So I asked her straight out if it was Samantha Greer."

"And what happened?" asked Cooke between sips.

"She was silent for more than a minute. She just stood there looking at me. Finally she said, 'Someone told you, didn't they?' And I said, 'Is that your name?' And she said, 'Yes, I'm Sammie Greer.'"

Tom stopped his story and looked over at his father. Cooke could see that the boy was scared.

"Tell him the rest," John Adair told his son.

Tom looked at Cooke, obviously struggling to speak but unable to. Then he blurted it out: "After that she vanished."

"Vanished?"

Tom looked down at his lap.

His father said, "The boy claims that she disappeared into thin air. Says she did it while he was standing there looking at her. One moment she was there, the next she wasn't. Just like that."

Cooke placed his cup of chocolate on the coffee table. The boy beside him was near collapse. Cooke placed his left hand on Tom's right shoulder and spoke his name. The boy lifted his head and looked at Cooke.

"Do you honestly believe," asked Cooke, "that you saw the ghost of Samantha Greer?"

Tom started to answer, choked on the words, and then managed to say: "Y-Yes. I-I don't wan-ta believe it, M-Mr. Cooke, but I saw it. I can't say I didn't when I did. Sh-She was there one second and gone the next. Like a m-mirage. I don't believe in ghosts, but—but what other explanation is there?"

Cooke nodded, then stared out the bay window that was on one side of the fireplace, in the same position as the book-case on the other side. He could see that it was still foggy outside, but the fog was being blown away by an ocean breeze. It would be gone soon. He hoped it would be com-pletely gone before he had to start back to Port Townsend.

"Do you believe me, Mr. Cooke?"

"I believe you saw what you say you saw."

"You do?" Tom's voice was filled with relief.

"Yes," said Cooke sadly. "But that doesn't mean that what you saw exists."

"Huh?"

Cooke faced the boy again. "I think you saw someone, but I don't think she was there."

"But that's impossible."

"No. It's the same as the mirage you mentioned."

Tom stared at Cooke for a moment, then looked down at his lap again. He was still trembling.

John Adair told his son to go into the kitchen to see if his mother needed help with anything.

"Well?" Adair asked Cooke when the kitchen door had shut. "Is my son going insane?"

Cooke swallowed hard. "Yes," he said.

John Adair sprang to his feet and began pacing the floor. Back and forth he walked, five times to and from the nearby fireplace, then he stopped in front of the fireplace with his back to Cooke. "What can I do?" he asked.

"I don't know," said Cooke. He started to reach for his cup, then decided it would be bad manners to sit sipping chocolate at such a time. "There's one thing that we've got to do, though."

"What?" Adair turned to face Cooke.

"We've got to make him see that what he thinks he saw and heard were only tricks of his mind. We must make him realize that. It may not cure him, but it might be a step in that direction. It might at least put him on guard against further hallucinations."

John Adair nodded. "Tom, come in here!" he shouted.

And so, for an hour, they worked on the boy. Cooke made him repeat every experience he'd had with the imaginary girl, then forced him to say after each recollection: "This did not happen. This is only something I made up in my own mind." At first Tom was reluctant, but after he'd renounced two or three memories he realized that Cooke and his father were right, that they were trying to help him, and he willingly did as instructed. Sweating like a malaria victim, yet also shivering despite the warmth of the room, Tom became anxious that he not forget any word that the

ghost had spoken to him, for he could not renounce it if he
failed to remember it. He denied the girl, denied the ghost,
and affirmed that everything was an invention of his own
mind, brought about by the loneliness of the farm and by
some deep sickness within his head that he hitherto had had
no knowledge of.

When all of this was accomplished, Cooke had the boy
put a coat over his sweat-drenched shirt, and together they
walked out to the big red barn. Only patches of the fog remained. The breeze from the strait was stronger now, as
cold and penetrating as the fog had been.

Inside the barn Cooke had the boy say: "I, Thomas
Adair, do hereby deny the existence of any ghosts or apparitions, most particularly any belonging to the late
Samantha Greer, and state that I do not know her, have
never known her, and have no wish to ever know her."

Tom was weak when Cooke led him out of the barn.
"I'm glad that's over," he said.

"It's not," said Cooke. "You've got to repeat those words
one other place."

"Where?"

"Tankard Cave."

The walk to the bluff seemed longer than the half mile it
actually was. They walked straight into the piercing cold
breeze. It wasn't a strong breeze, just powerful enough to
rustle the tips of the grass and the upper branches of the
spruce trees, but it didn't have to be strong when it was
cold. By the time they started down the bluff they both had
chattering teeth and were shivering.

Tankard Cave was twenty feet high and twenty-five feet
long, embedded in the green bluff that was the demarcation
between the Adair farm and the Strait of Juan de Fuca.
When Cooke and the boy arrived, the blue-grey waters of
the strait were snapping upon the grey sand a mere twenty
feet from the cave's entrance. Soon, the tide in, the water
would be up to the cave itself. Cooke looked at the sand in
front of it, seeking the footprints of Tom Adair. There were
none. Perhaps he had only imagined being at the cave yesterday. More likely he'd been there and the tide had washed

away his footprints, leaving in their stead only a few pieces of driftwood and a fisherman's floater.

"Repeat what you said inside the barn," Cooke told the boy.

Tom walked to the middle of the cave's mouth, stood erect with his arms hard against his sides, and, with his eyes clenched shut, he again renounced Samantha Greer.

A terrible chill went down Cooke's spine. He looked around him, then out to the strait. The other side of it was barely visible, a mere line of black riding above the liquid grey horizon. The waters were tossing and splashing; the breeze had become a wind. Everything—the sky, the water, the sand—was grey. And yet the fog was gone completely.

"How did I do?" asked Tom.

Cooke faced him and smiled. "You did fine, boy. Now let's get back."

They returned with the cold wind pushing them, with the trees and the grass shaking viciously around them, with the clouds outracing them. Cooke's legs were tired. But he hurried along faster than the boy, who was no longer weak, but, purged of his insane thoughts and reinforced with the enthusiasm of a convert, walked strong and happy. Occasionally the wind blowing through the trees created a howling sound, and when that happened Cooke could feel the hair rise on the back of his neck. He was scared. Spooked by talk of a ghost and by the breaking down of a boy whose brothers he had taught. He tried to think himself out of it. After all, he was a man of science. Ghosts did not exist; insanity, while unfortunate, happened to some people. It was all very sad but it was logical. Nothing to fear. He would almost convince himself, when suddenly the wind would create another howl and he would again feel the hairs on his neck stand on end.

Never had anyone been as happy to see the Adair house as James Palmer Cooke was that afternoon when it was finally back in view.

John Adair was grateful for Cooke's help. Profusely grateful. He put a bag of potatoes into Cooke's buggy. He invited Cooke to stay the night, pointing out that it would

be dark by the time he reached town if he left now, but
Cooke refused.

Cooke had started driving away when he heard the noise.
It was loud and came from the barn. It sounded like someone weeping. A woman or a girl.

He looked back toward the house. John and Molly Adair
had already gone inside with Tom. They were not making
the strange noise, nor would they be able to hear it inside.
Cooke could barely hear it. Although it had to be loud to be
heard where the buggy was (Cooke had stopped when he
heard the noise), he could barely distinguish it from the
howls of the wind.

He wrapped the reins around the brake handle and
stepped down. He walked toward the barn. The front doors
were open. The barn loomed larger as Cooke walked
closer, big and red and huge against the black clouds racing
across the cheerless grey sky.

The closer he walked, the more distinctly the noise
sounded like a girl weeping.

He slowed his pace. His heart was pounding. He was hot.
His stomach was electric.

The weeping stopped.

For a moment he stood there, ten feet from the butterfly
doors of the big red barn, waiting for something to happen.
Nothing did. He heard only the howling of the wind and the
distant lowing of cattle. He saw only the black interior of
the barn—free of ghostly movements.

After a minute or more of standing there and waiting,
Cooke took a step forward. Then another, and another, and
another.

Finally he was inside the barn. It was dark because the
day was dark, but other than that there was nothing strange
there, nothing to distinguish it from a hundred other barns.
There was hay scattered on the wooden floor, empty stalls,
a pile of ropes, a few pieces of farm equipment, and a loft
with more hay, in bales.

He laughed out loud at his own foolishness. The boy's
insane imaginings had spooked him good.

He turned and walked toward the doors.

Suddenly—just as he reached the doors—he was physically struck by something cold, something that penetrated his clothes and his skin and that chilled his very bones, while at the same instant a loud, terrible wail assaulted his ears—the distinct, unmistakable weeping of a young woman.

He ran.

He didn't look back, didn't stop to investigate, didn't do anything else—just ran.

Cooke didn't stop running until he reached the buggy. Then, with the noise still coming from the barn, he undid the reins and used them to whip the horse into a gallop. *"Hyah! Hyah! Hyah!"* he cried at the top of his voice, whipping with the reins, terrifying the horse more than he himself was terrified, almost overturning the buggy as it cleared the Adair gate, speeding past Mr. Williams's wagon, which happened to be passing by, and causing Mr. Williams's horse to rear up and Mr. Williams to open his mouth in astonishment. Cooke continued at that breakneck speed all the way into Port Townsend.

Brown, at the livery stable, was furious. He demanded an extra two dollars as compensation for the added wear on his buggy and the condition of his horse. And Cooke, a miser if there ever was one, paid it without argument or complaint. He then left the livery and returned to his store.

It was observed by several people that Mr. Cooke's lights were on quite late that night. Also, they were on quite early the next morning. Someone wondered aloud if perhaps Mr. Cooke had left his lights on all night. But that was laughed at, for Cooke was not a man to waste money by having all his lights burning through the night. Even if he himself remained awake, surely one light would suffice.

The reason for the lights in Cooke's store was learned during the afternoon. A farmer named Samuel London had gone to visit his friend John Adair shortly before noon. London generally timed any visit for the noon hour in hopes of being invited to share the family lunch. What he found at the Adair house was not lunch, but rather something that ruined his appetite for the remainder of the week. London rushed into town to report what he'd found. The sheriff rode out to the farm with all his deputies except Cory Miller. And it was fortunate for Cooke that Miller had been left behind. Because, although London accompanied the sheriff back out to the Adair farm, word of his discovery swept through Port Townsend like indigestion on a feast day. Within minutes everyone knew. And within half an hour, Williams had remembered and told everyone who would listen how he had been driving his wagon past Adair's gate the previous day along about dusk and how that crazy man James Cooke had come out like he was being chased by a stampede of buffaloes. When folks put that information together with their natural dread and distrust of Cooke, and the fact his lights had burned all night (a guilty conscience, they said), they realized that the perpetrator had to be James Cooke. There was no doubt about it. Word spread. A mob formed.

Cory Miller took his duties seriously. He had been sworn to uphold the law, and as a good Christian, he did not take an oath lightly. When he was told that a mob was gathering in front of James Cooke's store, he grabbed a carbine and went outdoors, out into the piercing cold wind that was blowing from the strait, and walked toward the mob, to put himself and his weapon between them and the man that even he now believed to be the perpetrator.

Cory Miller faced down the mob that day. He spoke to the crowd, called the individuals who composed it by their first names, and told them that if they planned to lynch James Cooke, they'd have to kill him first. He reminded them that Port Townsend was not a lynch town, but a place where the law was upheld and order was respected. He called upon them to disperse, and assured them that if they found Cooke guilty he would surely hang by his neck until he was dead, dead, dead. The men were less than satisfied, but they were unwilling to murder Miller in order to string up James Cooke. They dispersed.

Miller then turned and knocked loudly upon the locked door of the store until it was opened.

Cooke was there, peeking out at Miller, sweat on his brow and fear in his green eyes. "What's going on?" he asked. "Why were they after me?"

"I think you'd better come with me," said Miller.

"Why?"

"For one thing, you'll be safer in jail than you will here. Those men are angry. They might come back."

"Yes . . . yes, of course." Cooke opened the door wide so that Miller could step inside. "I'll get my hat and be right with you."

"Good."

A moment later Cooke had returned from his back room. He wore his faded black suit and derby. He looked terrified. "Am I under arrest?" he asked.

"Yes," said Miller. "If the sheriff finds something that implicates someone else, then we can always let you go later."

"Implicates someone else in what?"

"Sam London found the Adairs dead this morning. Slaughtered. Blood all over the place. We know that you were out there late yesterday, so it's murder we're thinking about."

More than two hundred people attended the funeral of the Adairs. Many mere acquaintances were there, and all of their friends except James Palmer Cooke. Everyone on the peninsula was shocked by the triple slayings. No less shocking was the manner in which it was done. John Adair had been stabbed five times with a butcher knife, every wound in his back; his wife Molly had several wounds on her hands, but the fatal wounds were in her heart and neck; young Tom bore a single stab wound in his heart, where the butcher knife was lodged upside down. Blood was all over the living room, where the bodies were found.

A hearing was held soon afterward in the Jefferson County courthouse to determine if there was sufficient evidence to bind over James Palmer Cooke for trial. There was. His lawyer, Zeb Whitney, requested a change of location, arguing that public opinion was so hostile that Cooke could not possibly receive a fair trial in Port Townsend or anywhere on the Olympic Peninsula. Judge

Carter granted the request. Seattle was chosen as the place of trial.

The Seattle courtroom of Judge Winslow Singleton was crowded with spectators when the trial started at winter's end. Among the spectators were several dozen from Port Townsend, almost all against Cooke, and the two sons of John and Molly who had been living in Oregon. Singleton kept the crowd quiet throughout the trial, less because of any sense of judicial duty than to impress the reporters. The judge, a tall, white-haired man with a ruler-straight back and a huge, positively wild mustache, wanted to be governor of Washington someday and wasn't above catering to popular whim. He knew that public opinion was against Cooke; his rulings were lopsided in the prosecution's favor. The reporters wrote what a splendid and even-handed job Judge Singleton was doing, and the public parroted this praise. Likewise the courtroom crowd, aware that Singleton was doing a "good job" on most of the rulings he made, were less upset by those few he made that favored the defense.

Prosecuting the case was a fat, short little man with a pockmarked face, Henry Grant. Grant called Cooke a murderer, a savage, a "vile, wicked creature fit only to retrieve garbage from the slums of European cities." Despite his invective, however, the crux of Grant's case was the testimony of witnesses. Williams told how Cooke had shot out of the Adair gate on the fatal day, Brown about the state of the rented buggy and horse, and other witnesses recollected how Cooke's store lights were on for an entire night, in violation of every miserly principle held dear by the man.

Zeb Whitney countered by calling the sheriff and Cory Miller. Both of these lawmen testified that no blood had been found on the person or clothes or in the abode of Cooke, and gave it as their expert opinion that had he committed the crime there would have been blood on his clothes and shoes. This was convincing testimony. It might have saved the neck of Cooke had he not insisted upon being allowed to tell his side of the story.

What Cooke told was a ghost story. He repeated to the

jury everything that had happened, including the wail from the barn. His lawyer's face was a picture of honest misery.

Henry Grant rose from his chair and approached the witness stand. "Are you telling us, Mr. Cooke," he asked, "that the ghost of Samantha Greer murdered the Adairs?"

"I know it sounds ridiculous, and as a man of science I—"

"Just answer the question."

"Very well. I know what I heard, Mr. Grant. And I know what the poor Adair boy told me. I refused to believe Tom, but then I heard the weeping of that girl."

"Of the ghost?"

"Yes."

"I repeat," said Grant. "Are you asking us to believe that John, Molly, and Tom Adair were murdered by the ghost of a girl who committed suicide a dozen years ago?"

Cooke's Adam's apple shot up, then down. "Yes," he said.

Grumbles and moans spread through the courtroom. Judge Singleton demanded order, but frowned at Cooke to show where his sympathies lay. Cooke looked shocked by the angry reaction. Zeb Whitney, a good country lawyer who seldom believed in his clients but who did believe in Cooke, slumped in his chair, resting his chin on his upturned hands.

Henry Grant walked back to the prosecution table, saying, "No further questions of this murderer, your Honor."

In his closing argument Zeb Whitney concentrated upon the lack of blood on Cooke's clothes and other possessions. He ignored his client's claims about why he'd gone out to the Adair farm (the two surviving Adairs had testified that their brother had always been mentally sound) and Cooke's belief that a girl's ghost had murdered the family in revenge for Tom's renouncing her. He insisted that they ignore Grant's earlier closing argument—in which the prosecutor had branded Cooke "a twisted, evil fiend of a creature whose mind is filled with apparitions and murder"—and remember only the evidence. The testimony of Williams and Brown, he said, was circumstantial and meant nothing, but that of the sheriff and his deputy was expert and meant everything.

The jury was out for twenty minutes. Their verdict: guilty of murder, three counts. Judge Singleton thanked the jury members "for doing a difficult job exceedingly well."

The grass was green, the sky was blue, and the air was warm that day in mid-June of 1902 when James Palmer Cooke mounted the gallows inside the grey stone walls of the Washington State Prison. "I am innocent," he said, and then the trap door sprang and he was dead.

No one in Port Townsend actually celebrated the hanging of Cooke, but many people there did feel relief that the dirty business was over and done with. Almost everyone believed that another murderer had received his just deserts. Most of them were also pleased that the sinister man who had for so long haunted their community was gone. But a few people continued to admire Cooke and to defend his memory. They claimed he had been wrongly accused, that even if there was no ghost at the Adair farm it had not been James Cooke who murdered the family.

The elder sons of John and Molly Adair inherited their parents' farm. They took a careful inventory, found nothing missing, and declared that to be further proof that Cooke had been the murderer and not some thief or passing tramp. They put the farm up for sale. Times were hard in the area and they had to cut the price more than once, but eventually they sold it to a family named Peterson. They used the money to buy a second troller and an interest in a fish processing plant.

Late in the fall of 1916 Hans Peterson was leaving the big red barn with his work mules when there came from the building a loud noise, identical in sound to the weeping of a young woman. The mules were startled, panicked, and one broke free from Peterson's strong grip. The animal was found an hour later munching on grass near the rail fence that separated the Peterson and McEwen farms. Peterson managed to restrain the other mule, led him away from the barn and around the house, where he tied him to a cedar tree. Then he walked back to the barn and, with the wail still coming from it, entered the open butterfly doors. For a moment Peterson stood motionless, listen-

ing to the loud noise and trying to determine where it
came from. When at last he decided that it originated in
the loft, he climbed the ladder that led there, and then
walked across it in search of the source. What he eventually found was a small hole (one foot high and less than
an inch wide) in the side of the barn, through which the
strong wind from the strait entered. The shape of the hole,
combined with a splinter that divided it in half, produced
the noise in much the same way the sound of a whistle is
created. Peterson stuffed hay in the crack, and the weeping sound stopped dead.

When Peterson told about the noise and its source in Port
Townsend, people who had believed Cooke said, "You see,
he told the truth. That boy just got him spooked and Cooke
forgot his scientific training. His crime was not trusting his
own knowledge."

In 1983, Howard Percell agreed. Percell, a historian,
was compiling a book about the great true Washington
murder mysteries. He intended to include the Adair case.
He examined the transcript of the trial and all the other
documents he was able to locate relating to the case.
When Percell had completed this phase of his investigation he told a friend who was interested in the case: "The
solution was right there before Cooke, if only he hadn't
been such an egotist about his scientific and other abili-
ties. Thinking he cured Tom Adair. Well, he didn't. And
his story about a ghost discredited him so badly that no
one believed him when he testified that the boy had been
insane."

The next phase of Percell's investigation was an on-site
inspection of the old Adair farm. He went through the
house, and out to where Tankard Cave used to be before it
collapsed in 1937. It gave him a feeling for the area but did
not increase his knowledge of the murders. And the wind
was not blowing, so he couldn't be sure what it was like for
James Palmer Cooke that terrible day. He walked back to
the house.

Then he examined the ground where the barn used to

stand before it was torn down in 1959. He stood where it had stood and thought deeply about the murders.

That was when he heard—

"Oh no!"

He ran away.

The Adair case is not mentioned in the book, which was published last week. In fact, Port Townsend itself is mentioned only once—in the dedication: "To four victims of an insane murderer at Port Townsend."

THE POND

PATRICIA HIGHSMITH

Elinor Sievert stood looking down at the pond. Was it safe? For Chris? The real-estate agent had said it was four feet deep. It was certainly full of weeds, its surface nearly covered with algae or whatever they called the little oval green things that floated. Well, four feet was enough to drown a four-year-old. She must warn Chris.

She lifted her head and walked back toward the white two-story house. She had just rented the house, and had been here only since yesterday. She hadn't entirely unpacked. Hadn't the agent said something about draining the pond, that it wouldn't be too difficult or expensive? Was there a spring under it? Elinor hoped not, because she'd taken the house for six months.

It was two in the afternoon, and Chris was having his nap. There were more kitchen cartons to unpack, also the record player in its neat taped carton. Elinor fished the record player out, connected it, and chose an LP of New Orleans jazz to pick her up. She hoisted another load of dishes up to the long drainboard.

The doorbell rang.

Elinor was confronted by the smiling face of a woman about her own age.

"Hello. I'm Jane Caldwell—one of your neighbors. I just wanted to say hello and welcome. We're friends of Jimmy Adams, the agent, and he told us you'd moved in here."

"Yes. My name's Elinor Sievert. Won't you come in?" Elinor held the door wider. "I'm not quite unpacked as yet—but at least we could have a cup of coffee in the kitchen."

Within a few minutes they were sitting on opposite sides of the wooden table, cups of instant coffee before them. Jane said she had two children, a boy and a girl, the girl just starting school, and that her husband was an architect and worked in Hartford.

"What brought you to Luddington?" Jane asked.

"I needed a change—from New York. I'm a freelance journalist, so I thought I'd try a few months in the country. At least I call this the country, compared to New York."

"I can understand that. I heard about your husband," Jane said on a more serious note. "I'm sorry. Especially since you have a small son. I want you to know we're a friendly batch around here, and at the same time we'll let you alone, if that's what you want. But consider Ed and me neighbors, and if you need something, just call on us."

"Thank you," Elinor said. She remembered that she'd told Adams that her husband had recently died, because Adams had asked if her husband would be living with her. Now Jane was ready to go, not having finished her coffee.

"I know you've got things to do, so I don't want to take any more of your time," said Jane. She had rosy cheeks, chestnut hair. "I'll give you Ed's business card, but it's got our home number on it too. If you want to ask any kind of question, just call us. We've been here six years. —Where's your little boy?"

"He's—"

As if on cue Chris called, "Mommy!" from the top of the stairs.

Elinor jumped up. "Come down, Chris. Meet a nice new neighbor."

Chris came down the stairs a bit timidly, holding onto the banister.

Jane stood beside Elinor at the foot of the staircase. "Hello, Chris. My name's Jane. How are you?"

Chris's blue eyes examined her seriously. "Hello."

Elinor smiled. "I think he just woke up and doesn't know where he is. Say 'How do you do,' Chris."

"How do you do," said Chris.

"Hope you'll like it here, Chris," Jane said. "I want you to meet my boy Bill. He's just your age. Bye-bye, Elinor. Bye, Chris." Jane went out the front door.

Elinor gave Chris his glass of milk and his treat—today a bowl of applesauce. Elinor was against chocolate cupcakes every afternoon, though Chris at the moment thought they were the greatest food ever invented. "Wasn't she nice? Jane?" Elinor said, finishing her coffee.

"Who is she?"

"One of our new neighbors." Elinor continued her unpacking. Her article-in-progress was about self-help with legal problems. She would need to go to the Hartford library, which had a newspaper department, for more research. Hartford was only a half hour away. Elinor had bought a good second-hand car. Maybe Jane would know a girl who could baby-sit now and then. "Isn't it nicer here than in New York?"

Chris lifted his blond head. "I want to go outside."

"But of course. It's so sunny you won't need a sweater. We've got a garden, Chris. We can plant—radishes, for instance." She remembered planting radishes in her grandmother's garden when she was small, remembered the joy of pulling up the fat red and white roots—edible. "Come on, Chris." She took his hand.

Chris's slight frown went away as he gripped his mother's hand.

Elinor looked at the garden with different eyes, Chris's eyes. Plainly no one had tended the garden for months. There were big prickly weeds between the jonquils that were beginning to open, and the peonies hadn't been cut last year. But there was an apple tree big enough for Chris to climb in.

"Our garden," Elinor said. "Nice and sloppy. All yours to play in, Chris, and the summer's just beginning."

"How big is this?" Chris asked. He had broken away and was stooped by the pond.

Elinor knew he meant how deep was it. "I don't know. Not very deep. But don't go wading. It's not like the seashore with sand. It's all muddy there." Elinor spoke quickly. Anxiety had struck her like a physical pain. Was she still reliving the impact of Cliff's plane against the mountainside—that mountain in Yugoslavia that she'd never see? She'd seen two or three newspaper photographs of it, blotchy black and white chaos, indicating, so the print underneath said, the wreckage of the airliner on which there had been no survivors of 107 passengers plus eight crewmen and stewardesses.

No survivors. And Cliff among them. Elinor had always thought air crashes happened to strangers, never to anyone you knew, never even to a friend of a friend. Suddenly it had been Cliff, on an ordinary flight from Ankara. He'd been to Ankara at least seven times before.

"Is that a snake? Look, Mommy!" Chris yelled, leaning forward as he spoke. One foot sank, his arms shot forward for balance, and suddenly he was in water up to his hips. "Ugh! Ha-ha!" He rolled sideways on the muddy edge and squirmed backward up to the level of the lawn before his mother could reach him.

Elinor set him on his feet. "Chris, I told you not to try wading! Now you'll need a bath. You see?"

"No, I won't!" Chris yelled, laughing, and ran off across the grass, his bare legs and sandals flying, as if the muddy damp on his shorts had given him a special charge.

Elinor had to smile. Such energy! She looked down at the pond. The brown and black mud swirled, stirring long tentacles of vines, making the algae undulate. It was at least seven feet in diameter, the pond. A vine had clung to Chris's ankle as she'd pulled him up. Nasty! The vines were even growing out onto the grass to a length of three feet or more.

Before five p.m. Elinor phoned the rental agent. She asked if it would be all right with the owner if she had the pond drained. Price wasn't of much concern to her, but she didn't tell Adams that.

"It might seep up again," said Adams. "The land's pretty low. Especially when it rains and—"

"I really don't mind trying it. It might help," Elinor said. "You know how it is with a small child. I have the feeling it isn't quite safe."

Adams said he would telephone a company tomorrow morning. "Even this afternoon, if I can reach them."

He telephoned back in ten minutes and told Elinor that the workmen would arrive the next morning, probably quite early.

The workmen came at eight a.m. After speaking with the two men, Elinor took Chris with her in the car to the library in Hartford. She deposited Chris in the children's book section, and told the woman in charge there that she would be back in an hour for Chris, and in case he got restless she would be in the newspaper archives.

When she and Chris got back home, the pond was empty but muddy. If anything, it looked worse, uglier. It was a crater of wet mud laced with green vines, some as thick as a cigarette. The depression in the garden was hardly four feet deep. But how deep was the mud?

"I'm sad," said Chris, gazing down.

Elinor laughed. "Sad? —The pond's not the only thing to play with. Look at the trees we've got! What about the seeds we bought? What do you say we clear a patch and plant some carrots and radishes—now?"

Elinor changed into blue jeans. The clearing of weeds and the planting took longer than she had thought it would, nearly two hours. She worked with a fork and a trowel, both a bit rusty, which she'd found in the toolshed behind the house. Chris drew a bucket of water from the outside faucet and lugged it over, but while she and Chris were putting the seeds carefully in, one inch deep, a roll of thunder crossed the heavens. The sun had vanished. Within seconds rain was pelting down, big drops that made them run for the house.

"Isn't that wonderful? Look!" Elinor held Chris up so he could see out a kitchen window. "We don't need to water our seeds. Nature's doing it for us."

"Who's nature?"

Elinor smiled, tired now. "Nature rules everything. Nature knows best. The garden's going to look fresh and new tomorrow."

The following morning the garden did look rejuvenated, the grass greener, the scraggly rosebushes more erect. The sun was shining again. And Elinor had her first letter. It was from Cliff's mother in Evanston. It said:

"Dearest Elinor,

"We both hope you are feeling more cheerful in your Connecticut house. Do drop us a line or telephone us when you find the time, but we know you are busy getting settled, not to mention getting back to your own work. We send you all good wishes for success with your next articles, and you must keep us posted.

"The color snapshots of Chris in his bath are a joy to us! You mustn't say he looks more like Cliff than you. He looks like both of you . . ."

The letter lifted Elinor's spirits. She went out to see if the carrot and radish seeds had been beaten to the surface by the rain—in which case she meant to push them down again if she could see them—but the first thing that caught her eye was Chris, stooped again by the pond and poking at something with a stick. And the second thing she noticed was that the pond was full again. Almost as high as ever!

Well, naturally, because of the hard rain. Or was it naturally? It had to be. Maybe there was a spring below. Anyway, she thought, why should she pay for the draining if it didn't stay drained? She'd have to ring the company today. Miller Brothers, it was called.

"Chris? What're you up to?"

"Frog!" he yelled back. "I *think* I saw a frog."

"Well, don't try to catch it!" Damn the weeds! They were back in full force, as if the brief draining had done them good. Elinor went to the toolshed. She thought she remembered seeing a pair of hedge clippers on the cement floor there.

Elinor found the clippers, rusted, and though she was eager to attack the vines she forced herself to go to the kitchen first and put a couple of drops of salad oil on the center screw of the clippers. Then she went out and started on the long grapevinelike stems. The clippers were dull, but better than nothing, and still faster than scissors.

"What're you doing that for?" Chris asked.

"They're nasty things," Elinor said. "Clogging the pond. We don't want a messy pond, do we?" *Whack whack!* Elinor's espadrilles sank into the wet bank. What on earth did the owners, or the former tenants, use the pond for? Gold-fish? Ducks?

A carp, Elinor thought suddenly. If the pond was going to stay a pond, then a carp was the thing to keep it clean, to nibble at some of the vegetation. She'd buy one.

"If you ever fall in, Chris—"

"What?" Chris, stooped on the other side of the pond now, flung his stick away.

"For goodness' sake, don't fall in, but if you do"—Elinor forced herself to go on—"grab hold of these vines. You see? They're strong and growing from the edges. Pull your-self out by them." Actually, the vines seemed to be growing from underwater as well, and pulling at those might send Chris deeper into the pond.

Chris grinned, sideways. "It's not deep. Not even deep as I am."

Elinor said nothing.

The rest of that morning she worked on her law article, then telephoned Miller Brothers.

"Well, the ground's a little low there, ma'am. Not to mention the old cesspool's nearby and it still gets the drain from the kitchen sink, even though the toilets've been put on the mains. We know that house. Pond'll get it too if you've got a washing machine in the kitchen."

Elinor hadn't. "You mean, draining it is hopeless?"

"That's about the size of it."

Elinor tried to force her anger down. "Then I don't know why you agreed to do it."

"Because you seemed set on it, ma'am."

They hung up a few seconds later. What was she going to do about the bill when they presented it? She'd perhaps make them knock it down a bit. But she felt the situation was inconclusive. And Elinor hated that.

While Chris was taking his nap, Elinor made a quick trip to Hartford, found a fish shop, and brought back a carp in a red plastic bucket which she had taken with her in the car. The fish flopped about in a vigorous way, and Elinor drove slowly, so the bucket wouldn't tip over. She went at once to the pond and poured the fish in.

It was a fat silvery carp. Its tail flicked the surface as it dove, then it rose and dove again, apparently happy in wider seas. Elinor smiled. The carp would surely eat some of the vines, the algae. She'd give it bread too. Carps could eat anything. Cliff had used to say there was nothing like carp to keep a pond or a lake clean. Above all, Elinor liked the idea that there was something *alive* in the pond besides vines.

She started to walk back to the house and found that a vine had encircled her left ankle. When she tried to kick her foot free, the vine tightened. She stooped and unwound it. That was one she hadn't whacked this morning. Or had it grown ten inches since this morning? Impossible.

But now as she looked down at the pond and at its border, she couldn't see that she had accomplished much, even though she'd fished out quite a heap. The heap was a few feet away on the grass, in case she doubted it. Elinor blinked. She had the feeling that if she watched the pond closely, she'd be able to see the tentacles growing. She didn't like that idea.

Should she tell Chris about the carp? Elinor didn't want him poking into the water, trying to find it. On the other hand, if she didn't mention it, maybe he'd see it and have some crazy idea of catching it. Better to tell him, she decided.

So when Chris woke up Elinor told him about the fish.

"You can toss some bread to him," Elinor said. "But don't try to catch him, because he likes the pond. He's going to help us keep it clean."

"You don't want ever to catch him?" Chris asked, with milk all over his upper lip.

He was thinking of Cliff, Elinor knew. Cliff had loved fishing. "We don't catch this one, Chris. He's our friend."

Elinor worked. She had set up her typewriter in a front corner room upstairs which had light from two windows. The article was coming along nicely. She had a lot of original material from newspaper clippings. The theme was to alert the public to free legal advice from small-claims offices which most people didn't know existed. Lots of people let sums like $250 go by the board, because they thought it wasn't worth the trouble of a court fight.

Elinor worked until 6:30. Dinner was simple tonight, macaroni and cheese with bacon, one of Chris's favorite dishes. With the dinner in the oven, Elinor took a quick bath and put on blue slacks and a fresh blouse. She paused to look at the photograph of Cliff on the dressing table—a photograph in a silver frame which had been a present from Cliff's parents one Christmas.

It was an ordinary black-and-white enlargement showing Cliff sitting on the bank of a stream, propped against a tree, an old straw hat tipped back on his head. The picture had been taken somewhere outside of Evanston, on one of their summer trips to visit his parents. Cliff held a straw or a blade of grass lazily between his lips. His denim shirt was open at the neck. No one, looking at the hillbilly image, would imagine that Cliff had had to dress up in white tie a couple of times a month in Paris, Rome, London, and Ankara. Cliff had been in the diplomatic service, assistant or deputy to American statesmen, and had been gifted in languages, gifted in tact.

What had Cliff done exactly? Elinor knew only sketchy anecdotes that he had told her. He had done enough, however, to be paid a good salary, to be paid to keep silent, even to her. It had crossed her mind that his plane had been wrecked to kill him, but she assured herself that was absurd. Cliff hadn't been that important. His death had been an accident, not due to the weather but to a mechanical failure in the plane.

What would Cliff have thought of the pond? Elinor smiled wryly. Would he have had it filled in with stones, turned it into a rock garden? Would he have filled it in with earth? Would he have paid no attention at all to the pond? Just called it "nature"?

Two days later, when Elinor was typing a final draft of her article, she stopped at noon and went out into the garden for some fresh air. She'd brought the kitchen scissors, and she cut two red roses and one white rose to put on the table at lunch. Then the pond caught her eye, a blaze of chartreuse in the sunlight.

"Good Lord!" she whispered.

The vines! The weeds! They were all over the surface.
And they were again climbing onto the land. Well, this was
one thing she could and would see to: she'd find an exterminator. She didn't care what poison they put down in the
pond, if they could clear it. Of course she'd rescue the carp
first and keep him in a bucket till the pond was safe again.

An exterminator was someone Jane Caldwell might
know about.

Elinor telephoned her before she started lunch. "This
pond," Elinor began and stopped, because she had so much
to say about it. "I had it drained a few days ago, and now
it's filled up again . . . No, that's not really the problem.
I've given up the draining, it's the unbelievable vines. The
way they grow! I wonder if you know a weed-killing company? I think it'll take a professional—I mean, I don't think
I can just toss in some liquid poison and get anywhere.
You'll have to see this pond to believe it. It's like a jungle!"

"I know just the right people," Jane said. "They're called
'Weed-Killer,' so it's easy to remember. You've got a
phone book there?"

Elinor had. Jane said Weed-Killer was very obliging and
wouldn't make her wait a week before they turned up.

"How about you and Chris coming over for tea this afternoon?" Jane asked. "I just made a coconut cake."

"Love to. Thank you." Elinor felt cheered.

She made lunch for herself and Chris, and told him they
were invited to tea at the house of their neighbor Jane, and
that he'd meet a boy called Bill. After lunch Elinor looked
up Weed-Killer in the telephone book and rang them.

"It's a lot of weeds in a pond," Elinor said. "Can you
deal with that?"

The man assured her they were experts at weeds in ponds
and promised to come over the following morning. Elinor
wanted to work for an hour or so until it was time to go to
Jane's, but she felt compelled to catch the carp now, or try
to. If she failed, she'd tell the men about it tomorrow, and
probably they'd have a net on a long handle and could

catch it. Elinor took her vegetable sieve which had a handle some ten inches long, and also some pieces of bread.

Not seeing the carp, Elinor tossed her bread onto the surface. Some pieces floated, others sank and were trapped among the vines. Elinor circled the pond, her sieve ready. She had half filled the plastic bucket and it sat on the bank.

Suddenly she saw the fish. It was horizontal and motionless, a couple of inches under the surface. It was dead, she realized, and kept from the surface only by the vines that held it under. Dead from what? The water didn't look dirty, in fact was rather clear. What could kill a carp? Cliff had always said—

Elinor's eyes were full of tears. Tears for the carp? Nonsense. Tears of frustration, maybe. She stooped and tried to reach the carp with the sieve. The sieve was a foot short, and she wasn't going to muddy her tennis shoes by wading in. Not now. Best to work a bit this afternoon and let the workmen lift it out tomorrow.

"What're you doing, Mommy?" Chris came trotting toward her.

"Nothing. I'm going to work a little now. I thought you were watching TV."

"It's no good. Where's the fish?"

Elinor took his wrist and swung him around. "The fish is fine. Now come back and we'll put on the TV again." Elinor tried to think of something else that might amuse him. It wasn't one of his napping days, obviously. "Tell you what, Chris, you choose one of your toys to take to Bill. Make him a present. All right?"

"One of *my* toys?"

Elinor smiled. Chris was generous enough by nature and she meant to nurture this trait. "Yes, one of yours. Even one you like—like your paratrooper. Or one of your books. You choose it. Bill's going to be your friend, and you want to start out right, don't you?"

"Yes." And Chris seemed to be pondering already, going over his store of goodies in his room upstairs.

Elinor locked the back door with its bolt, which was on a level with her eyes. She didn't want Chris going into the garden, maybe seeing the carp. "I'll be in my room, and I'll see you at four. You might put on a clean pair of jeans at four—if you remember to."

Elinor worked, and quite well. It was pleasant to have a tea date to look forward to. Soon, she thought, she'd ask Jane and her husband for drinks. She didn't want people to think she was a melancholy widow. It had been three months since Cliff's death. Elinor thought she'd got over the worst of her grief in those first two weeks, the weeks of shock. Had she really? For the past six weeks she'd been able to work. That was something. Cliff's insurance plus his pension made her financially comfortable, but she needed to work to be happy.

When she glanced at her watch it was ten to four. "Chris!" Elinor called to her half-open door. "Changed your jeans?"

She pushed open Chris's door across the hall. He was not in his room, and there were more toys and books on the floor than usual, indicating that Chris had been trying to select something to give to Bill. Elinor went downstairs where the TV was still murmuring, but Chris wasn't in the living room. Nor was he in the kitchen. She saw that the back door was still bolted. Chris wasn't on the front lawn either. Of course he could have gone to the garden by the front door. Elinor unbolted the kitchen door and went out.

"Chris?" She glanced everywhere, then focused on the pond. She had seen a light-colored patch in its center. *"Chris!"* She ran.

He was facedown, feet out of sight, his blond head nearly submerged. Elinor plunged in, up to her knees, her thighs, seized Chris's legs and pulled him out, slipped, sat down in the water, and got soaked as high as her breasts. She struggled to her feet, holding Chris by the waist. Shouldn't she try to let the water run out of his mouth? Elinor was panting.

She turned Chris onto his stomach, gently lifted his small body by the waist, hoping water would run from his nose and mouth, but she was too frantic to look. He was limp, soft in a way that frightened her. She pressed his rib cage, released it, raised him a little again. One had to do artificial respiration methodically, counting, she remembered. She did this . . . fifteen . . . sixteen . . . Someone should be telephoning for a doctor. She couldn't do two things at once.

"Help!" she yelled. "Help me, *please*!" Could the people next door hear? The house was twenty yards away, and was anybody home?

She turned Chris over and pressed her mouth to his cool lips. She blew in, then released his ribs, trying to catch a gasp from him, a cough that would mean life. He remained limp. She turned him on his stomach and resumed the artificial respiration. It was now or never, she knew. Senseless to waste time carrying him into the house for warmth. He could've been lying in the pond for an hour—in which case, she knew it was hopeless.

Elinor picked her son up and carried him toward the house. She went into the kitchen. There was a sagging sofa against the wall, and she put him there.

Then she telephoned Jane Caldwell, whose number was on the card by the telephone where Elinor had left it days ago. Since Elinor didn't know a doctor in the vicinity, it made as much sense to call Jane as to search for a doctor's name.

"Hello, *Jane!*" Elinor said, her voice rising wildly. "I think Chris has drowned! —Yes! *Yes!* Can you get a doctor? Right away?" Suddenly the line was dead.

Elinor hung up and went at once to Chris, started the rib pressing again, Chris now prone on the floor with his face turned to one side. The activity soothed her a little.

The doorbell rang and at the same time Elinor heard the latch of the door being opened. Then Jane called, "Elinor?"

"In the kitchen!"

The doctor had dark hair and spectacles. He lifted Chris a little, felt for a pulse. "How long—how long was he—"

"I don't know. I was working upstairs. It was the pond in the garden."

The rest was confused to Elinor. She barely realized when the needle went into her own arm, though this was the most definite sensation she had for several minutes. Jane made tea. Elinor had a cup in front of her. When she looked at the floor, Chris was not there.

"Where is he?" Elinor asked.

Jane gripped Elinor's hand. She sat opposite Elinor. "The doctor took Chris to the hospital. Chris is in good hands, you can be sure of that. This doctor delivered Bill. He's our family doctor."

But from Jane's tone Elinor knew it was all useless, and that Jane knew this too. Elinor's eyes drifted from Jane's face. She noticed a book lying on the cane bottom of the chair beside her. Chris had chosen his dotted-numbers book to give to Bill, a book that Chris rather liked. He wasn't half through doing the drawing. Chris could count and he was doing quite well at reading too. *I wasn't doing so well at his age,* Cliff had said not long ago.

Elinor began to weep.

"That's good. That's good for you," Jane said. "I'll stay here with you. Pretty soon we'll hear from the hospital. Maybe you want to lie down, Elinor? —I've got to make a phone call."

The sedative was taking effect. Elinor sat in a daze on the sofa, her head back against a pillow. The telephone rang and Jane took it. The hospital, Elinor supposed. She watched Jane's face, and knew. Elinor nodded her head, trying to spare Jane any words, but Jane said, "They tried. I'm sure they did everything possible."

Jane said she would stay the night. She said she had arranged for Ed to pick up Bill at a house where she'd left him.

In the morning Weed-Killer came, and Jane asked Elinor if she still wanted the job done.

"I thought you might've decided to move," Jane said.

Had she said that? Possibly. "But I do want it done."

The two Weed-Killer men got to work.

Jane made another telephone call, then told Elinor that a friend of hers named Millie was coming over at noon. When Millie arrived, Jane prepared a lunch of bacon and eggs for the three of them. Millie had blond curly hair, blue eyes, and was very cheerful and sympathetic.

"I went by the doctor's," Millie said, "and his nurse gave me these pills. They're a sedative. He thinks they'd be good for you. Two a day, one before lunch, one before bedtime. So have one now."

They hadn't started lunch. Elinor took one. The work-men were just departing, and one man stuck his head in the door to say with a smile, "All finished, ma'am. You shouldn't have any trouble any more."

During lunch Elinor said, "I've got to see about the fu-neral."

"We'll help you. Don't think about it now," Jane said. "Try to eat a little."

Elinor ate a little, then slept on the sofa in the kitchen. She hadn't wanted to go up to her own bed. When she woke up, Millie was sitting in the wicker armchair, reading a book.

"Feeling better? Want some tea?"

"In a minute. You're awfully kind. I do thank you very much." She stood up. "I want to see the pond." She saw Millie's look of uneasiness. "They killed those vines today. I'd like to see what it looks like."

Millie went out with her. Elinor looked down at the pond and had the satisfaction of seeing that no vines lay on the surface, that some pieces of them had sunk like drowned things. Around the edge of the pond were stubs of vines al-ready turning yellow and brownish, wilting. Before her eyes one cropped tentacle curled sideways and down, as if in the throes of death. A primitive joy went through her, a sense of vengeance, of a wrong righted.

"It's a nasty pond," Elinor said to Millie. "It killed a carp. Can you imagine? I've never heard of a carp being—"

"I know. They must've been growing like blazes. But they're certainly finished now." Millie held out her hand for Elinor to take. "Don't think about it."

Millie wanted to go back to the house. Elinor did not take her hand, but she came with Millie. "I'm feeling bet-ter. You mustn't give up all your time to me. It's very nice of you, since you don't even know me. But I've got to face my problems alone."

Millie made a polite reply.

Elinor really was feeling better. She'd have to go through the funeral next, Chris's funeral, but she sensed in herself a backbone, a morale—whatever it was called. After the ser-vice for Chris—surely it would be simple—she'd invite her

new neighbors, few as they might be, to her house for coffee or drinks or both. Food too.

Elinor realized that her spirits had picked up because the
pool was vanquished. She'd have it filled in with stones,
with the agent's and also the owner's permission of course.
Why should she retreat from the house? With stones showing just above the water it would look every bit as pretty,
maybe prettier, and it wouldn't be dangerous for the next
child who came to live here.

The service for Chris was held at a small local church.
The preacher conducted a short nondenominational ceremony. And afterward, around noon, Elinor did have a few
people to the house for sandwiches and coffee. The
strangers seemed to enjoy it. Elinor even heard a few
laughs among the group, which gladdened her heart.

She hadn't, as yet, phoned any of her New York friends
to tell them about Chris. Elinor realized that some people
might think that "strange" of her, but she felt that it would
only sadden her friends to tell them, that it would look like
a plea for sympathy. Better the strangers here who knew no
grief, because they didn't really know her or Chris.

"You must be sure and get enough rest in the next days,"
said a kindly middle-aged woman whose husband stood
solemnly beside her. "We all think you've been awfully
brave."

Elinor gave Jane the dotted-numbers book to take to Bill.

That night Elinor slept more than twelve hours and
awoke feeling better and calmer. She began to write the letters that she had to write—to Cliff's parents, to her own
mother and father, and to three good friends in New York.
Then she finished typing her article.

The next morning she walked to the post office and sent
off her letters, and also her article to her agent in New
York. She spent the rest of the day sorting out Chris's
clothing, his books and toys, and she washed some of his
clothes with a view to passing them on to Jane for Bill, pro-
viding Jane wouldn't think it unlucky. Elinor didn't think
Jane would. Jane telephoned in the afternoon to ask how
she was.

"Is anyone coming to see you? From New York? A friend, I mean?"

Elinor explained that she'd written to a few people, but she wasn't expecting anyone. "I'm really feeling all right, Jane. You mustn't worry."

By evening Elinor had a neat carton of clothing ready to offer Jane, and two more cartons of books and toys. If the clothes didn't fit Bill, then Jane might know a child they would fit. Elinor felt better for that. It was a lot better than collapsing in grief, she thought. Of course it was awful, a tragedy that didn't happen every day—losing a husband and a child in hardly more than three months. But Elinor was not going to succumb to it. She'd stay out the six months in the house here, come to terms with her loss, and emerge strong, someone able to give something to other people, not merely to take.

She had two ideas for future articles. Which to do first? She decided to walk out into the garden and let her thoughts ramble. Maybe the radishes had come up? She'd have a look at the pond. Maybe it would be glassy smooth and clear. She must ask the Weed-Killer people when it would be safe to put in another carp—or two carps.

When she looked at the pond she gave a short gasp. The vines had come *back*.

They looked stronger than ever—not longer, but more dense. Even as she watched, one tentacle, then a second, actually moved, curved toward the land and seemed to grow an inch. That hadn't been due to the wind.

The vines were growing visibly. Another green shoot poked its head above the water's surface. Elinor watched, fascinated, as if she beheld animate things, like snakes. Every inch or so along the vines a small green leaf sprouted, and Elinor was sure she could see some of these unfurling.

The water looked clean, but she knew that was deceptive. The water was somehow poisonous. It had killed a carp. It had killed Chris. And she could still detect, she thought, a rather acid smell of the stuff the Weed-Killer men had put in.

There must be such a thing as digging the roots out, Eli-

nor thought, even if Weed-Killer's stuff had failed. Elinor
got the fork from the toolshed, and the clippers. She
thought of getting her rubber boots from the house, but was
too eager to start to bother with them. She began by hack-
ing all round the edge with the clippers. Some fresh vine
ends cruised over the pond and jammed themselves amid
other growing vines. The stems now seemed tough as plastic clotheslines, as if the herbicide had fortified them. Some
had put down roots in the grass quite a distance from the
pond.

Elinor dropped the clippers and seized the fork. She had
to dig deep to get at the roots, and when she finally pulled
with her hands, the stems broke, leaving some roots still in
the soil. Her right foot slipped, she went down on her left
knee and struggled up again, both legs wet now. She was
not going to be defeated,.

As she sank the fork in, she saw Cliff's handsome, subtly
smiling eyes in the photograph in the bedroom, Cliff with
the blade of grass or straw between his lips, and he seemed
to be nodding ever so slightly, approving. Her arms began
to ache, her hands grew tired. She lost her right shoe in
dragging her foot out of the water yet again, and she didn't
bother trying to recover it. Then she slipped again and sat
down, water up to her waist.

Tired, angry, she still worked with the fork, trying to pry
roots loose, and the water churned with a muddy fury. She
might even be doing the damned roots good, she thought.
Aerating them or something. Were they invincible? Why
should they be? The sun poured down, overheating her,
bringing nourishment to the green, Elinor knew.

Nature knows. That was Cliff's voice in her ears. Cliff
sounded happy and at ease.

Elinor was half blinded by tears. Or was it sweat? *Chun-nk*
went her fork. In a moment, when her arms gave out, she'd
cross to the other side of the pond and attack there. She'd
got some roots out. She'd make Weed-Killer come again,
maybe pour kerosene on the pond and light it.

She got up on cramped legs and stumbled around to the
other side. The sun warmed her shoulders though her feet
were cold. In those few seconds that she walked, her

thoughts and her attitude changed, though she was not at once aware of this. It was neither victory nor defeat that she felt.

She sank the fork in again, again slipped and recovered. Again roots slid between the tines of the fork, and were not removed. A tentacle thicker than most moved toward her and circled her right ankle. She kicked, and the vine tightened, and she fell forward.

She went facedown into the water, but the water seemed soft. She struggled a little, turned to breathe, and a vine tickled her neck. She saw Cliff nodding again, smiling his kindly, knowing, almost imperceptible smile. It was nature. It was Cliff. It was Chris.

A vine crept around her arm—loose or attached to the earth she neither knew nor cared. She breathed in, and much of what she took in was water. *All things come from water,* Cliff had said once. Little Chris smiled at her with both corners of his mouth upturned. She saw him stooped by the pond, reaching for the dead carp which floated out of range of his twig. Then Chris lifted his face again and smiled.

THE GRIN REAPER

RICHARD F. McGONEGAL

Miss Alice was a "bumper." Whenever she wanted to get someone's attention, she bumped with her wheelchair. She bumped doors, shins, even other wheelchairs—including mine.

I was parked in the lobby, my favorite locale within the confines of Oak Forest Manor Care Center, on the Monday afternoon when Miss Alice bumped against the waist-high wall of Mrs. Wallace's work station.

Mrs. Wallace peered over the frames of her eyeglasses, over the wall of the work station, and down at Miss Alice. "Yes?" she said, obviously preoccupied with her duties. Despite the tortoise-shell eyeglasses, the hair pinned up beneath the nurse's cap, and the stiff, shapeless white uniform, Mrs. Wallace remained beautiful. Her smile revealed dainty dimples and her cheeks effused a rosy blush, enhanced of late by the crisp autumnal air. She was young, vibrant, and curvaceous, although she labored diligently to disguise those attributes. We suspected—and gossiped—that she tried to create an impression of professional efficiency. Her efforts, however, were hardly necessary. During her eight-year tenure as director of the nursing home, neither her professionalism nor her efficiency had ever been called into question.

"Is The Grin Reaper coming tonight?" Miss Alice asked, flashing a broad smile. Her smile, like her bumping, was habitual. It revealed rows of pristine white dentures which contrasted with her pale, shriveled lips and yellowing, wrinkled skin. She was wrapped in her customary lavender robe and seated on her chromium-frame wheelchair. The visual effect bordered on surrealism. I was compelled to consider that if Salvador Dali had ever selected old folks as subject matter, the finished canvas assuredly would bear a striking resemblance to Miss Alice.

"Yes, he's coming," Mrs. Wallace replied. "It's been posted on the board for a week," she added, motioning to the bulletin board on the wall across from her work station.

Miss Alice, however, was off and wheeling before Mrs. Wallace had finished her addendum. "Oh, I must tell the others. They'll be so thrilled," she said, as she rolled past me on her way out the Plexiglas-fronted recreation room. The automatic doors slid open as she announced: "News, everyone."

I resisted the temptation to call out that everyone already knew of the scheduled visit. It had been the talk of Oak Forest for the past week, and Miss Alice had certainly been among the talkers. Still, Miss Alice was nothing if not forgetful, and although it was often frustrating, we all tended to indulge her when she announced her "news."

The Grin Reaper was known on every day except Halloween as Zachariah Selby Peters, Jr. He earned his nickname when he first swept into the recreation room at Oak Forest Manor Care Center two Halloweens ago dressed as the harbinger of death.

His appearance had elicited a number of gasps—most noticeably from Miss Alice and Miroslav Miskov—but it was Zachariah Selby Peters, Jr., who turned out to be the most shocked and embarrassed of the group.

He confessed he had never even considered the impact his costume might have on an enclave of septuagenarians and octogenarians. He apologized profusely and offered to leave.

In an attempt to assuage our own embarrassment, we pleaded with him to stay, and the resulting party was so atypically enjoyable that we invited him to reprise his role on succeeding Halloweens. It was Miskov, the native of Estonia, who—with chance exactitude born of characteristic mispronunciation—dubbed our guest "The Grin Reaper."

Zachariah Selby Peters, Jr., was a chip off the old block, the old block being one of our fellow "tenants": Zachariah Selby Peters, Sr., known to us as "Big Pete."

I was stationed at my usual vantage point in the lobby on a sunny March day nearly two and a half years ago when Big Pete first hobbled through the doorway, followed by his son.

"Howdy, miss," the elder man had said, addressing Mrs. Wallace. "Name's Big Pete." He leaned his massive two-hundred-forty-pound, six-foot frame on his wooden crutches and offered her a large, calloused hand. She winced as she shook it.

"Howdy, pardner," he said, turning to me. "What ya in for?"

"Five to ten for arthritis," I said. He laughed and shook my hand gently; I smiled. I liked him immediately.

"Where's my manners?" he asked. "This here's my boy, but he don't take to being called 'Little Pete.' "

"Call me Zach," the son said. We—Zach, Mrs. Wallace, and I—exchanged handshakes. I liked Zach, too, and I sensed that Mrs. Wallace, despite her disapproving look, also liked them both.

I guessed Zach to be in his mid-thirties, about half his dad's age. Although father and son shared similar facial features, Zach was taller and much lankier—a younger, stretched-out version of his sire.

"Well, Zach," Big Pete intoned loudly as he hobbled around the lobby, "whaddya think?"

"Seems nice," Zach replied.

"Nice!" Big Pete bellowed. "Why, it's a gotdamn palace. Look at these floors, clean as a new ball bearin'; look at this glass." He rapped on the Plexiglas. "Why, it's clear as . . ." He shrugged. "Clear as glass." He paused and stared at Mrs. Wallace. "And I'll have this purdy lady to watch over me, keep me in line. Yep, I sure could get used to hangin' my hat in a place like this."

I knew immediately that Big Pete wouldn't "fit in" with the clientele at Oak Forest. We were, for the most part, the established "old money" elderly of the community. We were perceived as the sophisticated, the genteel, the wealthy, and the boring. I suspected Big Pete was none of the above. In short, he was everything we needed to add a little zest to our cloistered world.

Still, my better judgment told me Mrs. Wallace would never open our doors to a piker, particularly since Oak Forest was a private facility which received no government subsidies.

After overhearing Mrs. Wallace explain the rates to Big Pete, I learned that my earlier suspicions were only seventy-five percent correct. Although Big Pete was neither sophisticated, genteel, nor boring, he was wealthy.

"Why, that's peanuts, little lady," he roared in response, then went on to explain in detail how he had converted a back yard mechanic's shed into a thriving business, Big Pete's Farm Machinery Sales and Service.

Mrs. Wallace gave Big Pete the grand tour, he signed the required documents, and when he moved in a few days later, the fun began.

The first item on Big Pete's agenda was organizing a surreptitious late night poker game. Miss Alice, Miskov, Hortense Diekroeger, and I would all sneak into Big Pete's room after "lights out," Big Pete would jam a wadded-up towel beneath the door and duct-tape the doorframe to mask any telltale light, and the game would begin.

I had expected Big Pete would be a cagey card player, and Hortense, I knew, was a wily old bird, so I was counting on Miss Alice and Miskov to be the easy marks. Again, I was only seventy-five percent correct.

The first hand, dealt by Big Pete, was five card stud, nothing wild. Hortense and Miskov had folded, Miss Alice had a pair of eights, an ace, and a four showing, and Big Pete had a pair of jacks. I had one king up and one in the hole. Big Pete and I exchanged repeated raises, oblivious to Miss Alice, who seemed to be naively kicking in cash.

Finally, I called.

"You're lookin' at it—jacks," Big Pete said.

"Two kings," I announced, triumphantly, unearthing the buried monarch and reaching for the pot.

"Not so fast," Miss Alice countered. "Dead man's

hand—aces and eights," she proclaimed, flipping over her ace in the hole.

When the game concluded at two A.M., Miss Alice proved to be the big winner, a feat she duplicated in subsequent games.

Although our fivesome eagerly awaited the twice-weekly poker games, Big Pete remained restless. He would sit in the recreation room like a scolded three-year-old, his pent-up energy begging for release, watching us as we watched television or played checkers.

One spring afternoon about six weeks after his arrival, he rolled into the recreation room in a wheelchair, a basketball in his lap. "Who's up for a little hoop?" he asked, dribbling the ball beside the chair.

"I'm game," I said. "Where'd you get the wheelchair?"

"Commandeered it from the stockroom."

"What's hoop?" Miss Alice inquired.

"Basketball," Big Pete replied.

"We don't have a net," Miskov observed.

"We do now," Big Pete said, revealing a smile so broad it wrinkled the skin beneath his eyes.

We wheeled, hobbled, and walked into the parking lot, where Zach was standing on the roof of his pickup truck, busily fastening a net to the basketball rim and backboard he had screwed into the facade of Oak Forest Manor Care Center.

"Mrs. Wallace isn't going to like this," I ventured.

Big Pete dismissed my observation with a wave of the hand. "Miskov, Hortense, and the rest of you, go swipe some more wheelchairs and we'll get rollin'," he called out.

When we were all assembled and suitably seated, Big Pete designated Miss Alice and me as team captains, since we were the most proficient in maneuvering wheelchairs. We chose sides and Big Pete explained the rules. There were two, as follows: "Everything's legal except tippin' over someone else's chair, which constitutes a foul; and anyone who can figure out how to slam dunk a shot from one of these contraptions automatically wins the game for his or her team."

The game was a disaster. We bumped and thudded into

one another's chairs, knocked the wind out of our teammates with our passes, and lost the ball into the street fourteen times. But the laughter—never in my years at Oak Forest had I heard such an outpouring of childlike giggles or seen such tears of glee from our group.

Our boisterous merriment eventually drew Mrs. Wallace to the parking lot. She eyed us sternly at first, but quickly softened. The spirit of the scene was not lost on her, and before our game ended, she was cheering every basket. Under Zach's tutelage, Mrs. Wallace became our referee and, in our second season, we designated her as manager. She recently organized our first road game against Green Meadows Skilled Nursing Facility, which we won 26-14.

Big Pete's exuberance was contagious. Miss Alice, who talked incessantly about the fabulous desserts she once made for dinner guests, started a cooking class. Miskov, a jeweler prior to retirement, began fixing watches and repairing and resetting jewelry for the tenants. Hortense offered ballroom dancing instruction for those who were ambulatory, and I, a former banker, favored my avocation over my vocation and organized fishing trips.

Our ever-increasing activities gained not only Mrs. Wallace's blessing—which we required—but also her assistance. She and Herb, the handyman, either individually or collectively, served as our chauffeurs, aides, and cheerleaders.

Mrs. Wallace possessed a good heart, but her motivation was not entirely altruistic; she also reaped significant benefits from our rejuvenation. We suffered a few bumps and scrapes from the basketball games, an occasional bruised foot from Hortense's dancing lessons, and several minor burns from Miss Alice's cooking classes, but the major maladies, once so common among the tenants, all but disappeared.

My arthritis abated, Miskov's bad heart thumped with vigorous regularity, Miss Alice's bouts of forgetfulness improved a bit, and Big Pete—whose degenerative muscle disease should have confined him to bed months ago, according to his doctors—continued to hobble along ably on his crutches.

As a further testament to our regeneration, no one had passed away since Big Pete's arrival. Death, once commonplace at Oak Forest, had been temporarily exiled, if not banished. And the appearance of The Grin Reaper, which initially had shocked, was now eagerly awaited as cause for yet another festive evening.

Like expectant children lying awake on Christmas Eve listening for the sound of hoofbeats, we had gathered in the recreation room to greet The Grin Reaper.

Miss Alice and her protégés had baked Halloween cookies bedecked with orange and black icing and concocted the punch, spiked liberally by Big Pete; Hortense had selected the music, which ranged from Bobby "Boris" Pickett's "Monster Mash" to Michael Jackson's "Thriller"; and Miskov and I had constructed the decorations, a traditional assortment of witches, skeletons, and black cats, enhanced by scattered jack-o'-lanterns and orange and black streamers.

Nature had contributed a suitably "dark and stormy night," and Mrs. Wallace was at her work station, diligently watching us while appearing to be otherwise occupied.

The door—seemingly rent by the forces of the wind—sprang open. Miss Alice gasped. Amidst a fury of swirling leaves and rippling black robes, The Grin Reaper entered. He walked rapidly and authoritatively into the recreation room, robes flowing, skeletal face masked in the shadow of his dark hood.

We laughed, albeit nervously. Zach, I considered, had outdone himself. He looked genuinely malevolent.

Miskov patted him on the shoulder and The Grin Reaper turned his head, emitting a dull squeak. It sounded like the rasping of bone on bone. I shuddered.

Hortense offered him cookies and punch, which he brushed aside with a wave of his slender arm. She stepped back and eyed him curiously.

The Grin Reaper stared at her momentarily, then at me—seeing but remaining unseen. His face was a ghostly, featureless visage hidden in hooded shadow. His gaze held me entranced, chilling me.

He turned to Miskov, to Big Pete (who smiled proudly),

to another and another. When his stare finally settled on Miss Alice, he held it for what seemed a long time before he raised his arm and pointed a bony finger at her.

She wheeled toward him; he opened the door and followed her down the corridor.

"Gotdamn," Big Pete said. "Zach's doin' a hell of a job tonight. Even gave me the heebie-jeebies."

"Where're they going?" I asked, trying to mask the alarm that was battling to overcome my common sense.

"I dunno," Big Pete replied. His tone indicated he too harbored some concern.

"We go maybe and should check on them," Miskov offered.

"Oh, don't be silly," Hortense said. "We can't just . . . well, maybe if we had some kind of reason."

"What if we . . ." I began, halting in midsentence as the front door was flung open and The Grin Reaper entered anew. He walked confidently into the recreation room, black robes swirling, face masked in shadow.

"Where's Miss Alice?" Big Pete asked.

"What?" replied The Grin Reaper. He sounded confused.

"Miss Alice, where is she?" Big Pete repeated.

"Dunno," The Grin Reaper said. "I just got here."

A collective murmur arose, then quieted as Big Pete asked: "What do you mean 'you just got here'?"

"Damn lucky to be here, too," The Grin Reaper said. "Lost the accelerator spring on my pickup as I was comin' down Overlook Road. Ran off the road through the drainage ditch and came within about fifteen feet of goin' off that bluff. Look at me, I'm still shakin'." He extended his hand as visible proof.

"You bluffin' me?" Big Pete asked. He cocked his head in a threatening, but paternal gesture which demanded the truth.

"I'm serious, Pop." He scanned our faces. "What's goin' on?"

"C'mon!" Big Pete ordered. We funneled through the automatic sliding doors and spread out, moblike, across the corridor as we marched, wheeled, and hobbled to Miss Alice's room. Mrs. Wallace, firing questions at us, scurried alongside.

Big Pete halted outside Miss Alice's room, then flung the door open. The room was dark, but light from the corridor spilled inside and illuminated the outline of The Grin Reaper as he extended his hand toward Miss Alice's bosom.

"Out," Big Pete demanded. The Grin Reaper stopped in mid-reach and stared at us. Miss Alice remained immobile, apparently transfixed. "I said: Out!" Big Pete shouted.

Miss Alice turned, as if startled into consciousness. She wheeled herself into the corridor.

"You, too," Big Pete ordered.

The Grin Reaper stepped into the doorframe, filling it. Big Pete held his ground. He looked from The Grin Reaper in the doorframe to The Grin Reaper among us in the corridor.

"You cook this up, Zach?" he asked the latter.

Zach removed his hood, revealing a face encased in white makeup. Black circles surrounded his eye sockets and dark shadows accentuated his cheekbones. He shook his head.

"Then what the hell is goin' on?" Big Pete asked no one in particular, his tone fraught with exasperation.

"He needs . . ." Miss Alice began, her voice wavering, ". . . he needs to take someone from here. We used to have people going to him regularly, but we haven't had any for some time now. So he came to visit, to take someone. But he can take only one tonight. Only one. All he has to do is touch your heart. He can reach inside you and touch your heart, and then . . ." Her words trailed wearily off.

"You can take anyone?" Big Pete asked, addressing the hooded figure in the doorframe.

The Grim Reaper—whose aspect had become even more decidedly grim—nodded.

"Then I'm your man," Big Pete said, poking himself in the chest. "Take me."

The Grim Reaper stared.

"Go ahead," Big Pete challenged, dropping his arms to his sides.

The Grim Reaper advanced, then halted as Miskov

surged from the crowd and stepped in front of Big Pete. "I the person to take," he said. "I ready."

Hortense stepped ahead of Miskov. "Me," she said, defiantly.

Big Pete rolled his eyes. "This is gettin' ridiculous," he said.

The Grim Reaper gazed at each member of the trio, evidently confused by the spirit of volunteerism.

I rolled forward, making it a foursome. "I'm the one to take," I said.

"Gotdamn," I heard Big Pete say.

"Just a minute," Mrs. Wallace interrupted, advancing from the group. She stared at The Grim Reaper. "You can take only one person tonight, right?"

The Grim Reaper nodded.

"And you can only take that person by touching the heart, correct?"

Again The Grim Reaper nodded.

"Okay," she said, turning to us. "Since we have such an abundance of volunteers, the only way to settle this is to go back to the recreation room and find a way to choose democratically."

"Democratically?" Big Pete asked with a sarcastic chuckle.

"You have a better idea?" Mrs. Wallace said.

Big Pete shrugged.

"Okay," she said. "Then let's go."

We retraced our path down the corridor and funneled back into the recreation room. "You," Mrs. Wallace said, halting The Grim Reaper near her work station, "wait here." The Grim Reaper loomed at her threateningly, but he obliged.

When we tenants and Zach had assembled within the recreation room, Mrs. Wallace reached over the wall of her work station and flipped a switch. The automatic doors slid closed and sealed.

"Oh no," I whispered, stung by the immediate realization that Mrs. Wallace and The Grim Reaper were on the outside while all of us were locked inside.

Big Pete grabbed a chair and swung it at the Plexiglas, but it bounced back harmlessly. We shouted as he swung the chair again to no avail, then watched in silent horror as Mrs. Wallace closed her eyes, tilted her head back slightly and offered her bosom to The Grim Reaper.

The hooded figure reached, his bony fingers out-stretched. His hand seemed to dematerialize inside her chest, then his body pulsated as if lit by a strobelike X-ray, revealing a skeletal shape beneath the robes and hood.

The pulsations, hammering with the regularity of a heart-beat, magnified; the illuminations intensified; the bony jaw betrayed an agonized grimace.

The Grim Reaper withdrew his hand and scowled, some-how foiled. He clutched his robes and stormed out the front door.

Mrs. Wallace opened her eyes and smiled serenely. She flipped the switch to unlock the automatic doors and en-tered the recreation room.

We stared at her, mouths agape.

"What happened?" Big Pete asked.

"I tricked him," Mrs. Wallace said calmly. "He said he could take only one person and had to touch the heart," she explained. "But he couldn't take me without taking some-one else, and he couldn't take that someone else because there's no heart to touch yet."

I pondered a moment before the revelation struck me. "You're pregnant!" I shouted.

Mrs. Wallace nodded, evincing a girlish smile. "I've been meaning to tell you," she said. "I was just waiting for the right moment."

FATAL CORNER

PATRICIA McGERR

Gresham's Department Store where I sell women's budget dresses stays open until nine o'clock three nights a week. When they asked me to work late on Thursdays and Fridays, I hesitated. I live with my parents out in the country and it's nearly an hour's drive each way. But the change meant a raise in salary as well as every other Saturday off. So, after I checked the bus schedule and found there was one leaving at 9:05 P.M. that would get me home before ten, I accepted the offer.

When I boarded the bus that first Friday, it was crowded with late shoppers, but most of them got off before we passed the city limits. By the time we turned onto the narrow road that circles Pine Tree Canyon, there were only six passengers left. I was sitting beside Mrs. Ryan, who is salad maker in the store cafeteria. We were both tired and didn't feel much like conversation, so I was watching the road in front of the bus when it made a sharp turn.

Suddenly, the headlights caught a small girl on a bicycle. She appeared to be about eight or nine years old and was dressed in shorts and a T-shirt. Her fair hair hung down her back in pigtails tied with a bright-red ribbon. At the moment I saw her, she was riding across the road directly in front of the bus. I braced myself for the fast braking that would bring the vehicle to a screeching halt. Instead, as it was almost upon the child, we seemed to increase speed. I half rose in my seat, ready to cry out a warning, but Mrs. Ryan pressed her hand over my mouth and held me back.

"Hush yourself, dear," she whispered. "It's only a ghost."

"A what? You can't—" As I sputtered a protest, the bus passed over the spot where the child had been and Mrs. Ryan took her hand away. I strained to see through the darkness beside the road, sure the rider had by some miracle escaped collision. No one was there.

"Don't be upset," Mrs. Ryan soothed. "It's the little Barlow girl. You must have heard about the accident. She was killed right in that spot last summer."

"Are you saying that her ghost haunts this road? But that's crazy!" I looked around the bus. The man across the aisle was reading a newspaper. A couple in the front seat were having an animated discussion about prices. Behind us, Miss Wylie from the accounting department was knitting a sweater. "How can they be so calm? Are you and I the only ones who saw her?"

"No, dear. We all see her, but the rest of us are used to it. She's there every Friday. We try not to take any notice. For Mr. Johnson's sake." She gestured toward the driver. "It's very hard on him, poor man. You see, he was driving the bus when it happened."

Mrs. Ryan got off at the next stop, so I wasn't able to learn any more from her that night, but at breakfast the next morning I asked my folks if they knew anything about a bus hitting a little girl on a bike.

"Oh, yes," my mother answered. "It was very sad. Surely you remember, Sis. Everyone was talking about it."

"No, I don't. It must have happened while I was on vacation."

"That's right," my father confirmed. "You came back right after Labor Day and the accident was in the middle of August."

"It was a great tragedy," my mother said. "Her name was Janey Barlow—or was it Jenny? Nine years old and a pretty little thing to judge by the picture in the paper."

"With blonde pigtails tied with a bow?"

"Well, I don't recall the bow, but—" She frowned, think-

ing it over. "Yes, she was blonde and I believe there were
pigtails. Her family hadn't lived in the area very long. They
bought a house in that new development up above the
canyon. Overpriced but very nice. They sold mostly to
young couples with children. The Barlows still live there,
don't they, Frank?"

"As far as I know. The wife had a breakdown and had to
go away for a while, but I expect she's recovered and back
home again."

"Was it the bus driver's fault?"

"Not at all," my father said. "There was a hearing, of
course, but he was completely exonerated. The people on
the bus were all witnesses. They told how the little girl
came down a side road and was right in front of the bus
when it came round the corner. He jammed on the brakes
but couldn't get it stopped in time. She was thrown off the
bicycle and struck her head on a rock. She was killed instantly, the coroner said."

"*Mr. Barlow* blamed the driver, though," my mother
added. "The paper said he stood up in court and called him
a murderer. Well, you can understand his feelings. She was
their only child."

"The driver must have felt terrible, too."

"I'm sure he did," she agreed. "It must be an awful burden to know you killed someone, even if you couldn't help
it."

"The kid shouldn't have been out that late," my father
decreed. "They ought to have taught her never to ride her
bike on the highway."

"That's easy enough to say," my mother returned. "But
the way children are nowadays, what can you do?" She
shook her head. "You can't watch them all the time. I remember when you were that age, Sis. You were a regular
daredevil."

They took off on recollections of my reckless childhood
and no more was said about the Barlow girl. I thought of
telling them that I'd seen her ghost, but by daylight it
seemed absurd. Perhaps, I told myself, I'd dreamed the
whole episode—the sight on the highway, the exchange
with Mrs. Ryan. After coming back from last summer's va-

cation, I'd probably heard talk about the child's death and it had stayed in the back of my mind until last night when riding the late bus had brought it to the surface and turned it into the stuff of nightmare. It's queer how vivid dreams can be.

The following Thursday I rode the late bus again. It was an uneventful trip. By then I had nearly convinced myself that I had imagined or dreamed the phantom bicyclist.

The next night I sat beside a late shopper who got off shortly before we reached the old canyon road. Mrs. Ryan immediately slipped into the empty seat.

"We'll be seeing her soon," she said softly. "Just try to stay calm."

"Seeing whom?" I asked.

"The Barlow child. You saw her last week, remember? She's always there on Fridays. It's a pity the little mite can't find rest."

"I don't believe in ghosts, Mrs. Ryan," I said firmly.

"Don't you, dear?" Her tone was indulgent. "Then maybe you'd better shut your eyes at the next turn. It's hard not to believe in what you see."

Of course I kept my eyes open. I told myself that what I thought I'd seen the week before, what Mrs. Ryan described as a ghost, must be an optical illusion, a play of light on the rock formation that lined the road. Then the bus rounded the corner and there she was. A small girl leaning forward over the handlebars, pedaling furiously, her pigtails swinging as she rode her bicycle across the road. Again I felt the bus gain speed. Mrs. Ryan patted my hand as I suppressed an urge to cry out.

"Poor soul," she murmured. "If we could just find out what it is she wants and get it for her, then she'd be at peace."

I didn't answer. I couldn't think of anything to say and I was relieved when we reached her stop.

As soon as Mrs. Ryan was off the bus, Miss Wylie moved forward to sit beside me. "I suppose," she began,

"Mrs. Ryan has been filling your head with ghost stories. I hope you're not gullible enough to believe such nonsense."

"I did see something, though," I said reluctantly. "I saw it last week and again tonight. It looked like a girl on a bicycle and the bus went right through her. Mrs. Ryan told me it happens every week."

"That much is correct," she conceded. "No doubt you know about the accident."

"I didn't until last weekend. After seeing—what we saw—I asked my parents about it. They said a child was killed at that corner last August, but it wasn't the driver's fault. If that's true, I don't understand why he should be haunted."

"There's no haunting," Miss Wylie scoffed. "At least, not in the way that superstitious old woman means it."

"What is it we see then, if it's not a ghost?"

"I was at the hearing," she answered. "All of us who were on the bus that night were called to testify. Jenny Barlow's father sat through it with a terrible look on his face, staring the whole time at the driver. At the end, when the judge announced the finding of accidental death and said nobody was to blame, he went berserk. He yelled that his daughter had been murdered and her murderer would have to pay. It took two men to hold him back or he would have attacked Johnson right there in the courtroom."

"I can see how losing his child that way could make him pretty irrational. Do you think he has something to do with—these appearances?"

"He's a professional photographer," she explained. "Before they moved here, he worked in Hollywood on commercials and documentaries. They say he has part of his house fixed up as a studio and a darkroom. If you go to the movies much, you know what remarkable things they can do with special effects."

"Is that what you think we see on the road—some kind of trick photography?"

"He's an expert," she answered. "And he must have taken many pictures of his own daughter. What better way could he find to take revenge on the man who killed her?"

"But how cruel!" I looked at Mr. Johnson. With the accident scene behind us, he had settled back in the seat, but there was still tension in the set of his shoulders. "I can see how Mr. Barlow would be distraught at the time it happened. But that was months ago. To go on torturing a man like this week after week is unnatural. Can't somebody stop him?"

"They can't even prove he's doing it," Miss Wylie returned. "Oh, the police sent someone out to question him and the bus company made its own investigation. But whatever device Barlow has rigged up, it's well hidden and can be operated by remote control. He told them he knew nothing about it and insisted that his daughter wouldn't have to come out of her grave if justice had been done. And, since there's no law against showing pictures on a country road, that was the end of it as far as the authorities were concerned."

"Why doesn't Mr. Johnson transfer to another route?" I suggested. "Or he could at least stop driving on Friday nights if that's the only time she appears."

"I'm sure the bus company would let him," she agreed. "But in the beginning everybody assumed it would stop after a few weeks. No one could foresee that the father's madness would last for so many months. And now it seems to have become a kind of contest, a test of wills. Johnson knows he's innocent, and to ask for a different route, let Barlow win, might seem to be an admission of guilt. Call it pride or stubbornness or whatever, it's gone on too long now for either man to give in."

"How awful for them both."

"When you discussed the child's death with your parents, did you tell them you thought you'd seen her ghost?"

"No, it seemed too foolish. In fact, the next morning when I mentioned it to them I doubted if I'd really seen anything."

She nodded approval. "It's better not to talk about it. Even Mrs. Ryan has sense enough to realize that spreading this around could only do harm, especially to Mr. Johnson. Since there are so few of us who ride the bus this far, we've been able to keep it quiet. I hope you'll continue to be discreet."

"I will," I promised. "I certainly don't want to cause the driver any more trouble."

After that I began to take a book with me to work on Fridays. Reading it on the trip home was a way to keep from watching the road and seeing again and again the image, in living color, of the now dead girl. Even so, no matter how absorbing the story, I always felt the bus accelerate as we turned the fatal corner and I knew, without raising my eyes, that we had once more passed through the eerie presence.

As the weeks passed, I, like my fellow passengers, grew used to it. But I could never entirely put out of my mind those two tormented men. The father, deranged by grief, somewhere up in the hills listening for the bus to reach the place where he could, perhaps by the pressure of a button, cause a reenactment of what he believed had been his daughter's murder. And the driver, dogged by the reminder that he had, no matter how guiltlessly, ended a child's life, each week drawing near to that corner, anticipating what he would see, hands tight on the wheel, foot pressing hard on the gas pedal in order to get past it as quickly as possible. It can't go on forever, I told myself. Someday Mr. Barlow would dismantle his equipment and give them both a chance to forget.

Then one night I boarded the bus as usual and took a seat near the front. It was a fine spring evening, unseasonably warm, with the scent of early blossoms in the air. The woman beside me was laden with packages and bubbling with pleasure at the bargains she had found. The start of a three-day clearance sale had brought a rush of business and I was worn out. When she got off a short time before we reached the canyon, I relaxed in the seat, rotating my neck to ease the taut muscles and flexing my tired fingers. Tomorrow would be just as busy and Saturday was likely to be a mob scene.

I put up my hand to cover a yawn just as we turned what I now thought of as the Barlow corner. There, as always, the headlights revealed a bicycling child. And, as always, the bus increased speed.

Only it wasn't as always. Instead of blond pigtails, the short-cropped hair was dark brown. And today, I realized a second before I heard the sickening crunch of glass and metal, was Thursday. Wrong day. Wrong child.

EVIDENCE SEEN

JOHN C. BOLAND

It was a Victorian desk, with a fold-down leaf, a rack of tiny pigeonholes, and below, where a leg well otherwise would have been, three drawers. Someone in its history had painted it a bilious, semi-gloss green. Walt put a hand to his mouth and blew out his cheeks. "Ugh."

"Why, it's lovely," Mandy said. "Or will be, stripped and refinished. Look at the scrollwork at the top."

"I'm looking. Actually, it isn't bad." He was surprised as soon as he said it. He glanced down the churchyard, thinking that something else might catch his eye.

"It's not really an antique," said a tiny white-haired woman, coming close. She wore a sensible tweed skirt and a blue sweater against the shadows that were spreading up Farrowers Hill. "It's not an antique by our local standards. *I'm* not an antique by our local standards," she added with a smile. "Name's Meggy Gibb; I volunteered to help Pastor Combs with the sale."

Walt Darrow introduced himself and his wife, uneasy at the display of friendship.

Meggy Gibb nodded. "Of course. You two bought the Garroway place. I saw it last winter in the real-estate notices. How have you settled in?"

Walt and Mandy exchanged glances. "Pretty well," he said. "We've had lots of time."

He didn't care if his voice carried resentment. The town had offered not even a grudging welcome. No committees of housewives with time on their hands came to visit. No invitations arrived for Walt, who had made a living as a freelance journalist in New York, to sit on the Library Board. Yet he could think of no overt discourtesy that had been shown them; the town's response to their presence was indifference. While he blustered to Mandy about constipated minds, he secretly enjoyed his time and privacy.

Walt gestured to the desk. "How would you date this if it isn't an antique?"

"Oh, I'd say about 1890. It's an antique anywhere except here. Some houses in this town have sideboards that served King George. Rather a lot of them, really. This is worth about forty dollars. Does that sound fair?"

"It's fair, but I'm not sure we want it. Stripping the paint will take forever."

"I see your point. Why don't we say thirty dollars? We'll call it a belated welcome-to-town price."

A man from the sale helped them load it in the station wagon, but he wasn't along when they got home. Trundling it inside, as far as the sparely furnished front room, exhausted Walt's interest in the treasure. He went to the kitchen for a drink while Mandy admired the scrollwork under the feeble ceiling light. "Bring back a screwdriver— or better yet a knife," she called. "Let's get these drawers open."

"Hoping to find the last eccentric owner's stocks and bonds?" he asked.

She frowned at the "last." She said, "Not even we eccentrics paint the insides of drawers. I want to see what kind of wood we've got."

She went to work with the knife on the top drawer, flexing the blade between the lock and the frame. He heard the click as pressure on the bolt turned the lock. Scooting back a step, Mandy pulled.

"No stocks," she announced. "No nothing. Just solid cherry. Look at that! We got a bargain."

"If the rest of it's cherry," he said.

He left her working on the second drawer and went outside to lock the car. Traces of frost stiffened the grass, and he hurried. In the back seat he noticed a bag from Whistler's Pharmacy with typing paper and ribbons he had bought that afternoon. He grabbed the bag and slammed the door. And heard the shriek.

He found Mandy in the middle of the living room, eyes narrow, giggling. "False alarm, darling," she said. "Someone's played an awful joke on us." But when she took her hands down from her face, she was pale around the unconvincing grin. She stared at the writing desk with loathing— and from a distance.

He stepped forward and looked. The drawer contained a hand—small, white, and perfect.

"Is it real?" she gasped. Fear had backed her up, but curiosity put her on tiptoes.

"It's a mannequin's," he said quickly.

"No, it isn't."

He bent. It sure as hell wasn't.

Papier-mâché? his mind offered. An elaborate construction of tiny sticks, two of them, bleached white, protruding at the wrist, wrapped in tissue-thin parchment that looked so delicate and white it might be translucent.

"It's small enough to be a child's," he said without meaning to.

"Or a woman's," Mandy said, looking at her own right hand, which was almost as white, almost as delicate, although a month's yard labors had reddened the knuckles and broken nails. The nails on the dead hand were perfect, Walt noticed. He felt a sense of relief.

"It's real, isn't it?" his wife said.

"You'll have to ask whoever lost it."

"That's not funny."

"I know. I'm having an attack of the cutes." He got up, staring at the graceful thing in the drawer.

"You're more rattled than I am," Mandy said.

"You've got a burly husband to protect you in case the owner comes around."

"Well, he or she couldn't be very big. That's something. And it looks very old. Dried out, like a flower kept for years and years."

He closed the drawer gently.

The telephone sat on the floor in the kitchen. He pulled the directory from under it. It was the first time he had called the local police department, and he was mildly surprised when the line was answered at the police chief's home. Dewey, the town's only full-time officer, sounded annoyed, as if he doubted Walt's ability to identify a human part. "I was just sitting down to supper. I'll be by in forty-five minutes."

Walt had barely put down the receiver when Mandy called from the hallway. "There's someone at the front door!"

He walked out of the kitchen. *His* wife—nervous about answering the door? They went together.

Pastor Jacob Combs stood in the porch light. As the door opened, he offered a gaunt, horsey grin that was interrupted by a dry cough. Despite the chill, his overcoat was open and his white-bristled throat was bare. "Folks, we made a mistake. Sold you good people something that wasn't ours to sell. I come to buy it back."

Walt stepped back, letting the emaciated figure inside. "It wasn't yours to sell? We thought everything had been donated."

Combs ignored the question. "If you can just show me where it is, we'll get it out to my truck."

"I guess you mean that someone who donated it has decided he wants it back?"

Combs's eyes shifted to the hall. "Is it down here?"

Mandy began: "We bought—"

"I'll pay you back your price."

Annoyed, Walt said, "That isn't exactly the point. We bought it because we liked it. That hasn't changed."

"But you bought something that wasn't rightly for sale," the old man said. "Surely you can see that the church doesn't want to arouse bad feelings about these sales. We'd never get anyone to donate again."

"Of course," Mandy said. "But this piece is special."

The old man sighed, rubbing a knuckle under his nose. "You found something in it, didn't you? Something that in your innocent greed you're unwilling to give up."

Mandy shot her husband a frown. "I wouldn't say that."

"Money, perhaps?"

"You don't know?" Walt said. He pointed to the front room. "Come have a look."

Combs bent over the desk drawer, staring intently. When he straightened, it was with wide eyes. "What you've got there is a glory hand!"

Walt glanced at his wife.

"First one I've seen in ages." When he saw Walt's stare, Combs added, "Some folks call them witch hands."

"You mean that hand was cut off a witch?"

"No, no—course not. Wasn't cut off anything." His quick glance scouted the room. He plucked up the paring knife Mandy had used on the lock. "Never was attached. These things are like—like—you know what a will-o'-the-wisp is? Just a little puff of swamp gas. These is like that, except they're made out of something else."

He bent close, reaching out with the knife blade toward the pale object in the drawer. As the blade neared the back of the hand, Walt thought he saw a tiny spark jump.

It was gone.

Combs drew a hand down his long jaw. "Perhaps you folks had better hang onto the desk. I'll have a talk with the owner."

Chief Dewey was perturbed by the absence of a hand. He lit a cigar in the front room, mumbling, "I don't believe in spiritual things."

Walt didn't, either. "You could talk to Pastor Combs."

"Even the Lord's registered agents can go senile. Old Combs is a great believer in hoo-doo. It appears he's got a couple of apprentices."

"Hardly," Walt said.

Dewey shrugged. "Why would you folks who've gone to college, got a little money from the looks of it, want to mess around with foolishness?"

As she closed the door, Mandy flicked off the outside light before Dewey reached his car. "He won't get my vote."

"At least you've still got your desk," Walt tempered.

The next morning, the hand was in the middle of the living room floor. Watering pot gripped tightly, Mandy came and collected him from the kitchen. In the strong autumn light, it stood out against the dark oak like a porcelain sculpture.

"Another will-o'-the-wisp," Mandy said woodenly.

"Take it easy. Combs is playing tricks on us."

"Sure."

"If it makes you nervous, wait in the hall. I want to see something." He bent and, after he was alone, reached out tentatively. He expected the cold hardness of china. Instead, when pressed, the flesh gave way fractionally until his finger felt bone. He removed his finger, and a tiny depression quickly smoothed itself.

"For God's sake, what are you doing?"

"Bring me a screwdriver."

She stopped at the doorway, and he had to go and take it from her. He strode back quickly and swept the tool down almost as if the blow were lethal. There was a snap of electrical discharge.

"Don't let it rattle you," he said, patting her back. "You always figured New England would be haunted."

"But why a—a missing left hand?"

He didn't answer. The night before, he was certain, it had been a right hand.

Combs came that afternoon to collect the desk. "Hope there's no hard feelings. The owner lady don't believe in ghosts. Or in the hereafter, I 'spect."

"Just get it out," Mandy said. "You can keep the thirty dollars."

Walt helped the old man load the antique into the back of a pickup truck. "What's this glory hand made of?" he asked.

"Oh, hard to say. They got some psychics in Ipswich who say it's that supernatural material. What do you call it?"

For a moment Walt was at a loss.

Combs prompted: "The stuff that appears at séances."

"Ectoplasm?"

"That's it."

"Then it's not real."

It had felt real.

"I don't know about that," Combs said.

"How long has that desk been haunted?"

"Didn't know it was, till I saw the glory hand. Can't think why Mrs. Timberlane wants it back."

Maybe the hand belongs to a friend, Walt thought.

He brought in some firewood, dumped it near the hearth in the big room on the southwest. It was the only one that got really good sunlight, and there wasn't much of it today. "Sit tight, I'll get the wine."

The kitchen, for all its country charm, had the coldest floor in the house. He pulled a bottle of burgundy, grabbed glasses and a corkscrew. The fire had taken hold behind the screen. He sat down close to her on the sofa.

She took her shoes off, tucked her feet under. "We're going to have to be more selective about flea markets."

"Right. No more on church lawns. We'll wait till the witches' coven has its annual fundraiser."

She raised a questioning eyebrow. "What did Chief Dewey say Pastor Combs was into? Hoo-doo? Like the rhyme in the old movie. A man with the power. Do you want cheese?"

"I've got the power," Walt said, suddenly amorous.

"You wait here. I'll get the cheese." She got up barefoot and ran across the floor. He heard her rattling in a drawer, then the grunt of the refrigerator door. An instant later came an explosive clatter and silence.

He got up slowly and went into the kitchen.

Cutting board, knife, and cheddar had hit the aged quarry tiles and scattered.

His wife stood with her backside pressed so hard against the sink that her denim jeans bulged at either hip. Her arms folded loosely, she stared at the corner behind him. He turned.

And looked.

After the delicacy of the hands, the sight jarred him. Pink ribbons of flesh and a jutting white bone stuck from the end of the foot, as if it had been hacked and ripped loose by someone in a frenzy. If the thing had bled, it hadn't been here. His stomach bucked like a wild horse, and only anger saved him. He cursed Combs.

Pushing hard, he got Mandy past the relic and into the southwest room. He lowered her onto the couch. Beneath his hands, she vibrated like a leaf caught in the wind. He felt that way himself.

"Call Dewey," she said.

"I'd rather call Combs. He was supposed to take this *away*."

"Let Dewey call him. We need help."

As the police chief, paunchy and soft, stared at the thing in the kitchen, blood clogged his face. "So you couldn't resist."

"We—"

Dewey rounded on them. He licked his lips. "Have you joined a coven yet? There's a nice one nearby."

"We haven't joined anything or done anything. We want help," Walt said.

Dewey said softly, "You got yourselves into it. Find your own way out." He strode for the door. Holding it wide, with the autumn chill sliding in, he pointed a thick finger at Walt. "Don't you call me again. Not for a burglar. Not for anything."

He closed the door, almost gently.

"What gives him—" Mandy began. "He should be fired."

Walt smiled. "I wouldn't mind. But it won't happen on our say-so. Not unless you want to be the one to tell the Board of Selectmen that the chief is afraid of glory hands."

"They'd laugh us out of the village."

"This is Massachusetts, remember? They used to be pretty rough on hoo-dooers." He went back into the kitchen for a paring knife to destroy the evidence.

"It's the next turnoff," Mandy said. She sat beside him. The headlights picked out the white clapboard church from the early dusk. The lawn stood empty this afternoon, except for tangles of thick grass and wildflowers. He pulled into the shell driveway between the stern-façaded worship hall and the ramshackle parsonage. Wisteria clung to gap-toothed latticework, leaves long dead on the vine. Walt could smell the salt marsh that started at the bottom of Farrowers Hill and reached to the bay.

Pastor Combs shuffled out onto the porch, a pale claw wrapped around a tumblerful of whisky. "Figured you'd be showing up. Curious about the glory hand, aren't you?"

"Yes, sir," Walt said.

"Afraid I don't know much." He tucked his eyes toward his drink, lifted the glass toward his lips. "My Uncle Cabot used to discover 'em all the time. Little boys' hands, way back before the war. That's when he was killed, 1940."

Mandy came onto the porch reluctantly. "Pastor Combs, is the glory hand like a haunting?"

His sharp little eyes had a secret to keep. "Expect it could be. Houses are haunted, aren't they?"

"But the ghost stays with the haunted object—the house, or the desk. Is that right?"

"Sounds reasonable." The eyes suspected something.

Walt said, "Why would Mrs. Timberlane's desk carry a glory hand?"

"She's an old widow. Soft in the noggin, or she wouldn't let the deacons take that desk when she wanted to keep it."

"You mentioned a group of psychics in Ipswich."

"May have."

"I was thinking there might be a good magazine article in this. . . ."

"No one'd print it."

"I was thinking of one of the Boston papers."

"You go ahead if you want. Them folks in Ipswich are fools, playing with something they don't understand. Make no mistake, the glory hand is nothing to meddle with."

"Is Mrs. Timberlane a member of the psychics group?" Walt asked.

"I don't know," Combs said.

Walt scouted the house before letting his wife enter. Then he brought out the bottle of wine that had been interrupted.

"Why didn't those visions go home with the desk?" Mandy asked.

He shook his head.

"Are you going to call that man with the psychics? What's his name?"

"Procter Gentry." Having wheedled the name of the psychics' leader out of Combs, he was reluctant to follow through. He wanted to keep their ghosts to himself. "Remember that house on Long Island?" he told her. "Once ghosts were reported, it became a tourist hangout."

In the end, he approached it circumspectly. He told Gentry by telephone that he was a writer interested in the occult and wanted to talk about the Ipswich group's work. When he drove there the next morning, Gentry turned out to be a large, wispy-haired man with a scientific frown.

"There's a local superstition about a 'glory hand,' " Walt said. "Does it ring a bell with you?"

Procter Gentry stirred tea. From their window table at the diner, the village seemed oddly empty for such a bright autumn morning. Off covening, Walt thought.

"It's no superstition," Gentry said. "I've seen one myself. It followed the murderer around like a puppy dog, forty-five or more years ago, I guess. He broke and confessed and they hanged him. It usually happens that way."

No wonder Mrs. Timberlane had wanted the desk returned.

"A murderer," Walt repeated. "Was the hand like a ghost haunting the killer?"

"More like his conscience," said Gentry. "What do you know about ectoplasm, Mr. Darrow? Not much? The mystics like to think it's something that has crossed from another plane, a dead loved one's transfigured substance, slipping from world to world just for the sake of shaking a table. Purest baloney! Ectoplasm stays right in the world where it's manufactured by loneliness, fear, guilt—any strong emotional energy."

"You mean it's imaginary?"

"It's thought to be real enough. You may have read about it in Richard Matheson's *Hell House,* for instance. The composition makes perfect sense once you think about it. The stuff is made up of bits and pieces of everything imaginable, like dust off the table next to you, a little bit of

your dandruff, cigarette ashes, nostril mucus, nap from
your coat—anything handy that a person with just normal
latent psychic powers could mold into the desired shape.
That's why a person who's good at calling up spirit forms
usually tests high on telekinetic skills—the ability to move
objects with the mind; they've been doing it all along. Just
like old Cabot Combs—that's the fellow they hanged—
that's what old Cabot was doing, though he didn't know it.
He was sure the glory hands belonged to those two little
boys he'd murdered. But it was just his subconscious re-
minding him what he'd done."

Walt managed to swallow the jolt the name gave him.
Whose word—he asked over the thumping in his chest—
did they have that the desk belonged to a Mrs. Timberlane?

Only Pastor Combs's.

Whose Uncle Cabot had seen glory hands back before
the war.

"That can't be the extent of your curiosity," Gentry said
with a prodding smile.

"So it isn't just the killer who sees the, uh, vision?"

"Manifestation. No, because it's not an hallucination. It
really exists, sort of like a dust ball somebody has sculptured." He seemed pleased with the analogy.

"I touched one," Walt said. "It felt like flesh."

"You're a brave man. Not many people would do that
unless they knew what they were dealing with. And you
know how to disperse the manifestation—the 'exorcism,' if
you will?"

"The touch of metal."

Gentry nodded. "Any metal that can carry a magnetic
charge, even a small one." He considered his tea, squinted
at the sunlight. "Though some manifestations may be difficult to discharge. It depends on the static power that put
them together."

"It varies?"

"Wouldn't you expect that? Some thunderstorms are
mild, some ferocious. Some electrical generators produce a
stronger magnetic field than others. That's all you're really
dealing with. So you saw and touched a glory hand, Mr.

Darrow. Can I assume your interest is not entirely journal-istic?"

"An acquaintance of mine bought a piece of furniture," Walt said. "The glory hand seemed to come with it."

Gentry's scientific squint sharpened. He shook his head. "Sorry, young man. It doesn't work that way. Now you're talking about what mystical folks call an 'aura,' a spiritual or emotional resonance left on an object. A haunting of a house, for instance, or an automobile that has a reputation as unlucky."

"What's the difference?"

"Science versus witchcraft, that's what! I don't believe auras or hauntings exist. Oh, I've been in houses that felt wrong, as if something unhappy had happened there, some-thing rotten to the soul, and the place remembered. But that's a poetic description, not scientific. I could never find any evidence that a previous occupant had left any de-tectable charge on the place. And, God help me, I've never seen a ghost!"

Procter Gentry waved a hand at the coffeeshop, which held a few late breakfast-eaters. "Some folks in town are certain that a member of the Psychical Inquiry Society must believe in every sort of nonsense—have hobgoblins in the belfry, ha ha! I only believe in what I have seen and can document—which means, measure objectively. I've seen a glory hand. I've got friends in Brighton who hooked an ampmeter to an icepick and got a faint reading when discharging a manifestation. But auras? No evi-dence."

"I've seen these hands," Walt insisted, slipping into the plural. "In a desk drawer."

"I take your word for it. I'm just saying you shouldn't as-sume the manifestation came 'with' a piece of furniture. It was created by somebody, most likely as an expression of profound guilt. Has your friend murdered anybody?"

"Of course not!"

"Perhaps somebody close to your friend, a visitor, has a guilty secret."

"Could a visitor create a manifestation from a distance?"

Gentry looked troubled. "I don't know. It would have to be a forceful mind at work—and a powerful guilt."

He paid the check and used a pay phone, watching Gentry cross the street huddling in the sunlight. "If Combs stops by, or anybody else, don't let them in," he told his wife.

He tried the operator and got a number for Edith Timberlane on the west side. He dialed, thinking he knew the answer—the desk belonged to Combs.

A young woman answered and said she was Joyce Timberlane. Her mother was at her Tuesday bridge club. Did he want to leave a message? Walt left his home number.

"Darrow," she repeated. "I think we know each other. You're the writer who comes into Whistler's Pharmacy for stationery? New in town? I'm the Joyce who waits on you. You were in on Saturday."

His mind dredged up a compact brunette in her twenties, pretty, bored with the village, who had gotten him talking once or twice about New York. A natural flirt, he had thought with approval. He was wary about flirting in a small town.

"Hi, I remember," he said, unable to summon any small talk. "Could you ask your mother to call this evening?"

He left the phone, shaking his head. He had all but forgotten the weekend up to the point of that damned church market.

He drove home and made himself a drink, stronger than usual. Calling Dewey was out of the question. The police chief wouldn't tell him whether any young woman had been murdered in the village in recent years.

The phone rang and a frail voice said, "This is Edith Timberlane, and I'm so sorry about the desk. My daughter thought I wanted to get rid of it because it's so ugly. But it was my mother's and I couldn't bear to."

He set down the phone and went back to the kitchen.

He grew aware of Mandy watching him from the doorway. She wouldn't come into the kitchen. Dramatizing or actually afraid—he wasn't sure which.

"What did Mr. Gentry have to say?"

"He said the things are demons of the mind."

"Whose mind?"

"Combs's. That Uncle Cabot he was so fond of killed two young boys before the war. That's why Cabot was seeing glory hands. It must run in the family."

"And just now?"

"The old woman changed her mind about the desk, just as Combs said."

She folded her arms tightly, shrinking within the faded plaid shirt that had been his. "Why don't you come along to the couch?" The invitation—and her strained smile said it was an invitation—was rare.

"In a little while." He sipped his drink and she went away. She *was* afraid of the kitchen, site of the raggedly butchered foot.

Idly, he glanced at the spot to the right of the doorway—

And saw it, pink-edged and ringed by crimson berries, the left foot this time. Dainty as the other had been, this was less ethereal, much less ethereal, a toenail broken, a hint of a tiny bunion, flesh bruised around the ghastly stump that ended at the shin.

The sense of revulsion hit him belatedly, driving him to the sink for a knife, the first slight touch of which exorcised the ghost. He stood trembling against the sink. What he needed was another drink. He reached to the overhead cabinet. As the door swung wide, he choked off a scream.

On the shelf directly before him, it occupied the spot where the Old Taylor would have been, a tangle of brown hair falling across the forehead. He couldn't see the features until he brushed the hair aside. The action was almost a caress, because he understood. If a guilty mind accused itself of a horrendous crime, what difference was time? Past or future would be a blur to the conscience. He noticed that he still gripped the kitchen knife. He set it down.

"Walt?" his wife called from the living room.

He breathed deeply, making sure his voice was under control. "I'll be there."

He knew, looking at the dead face, that whether he wanted to or not he would soon arrange a secret date with the brunette at the pharmacy. Now that he understood, he felt the time was almost right.

THE AVENGING OF
ANN LEETE

MARJORIE BOWEN

This is a queer story, the more queer for the interpretation of passions of strong human heat that have been put upon it, and for glimpses of other motives and doings, not, it would seem, human at all.

The whole thing is seen vaguely, brokenly, a snatch here and there; one tells the tale, strangely another exclaims amaze, a third points out a scene, a fourth has a dim memory of a circumstance, a nine-days' (or less) wonder, an old print helps, the name on a mural tablet in a deserted church pinches the heart with a sense of confirmation, and so you have your story. When all is said it remains a queer tale.

It is seventy years odd ago, so dating back from this present year of 1845 you come to nearly midway in the last century, when conditions were vastly different from what they are now.

The scene is in Glasgow, and there are three points from which we start, all leading us to the heart of our tale.

The first is the portrait of a woman that hangs in the parlour of a respectable banker. He believes it to be the likeness of some connexion of his wife's, dead this many a year, but he does not know much about it. Some while ago it was discovered in a lumber-room, and he keeps it for the pallid beauty of the canvas, which is much faded and rubbed.

Since, as a young man, I first had the privilege of my worthy friend's acquaintance, I have always felt a strange interest in this picture; and, in that peculiar way that the

imagination will seize on trifles, I was always fascinated by
the dress of the lady. This is of dark green, very fine silk;
an uncommon colour to use in a portrait, and, perhaps, in a
lady's dress. It is very plain, with a little scarf of a striped
Roman pattern, and her hair is drawn up over a pillow in
the antique mode. Her face is expressionless, yet strange,
the upper lip very thin, the lower very full, the light brown
eyes set under brows that slant. I cannot tell why this picture was always to me full of such a great attraction, but I
used to think of it a vast deal, and often to note, secretly,
that never had I chanced to meet in real life, or in any other
painting, a lady in a dark green silk dress.

In the corner of the canvas is a little device, put in a diamond as a gentlewoman might bear arms, yet with no pre-
tensions to heraldry, just three little birds, the topmost with
a flower in its beak.

It was not so long ago that I came upon the second clue
that leads into the story, and that was a mural tablet in an
old church near the Rutherglen Road, a church that has
lately fallen into disrepute or neglect, for it was deserted
and impoverished. But I was assured that a generation ago
it had been a most famous place of worship, fashionable
and well frequented by the better sort.

The mural tablet was to one "Ann Leete," and there was
just the date (seventy-odd years old), given with what
seemed a sinister brevity.

And underneath the lettering, lightly cut on the time-
stained marble, was the same device as that on the portrait
of the lady in the green silk dress.

I was curious enough to make inquiries, but no one
seemed to know anything of, or wished to talk about, Ann
Leete.

It was all so long ago, I was told, and there was no one
now in the parish of the name of Leete.

And all who had been acquainted with the family of
Leete seemed to be dead or gone away. The parish register
(my curiosity went so far as an inspection of this) yielded
me no more information than the mural tablet.

I spoke to my friend the banker, and he said he thought
that his wife had had some cousins by the name of Leete,

and that there was some tale of a scandal or great misfortune attached to them which was the reason of a sort of ban on their name so that it had never been mentioned.

When I told him I thought the portrait of the lady in the dark green silk might picture a certain Ann Leete he appeared uneasy and even desirous of having the likeness removed, which roused in me the suspicion that he knew something of the name, and that not pleasant. But it seemed to me indelicate and perhaps useless to question him.

It was a year or so after this incident that my business, which was that of silversmith and jeweller, put into my hands a third clue. One of my apprentices came to me with a rare piece of work which had been left at the shop for repair.

It was a thin medal of the purest gold, on which was set in fresh water pearls, rubies and cairngorms the device of the three birds, the plumage being most skillfully wrought in the bright jewels and the flower held by the topmost creature accurately designed in pearls.

It was one of these pearls that was missing, and I had some difficulty in matching its soft lustre.

An elderly lady called for the ornament, the same person who had left it. I saw her myself, and ventured to admire and praise the workmanship of the medal.

"Oh," she said, "it was worked by a very famous jeweller, my great-uncle, and he has a peculiar regard for it—indeed I believe it has never before been out of his possession, but he was so greatly grieved by the loss of the pearl that he would not rest until I offered to take it to be repaired. He is, you will understand," she added with a smile, "a very old man. He must have made that jewellery—why—seventy-odd years ago."

Seventy-odd years ago—that would bring one back to the date on the tablet to Ann Leete, to the period of the portrait.

"I have seen this device before," I remarked, "on the likeness of a lady and on the mural inscription in memory of a certain Ann Leete." Again this name appeared to make an unpleasant impression.

My customer took her packet hastily.

"It is associated with something dreadful," she said quickly. "We do not speak of it—a very old story. I did not know anyone had heard of it—"

"I certainly have not," I assured her. "I came to Glasgow not so long ago, as apprentice to this business of my uncle's which now I own."

"But you have seen a portrait?" she asked.

"Yes, in the house of a friend of mine."

"This is queer. We did not know that any existed. Yet my great-uncle does speak of one—in a green silk dress."

"In a green silk dress," I confirmed.

The lady appeared amazed.

"But it is better to let the matter rest," she decided. "My relative, you will realize, is very old—nearly, sir, a hundred years old, and his wits wander and he tells queer tales. It was all very strange and horrible, but one cannot tell how much my old uncle dreams."

"I should not think to disturb him," I replied.

But my customer hesitated.

"If you know of this portrait—perhaps he should be told; he laments after it so much, and we have always believed it an hallucination—"

She returned the packet containing the medal.

"Perhaps," she added dubiously, "you are interested enough to take this back to my relative yourself and judge what you shall or shall not tell him?"

I eagerly accepted the offer, and the lady gave me the name and residence of the old man who, although possessed of considerable means, had lived for the past fifty years in the greatest seclusion in that lonely part of the town beyond the Rutherglen Road and near to the Green, the once pretty and fashionable resort for youth and pleasure, but now a deserted and desolate region. Here, on the first opportunity, I took my way, and found myself well out into the country, nearly at the river, before I reached the lonely mansion of Eneas Bretton, as the ancient jeweller was called.

A ferocious dog troubled my entrance in the dark, over-grown garden where the black glossy laurels and bays strangled the few flowers, and a grim woman, in an old-fashioned mutch or cap, at length answered my repeated peals at the rusty chain bell.

It was not without considerable trouble that I was admitted into the presence of Mr. Bretton, and only, I think, by the display of the jewel and the refusal to give it into any hands but those of its owner.

The ancient jeweller was seated on a southern terrace that received the faint and fitful rays of the September sun.

He was wrapped in shawls that disguised his natural form, and a fur and leather cap was fastened under his chin.

I had the impression that he had been a fine man, of a vigorous and handsome appearance; even now, in the extreme of decay, he showed a certain grandeur of line and carriage, a certain majestic power in his personality. Though extremely feeble, I did not take him to be imbecile nor greatly wanting in his faculties.

He received me courteously, though obviously ill-used to strangers.

I had, he said, a claim on him as a fellow-craftsman, and he was good enough to commend the fashion in which I had repaired his medal.

This, as soon as he had unwrapped, he fastened to a fine gold chain he drew from his breast, and slipped inside his heavy clothing.

"A pretty trinket," I said, "and of an unusual design."

"I fashioned it myself," he answered, "over seventy years ago. The year before, sir, she died."

"Ann Leete?" I ventured.

The ancient man was not in the least surprised at the use of this name.

"It is a long time since I heard those words with any but my inner ear," he murmured; "to be sure, I grow very old. You'll not remember Ann Leete?" he added wistfully.

"I take it she died before I was born," I answered.

He peered at me.

"Ah, yes, you are still a young man, though your hair is grey."

I noticed now that he wore a small tartan scarf inside his coat and shawl; this fact gave me a peculiar, almost unpleasant shudder.

"I know this about Ann Leete—she had a dark green silk dress. And a Roman or tartan scarf."

He touched the wisp of bright-coloured silk across his chest.

"This is it. She had her likeness taken so—but it was lost."

"It is preserved," I answered. "And I know where it is. I might, if you desired, bring you to a sight of it."

He turned his grand old face to me with a civil inclination of his massive head.

"That would be very courteous of you, sir, and a pleasure to me. You must not think," he added with dignity, "that the lady has forsaken me or that I do not often see her. Indeed, she comes to me more frequently than before. But it would delight me to have the painting of her to console the hours of her absence."

I reflected what his relative had said about the weakness of his wits, and recalled his great age, which one was apt to forget in face of his composure and reasonableness.

He appeared now to doze and to take no further notice of my presence, so I left him.

He had a strange look of lifelessness as he slumbered there in the faintest rays of the cloudy autumn sun.

I reflected how lightly the spirit must dwell in this ancient frame, how easily it must take flight into the past, how soon into eternity.

It did not cost me much persuasion to induce my friend, the banker, to lend me the portrait of Ann Leete, particularly as the canvas had been again sent up to the attics.

"Do *you* know the story?" I asked him.

He replied that he had heard something; that the case had made a great stir at the time; that it was all very confused and amazing, and that he did not desire to discuss the matter.

I hired a carriage and took the canvas to the house of Eneas Bretton.

He was again on the terrace, enjoying with a sort of calm eagerness the last warmth of the failing sun.

His two servants brought in the picture and placed it on a chair at his side.

He gazed at the painted face with the greatest serenity.

"That is she," he said, "but I am glad to think that she looks happier now, sir. She still wears that dark green silk. I never see her in any other garment."

"A beautiful woman," I remarked quietly, not wishing to agitate or disturb his reflections, which were clearly detached from any considerations of time and space.

"I have always thought so," he answered gently, "but I, sir, have peculiar faculties. I saw her, and see her still as a spirit. I loved her as a spirit. Yet our bodily union was necessary for our complete happiness. And in that my darling and I were balked."

"By death?" I suggested, for I knew that the word had no terrors for him.

"By death," he agreed, "who will soon be forced to unite us again."

"But not in the body," I said.

"How, sir, do you know that?" he smiled. "We have but finite minds. I think we have but little conception of the marvellous future."

"Tell me," I urged, "how you lost Ann Leete."

His dim, heavy-lidded, many-wrinkled eyes flickered a glance over me.

"She was murdered," he said.

I could not forbear a shudder.

"That fragile girl!" I exclaimed. My blood had always run cool and thin, and I detested deeds of violence; my even mind could not grasp the idea of the murder of women save as a monstrous enormity.

I looked at the portrait, and it seemed to me that I had always known that it was the likeness of a creature doomed.

"Seventy years ago and more," continued Eneas Bretton, "since when *she has wandered lonely betwixt time and eternity,* waiting for me. But very soon I shall join her, and then, sir, we shall go where there is no recollection of the evil things of this earth."

By degrees he told me the story, not in any clear sequence, nor at any one time, nor without intervals of sleep and pauses of dreaming, nor without assistance from his

servants and his great-niece and her husband, who were his
frequent visitors.

Yet it was from his own lips and when we were alone together that I learned all that was really vital in the tale.

He required very frequent attendance; although all
human passion was at the utmost ebb with him, he had, he
said, a kind of regard for me in that I had brought him his
lady's portrait, and he told me things of which he had never
spoken to any human being before. I say human on purpose
because of his intense belief that he was, and always had
been, in communication with powers not of this earth.

In these words I put together his tale.

As a young man [said Eneas Bretton] I was healthy,
prosperous and happy.

My family had been goldsmiths as long as there was any
record of their existence, and I was an enthusiast in this
craft, grave, withal, and studious, over-fond of books and
meditation. I do not know how or when I first met Ann
Leete.

To me she was always there like the sun; I think I have
known her all my life, but perhaps my memory fails.

Her father was a lawyer and she an only child, and
though her social station was considered superior to mine, I
had far more in the way of worldly goods, so there was no
earthly obstacle to our union.

The powers of evil, however, fought against us; I had
feared this from the first, as our happiness was the complete circle ever hateful to fiends and devils who try to
break the mystic symbol.

The mistress of my soul attracted the lustful attention of
a young doctor, Rob Patterson, who had a certain false
charm of person, not real comeliness, but a trick of colour,
of carriage and a fine taste in clothes.

His admiration was whetted by her coldness and his intense dislike of me.

We came to scenes in which he derided me as no gentleman, but a beggarly tradesman, and I scorned him as an
idle voluptuary designing a woman's ruin for the crude
pleasure of the gratification of fleeting passions.

For the fellow made not even any pretence of being able to support a wife, and was of that rake-helly temperament that made an open mock of matrimony.

Although he was but a medical student, he was of what they call noble birth, and his family, though decayed, possessed considerable social power, so that his bold pursuit of Ann Leete and his insolent flaunting of me had some license, the more so that he did not lack tact and address in his manner and conduct.

Our marriage could have stopped this persecution, or given the right to publicly resent it, but my darling would not leave her father, who was of a melancholy and querulous disposition.

It was shortly before her twenty-first birthday, for which I had made her the jewel I now wear (the device being the crest of her mother's family and one for which she had a great affection), that her father died suddenly. His last thoughts were of her, for he had this very picture painted for her birthday gift. Finding herself thus unprotected and her affairs in some confusion, she declared her intention of retiring to some distant relative in the Highlands until decorum permitted of our marriage.

And upon my opposing myself to this scheme of separation and delay she was pleased to fall out with me, declaring that I was as importunate as Dr. Patterson, and that I, as well as he, should be kept in ignorance of her retreat.

I had, however, great hopes of inducing her to change this resolution, and, it being then fair spring weather, engaged her to walk with me on the Green, beyond the city, to discuss our future.

I was an orphan like herself, and we had now no common meeting-place suitable to her reputation and my respect.

By reason of a pressure of work, to which by temperament and training I was ever attentive, I was a few moments late at the tryst on the Green, which I found, as usual, empty; but it was a lovely afternoon of May, very still and serene, like the smile of satisfied love.

I paced about, looking for my darling.

Although she was in mourning, she had promised me to

wear the dark green silk I so admired under her black cloak, and I looked for this colour among the brighter greens of the trees and bushes.

She did not appear, and my heart was chilled with the fear that she was offended with me and therefore would not come, and an even deeper dread that she might, in vexation, have fled to her unknown retreat.

This thought was sending me hot-foot to seek her at her house, when I saw Rob Patterson coming across the close-shaven grass of the Green.

I remember that the cheerful sun seemed to me to be at this moment darkened, not by any natural clouds or mists, but as it is during an eclipse, and that the fresh trees and innocent flowers took on a ghastly and withered look.

It may appear a trivial detail, but I recall so clearly his habit, which was of a luxury beyond his means—fine grey broadcloth with a deep edging of embroidery in gold thread, little suited to his profession.

As he saw me he cocked his hat over his eyes, but took no other notice of my appearance, and I turned away, not being wishful of any encounter with this gentleman while my spirit was in a tumult.

I went at once to my darling's house, and learnt from her maid that she had left home two hours previously.

I do not wish to dwell on this part of my tale—indeed, I could not, it becomes very confused to me.

The salient facts are these—that no one saw Ann Leete in bodily form again.

And no one could account for her disappearance; yet no great comment was aroused by this, because there was no one to take much interest in her, and it was commonly believed that she had disappeared from the importunity of her lovers, the more so as Rob Patterson swore that the day of her disappearance he had had an interview with her in which she had avowed her intention of going where no one could discover her. This, in a fashion, was confirmed by what she had told me, and I was the more inclined to believe it, as my inner senses told me that she was not dead.

Six months of bitter search, of sad uneasiness, that remain in my memory blurred to one pain, and then, one autumn evening, as I came home late and dispirited, I saw her before me in the gloaming, tripping up the street, wearing her dark green silk dress and tartan or Roman scarf.

I did not see her face as she disappeared before I could gain on her, but she held to her side one hand, and between the long fingers I saw the haft of a surgeon's knife.

I knew then that she was dead.

And I knew that Rob Patterson had killed her.

Although it was well known that my family were all ghostseers, to speak in this case was to be laughed at and reprimanded.

I had no single shred of evidence against Dr. Patterson.

But I resolved that I would use what powers I possessed to make him disclose his crime.

And this is how it befell.

In those days, in Glasgow, it was compulsory to attend some place of worship on the Sabbath, the observation of the holy day being enforced with peculiar strictness, and none being allowed to show themselves in any public place during the hours of the church services, and to this end inspectors and overseers were employed to patrol the streets on a Sabbath and take down the names of those who might be found loitering there.

But few were the defaulters, Glasgow on a Sunday being as bare as the Arabian desert.

Rob Patterson and I both attended the church in Rutherglen Road, towards the Green and the river.

And the Sunday after I had seen the phantom of Ann Leete, I changed my usual place and seated myself behind this young man.

My intention was to so work on his spirit as to cause him to make public confession of his crime. And I crouched there behind him with a concentration of hate and fury, forcing my will on his during the whole of the long service.

I noticed he was pale, and that he glanced several times behind him, but he did not change his place or open his lips; but presently his head fell forward on his arms as if he was praying, and I took him to be in a kind of swoon brought on by the resistance of his spirit against mine.

I did not for this cease to pursue him. I was, indeed, as if in an exaltation, and I thought my soul had his soul by the throat, somewhere above our heads, and was shouting out: "Confess! Confess!"

One o'clock struck and he rose with the rest of the congregation, but in a dazed kind of fashion. It was almost side by side that we issued from the church door.

As the stream of people came into the street they were stopped by a little procession that came down the road.

All immediately recognized two of the inspectors employed to search the Sunday streets for defaulters from church attendance, followed by several citizens who appeared to have left their homes in haste and confusion.

These people carried between them a rude bundle which some compassionate hand had covered with a white linen cloth. Below this fell a swathe of dark green silk and the end of a Roman scarf.

I stepped up to the rough bier.

"You have found Ann Leete," I said.

"It is a dead woman," one answered me. "We know not her name."

I did not need to raise the cloth. The congregation was gathering round us, and amongst them was Rob Patterson.

"Tell me, who was her promised husband, how you found her," I said.

And one of the inspectors answered:

"Near here, on the Green, where the wall bounds the grass, we saw, just now, the young surgeon, Rob Patterson, lying on the sward, and put his name in our books, besides approaching him to inquire the reason of his absence from church. But he, without excuse for his offence, rose from the ground, exclaiming: 'I am a miserable man! Look in the water!'

"With that he crossed a stile that leads to the river and disappeared, and we, going down to the water, found the dead woman, deep tangled between the willows and the weeds—"

"And," added the other inspector gravely, "tangled in her clothes is a surgeon's knife."

"Which," said the former speaker, "perhaps Dr. Patterson can explain, since I perceive he is among this congregation—he must have found some quick way round to have got here before us."

Upon this all eyes turned to the surgeon, but more with amaze than reproach.

And he, with a confident air, said:

"It is known to all these good people that I have been in the church the whole of the morning, especially to Eneas Bretton, who sat behind me, and, I dare swear, never took his eyes from me during the whole of the service."

"Ay, your *body* was there," I said.

With that he laughed angrily, and mingling with the crowd passed on his way.

You may believe there was a great stir; the theory put abroad was that Ann Leete had been kept a prisoner in a solitary, ruined hut there was by the river, and then, in fury or fear, slain by her jailer and cast into the river.

To me all this is black. I only know that she was murdered by Rob Patterson.

He was arrested and tried on the circuit.

He there proved, beyond all cavil, that he had been in the church from the beginning of the service to the end of it; his alibi was perfect. But the two inspectors never wavered in their tale of seeing him on the Green, of his self-accusation in his exclamation; he was very well known to them, and they showed his name written in their books.

He was acquitted by the tribunal of man, but a higher power condemned him.

Shortly after he died by his own hand, which God armed and turned against him.

This mystery, as it was called, was never solved to the public satisfaction, but I know that I sent Rob Patterson's soul out of his body to betray his guilt, and to procure my darling Christian burial.

This was the tale Eneas Bretton, that ancient man, told me, on the old terrace, as he sat opposite the picture of Ann Leete.

"You must think what you will," he concluded. "They will tell you that the shock unsettled my wits, or even that I was always crazed. As they would tell you that I dream when I say that I see Ann Leete now, and babble when I talk of my happiness with her for fifty years."

He smiled faintly; a deeper glory than that of the autumn sunshine seemed to rest on him.

"Explain it yourself, sir. *What was it those inspectors saw on the Green?*"

He slightly raised himself in his chair and peered over my shoulder.

"*And what is this,*" he asked triumphantly, in the voice of a young man, "*coming towards us now?*"

I rose; I looked over my shoulder.

Through the gloom I saw a dark green silk gown, a woman's form, a pale hand beckoning.

My impulse was to fly from the spot, but a happy sigh from my companion reproved my cowardice. I looked at the ancient man whose whole figure appeared lapped in warm light, and as the apparition of the woman moved into this glow, which seemed too glorious for the fading sunshine, I heard his last breath flow from his body with a glad cry. I had not answered his questions; I never can.

MY LATE AUNT HATTIE

TIM MYERS

I have never been more terrified in my life than the night Aunt Hattie walked into the living room. It doesn't sound like I had much reason for alarm, except for the fact that she had been dead for eight months. I never expected to see her again, and I was so surprised by her sudden appearance that I forgot to ask her about the five hundred silver dollars she had always promised me when she "passed over." Aunt Hattie didn't have much to say, her vocal cords having long ago rotted into the moist, damp soil that surrounded her body. We had been too poor at the time of her death to afford much more than the economy model of casket. Evidently it hadn't held up very well under the effects of the rain, the snow, and the gophers. In fact, the parts of Aunt Hattie that *were* there had two major problems; they smelled like ripe roadkill, and they had a difficult time staying attached. As soon as I saw the hall rug, I knew it was a total loss. There are some things that even Stanley Steamer can't get out of your carpet.

Aunt Hattie appeared on Halloween last year, about twenty minutes before midnight. She manifested suddenly in the entryway, the screen door still firmly latched. As she shuffled toward me, I noticed that her cotton print burial shroud had not held up well, either. She had always been a fussy woman about her appearance, but I guess she just didn't notice how unkempt she had become. Her hair had turned into an unruly mess, filled with knots and tangles. The fingernails, painted a subdued red at the time of her interment, had grown ragged and coarse, the flecks of chipped polish flickering in the light of the fireplace. Her face was not for the weak-hearted. It had wrinkled and puckered into a tight mask, the main features atrophied away. Out of the general area of her mouth came a low, gurgling noise that had to be words. It was tough to understand, but it sounded like she was saying "A&P." Now, Aunt Hattie always had loved market day, but this was carrying things a little too far. It took a few minutes before I realized she didn't really want to go shopping at all. She was trying to say "Follow me." It must be like when children first learn to talk. No one can understand them but their parents. Aunt Hattie and I had always been close, but she was a little closer now than I cared to have her.

The air in the room was permeated with her wretched scent, so I decided to follow her as she motioned me outside. Out in the yard, I was so nervous I wasn't watching where I was going and slipped in a little of Aunt Hattie. Darn, my brand-new tennis shoes wouldn't be fit for mowing the lawn when this was over. I followed her from a distance, but the smell was still a gagging presence, hovering over everything around me. It reminded me of the time I had put out a mousetrap and had promptly forgotten about it. Until I noticed that my refrigerator had acquired a funny smell, that is. After checking all the interior contents, I decided it must have come from under the appliance. *Then* I remembered the long-forgotten mouse trap. The remains I found in that trap smelled like roses compared to Aunt Hattie's bouquet.

I followed her through the yard and straight to her favorite rosebushes. Those roses had been her pride and joy when she was alive, so I figured she was just taking a quick peek at them while she was in the neighborhood. Instead of moving on, she parked her decaying carcass right in front of those roses and kept saying, "Big. Big."

Now, I had watered and pruned those roses faithfully after Aunt Hattie died. I knew how much they meant to her. It was my own secret memorial. I swelled with pride as she continued praising their growth since she had last seen them. But after a few minutes of her compliments, I grew tired of her moaning speech. My fidgeting must have attracted her attention. There wasn't much left in the way of eyeballs, but she somehow managed to convey the message that I was dumber than the horse manure she had always used to fertilize those bushes.

She finally gave up trying to speak and stumbled over to the barn, where we kept our tools. It looked to me like she was going to take a tour of the whole place, but I was in no position to protest. Just as she reached for the shovel, she started moaning, "Big, big," again, and pointing to those darned bushes. Dead or not, I was getting tired of her grunts and groans. As she reached out to whop me—a reaction I always seemed to evoke in her—the bells of Saint Thomas the Divine Catholic Church started ringing, declaring the beginning of All Saints' Day and banishing the spirits of the dead to another year of exile. As the last chime pealed, Aunt Hattie did the most unusual thing she had done since she had walked into my living room earlier that night, she disappeared. Poof. No more Aunt Hattie and no more smell. I ran back to the house, more frightened by her vanishing act than her reappearance. I was stunned and looked at my rug. I couldn't believe it, but it was just as clean as it had been before her visit. Looking down, I saw that my tennis shoes were spotless, too—except for the dog poo that I had somehow picked up in the yard following her cadaver around.

About a year has passed since Aunt Hattie first visited me in the living room, and I am ready for her if she should decide to make a return visit this Halloween. The rosebushes are as pretty as ever, and I polished up the shovel in case she wants to see it again. I can't help thinking she was trying to tell me something last year, and if I can remember, I'm going to find out about those coins, too. Oh well. I'll ask her the next time I see her.

THE HAUNTED DOLLS' HOUSE

M. R. JAMES

"I suppose you get stuff of that kind through your hands pretty often?" said Mr. Dillet, as he pointed with his stick to an object which shall be described when the time comes: and when he said it, he lied in his throat, and knew that he lied. Not once in twenty years—perhaps not once in a lifetime—could Mr. Chittenden, skilled as he was in ferreting out the forgotten treasures of half a dozen counties, expect to handle such a specimen. It was collectors' palaver, and Mr. Chittenden recognized it as such.

"Stuff of that kind, Mr. Dillet! It's a museum piece, that is."

"Well, I suppose there are museums that'll take anything."

"I've seen one, not as good as that, years back," said Mr. Chittenden thoughtfully, "but that's not likely to come into the market: and I'm told they 'ave some fine ones of the period over the water. No, I'm only telling you the truth, Mr. Dillet, when I say that if you was to place an unlimited order with me for the very best that could be got—and you know I 'ave facilities for getting to know of such things, and a reputation to maintain—well, all I can say is, I should lead you straight up to that one and say, 'I can't do any better for you than that, sir.'"

"Hear, hear!" said Mr. Dillet, applauding ironically with the end of his stick on the floor of the shop. "How much are you sticking the innocent American buyer for it, eh?"

"Oh, I shan't be over hard on the buyer, American or

otherwise. You see, it stands this way, Mr. Dillet—if I knew just a bit more about the pedigree—"

"Or just a bit less," Mr. Dillet put in.

"Ha, ha! You will have your joke, sir. No, but as I was saying, if I knew just a little more than what I do about the piece—though anyone can see for themselves it's a genuine thing, every last corner of it, and there's not been one of my men allowed to so much as touch it since it came into the shop—there'd be another figure in the price I'm asking."

"And what's that: five and twenty?"

"Multiply that by three and you've got it, sir. Seventy-five's my price."

"And fifty's mine," said Mr. Dillet.

The point of agreement was, of course, somewhere between the two, it does not matter exactly where—I think sixty guineas. But half an hour later the object was being packed, and within an hour Mr. Dillet had called for it in his car and driven away. Mr. Chittenden, holding the cheque in his hand, saw him off from the door with smiles, and returned, still smiling, into the parlour where his wife was making the tea. He stopped at the door.

"It's gone," he said.

"Thank God for that!" said Mrs. Chittenden, putting down the teapot. "Mr. Dillet, was it?"

"Yes, it was."

"Well, I'd sooner it was him than another."

"Oh, I don't know; he ain't a bad feller, my dear."

"Maybe not, but in my opinion he'd be none the worse for a bit of a shake-up."

"Well, if that's your opinion, it's my opinion he's put himself into the way of getting one. Anyhow, *we* shan't have no more of it, and that's something to be thankful for."

And so Mr. and Mrs. Chittenden sat down to tea.

And what of Mr. Dillet and of his new acquisition? What it was, the title of this story will have told you. What it was like, I shall have to indicate as well as I can.

There was only just room enough for it in the car, and Mr. Dillet had to sit with the driver: he had also to go slow, for though the rooms of the dolls' house had all been stuffed carefully with soft cotton wool, jolting was to be avoided, in view of the immense number of small objects which thronged them; and the ten-mile drive was an anxious time for him, in spite of all the precautions he insisted upon. At last his front door was reached, and Collins, the butler, came out.

"Look here, Collins, you must help me with this thing—it's a delicate job. We must get it out upright, see? It's full of little things that mustn't be displaced more than we can help. Let's see, where shall we have it? (After a pause for consideration.) Really, I think I shall have to put it in my own room, to begin with at any rate. On the big table—that's it."

It was conveyed—with much talking—to Mr. Dillet's spacious room on the first floor, looking out on the drive. The sheeting was unwound from it, and the front thrown open, and for the next hour or two Mr. Dillet was fully occupied in extracting the padding and setting in order the contents of the rooms.

When this thoroughly congenial task was finished, I must say that it would have been difficult to find a more perfect and attractive specimen of a dolls' house in Strawberry Hill Gothic than that which now stood on Mr. Dillet's large kneehole table, lighted up by the evening sun which came slanting through three tall sash-windows.

It was quite six feet long, including the chapel or oratory which flanked the front on the left as you faced it, and the stable on the right. The main block on the house was, as I have said, in the Gothic manner: that is to say, the windows had pointed arches and were surmounted by what are called ogival hoods, with crockets and finials such as we see on the canopies of tombs built into church walls. At the angles were absurd turrets covered with arched panels. The chapel had pinnacles and buttresses, and a bell in the turret and coloured glass in the windows. When the front of the house was open you saw four large rooms, bedroom, dining room, drawing room, and kitchen, each with its appropriate furniture in a very complete state.

The stable on the right was in two storeys, with its proper

complement of horses, coaches, and grooms, and with its
clock and Gothic cupola for the clock bell.

Pages, of course, might be written on the outfit of the
mansion—how many frying pans, how many gilt chairs,
what pictures, carpets, chandeliers, fourposters, table linen,
glass, crockery, and plate it possessed; but all this must be
left to the imagination. I will only say that the base of
plinth on which the house stood (for it was fitted with one
of some depth which allowed of a flight of steps to the front
door and a terrace, partly balustraded) contained a shallow
drawer or drawers in which were neatly stored sets of em-
broidered curtains, changes of raiment for the inmates, and,
in short, all the materials for an infinite series of variations
and refittings of the most absorbing and delightful kind.

"Quintessence of Horace Walpole, that's what it is: he
must have had something to do with the making of it."
Such was Mr. Dillet's murmured reflection as he knelt before it in a reverent ecstasy. "Simply wonderful! This is my
day and no mistake. Five hundred pounds coming in this
morning for that cabinet which I never cared about, and
now this tumbling into my hands for a tenth, at the very
most, of what it would fetch in town. Well, well! It almost
makes one afraid something'll happen to counter it. Let's
have a look at the population, anyhow."

Accordingly, he set them before him in a row. Again,
here is an opportunity, which some would snatch at, of
making an inventory of costume: I am incapable of it.

There was a gentleman and lady, in blue satin and brocade respectively. There were two children, a boy and a
girl. There was a cook, a nurse, a footman, and there were
the stable servants, two postilions, a coachman, two
grooms.

"Anyone else? Yes, possibly."

The curtains of the fourposter in the bedroom were
closely drawn round all four sides of it, and he put his finger in between them and felt in the bed. He drew the finger
back hastily, for it almost seemed to him as if something
had—not stirred, perhaps, but yielded—in an odd live way
as he pressed it. Then he put back the curtains, which ran
on rods in the proper manner, and extracted from the bed a

white-haired old gentleman in a long linen nightdress and cap, and laid him down by the rest. The tale was complete.

Dinnertime was now near, so Mr. Dillet spent but five minutes in putting the lady and children into the drawing room, the gentleman into the dining room, the servants into the kitchen and stables, and the old man back into his bed. He retired into his dressing room next door, and we see and hear no more of him until something like eleven o'clock at night.

His whim was to sleep surrounded by some of the gems of his collection. The big room in which we have seen him contained his bed: bath, wardrobe, and all the appliances of dressing were in a commodious room adjoining: but his fourposter, which itself was a valued treasure, stood in the large room where he sometimes wrote, and often sat, and even received visitors. Tonight he repaired to it in a highly complacent frame of mind.

There was no striking clock within earshot—none on the staircase, none in the stable, none in the distant church tower. Yet it is indubitable that Mr. Dillet was startled out of a very pleasant slumber by a bell tolling one.

He was so much startled that he did not merely lie breathless with wide-open eyes, but actually sat up in his bed.

He never asked himself, till the morning hours, how it was that, though there was no light at all in the room, the dolls' house on the kneehole table stood out with complete clearness. But it was so. The effect was that of a bright harvest moon shining full on the front of a big white stone mansion—a quarter of a mile away it might be, and yet every detail was photographically sharp. There were trees about it, too—trees rising behind the chapel and the house. He seemed to be conscious of the scent of a cool, still September night. He thought he could hear an occasional stamp and clink from the stable, as of horses stirring. And with another shock he realised that, above the house, he was looking, not at the wall of his room with its pictures, but into the profound blue of a night sky.

There were lights, more than one, in the windows, and he quickly saw that this was no four-roomed house with a movable front, but one of many rooms, and staircases—a real house, but seen as if through the wrong end of a telescope. "You mean to show me something," he muttered to himself, and he gazed earnestly on the lighted windows. They would in real life have been shuttered or curtained, no doubt, he thought; but, as it was, there was nothing to intercept his view of what was being transacted inside the rooms.

Two rooms were lighted—one on the ground floor to the right of the door, one upstairs, on the left—the first brightly enough, the other rather dimly. The lower room was the dining room: a table was laid, but the meal was over, and only wine and glasses were left on the table. The man of the blue satin and the woman of the brocade were alone in the room, and they were talking very earnestly, seated close together at the table, their elbows on it: every now and again stopping to listen, as it seemed. Once *he* rose, came to the window and opened it, and put his head out and his hand to his ear. There was a lighted taper in a silver candlestick on a sideboard. When the man left the window he seemed to leave the room also; and the lady, taper in hand, remained standing and listening. The expression on her face was that of one striving her utmost to keep down a fear that threatened to master her—and succeeding. It was a hateful face, too; broad, flat, and sly. Now the man came back and she took some small thing from him and hurried out of the room. He, too, disappeared, but only for a moment or two. The front door slowly opened and he stepped out and stood on the top of the perron, looking this way and that; then turned towards the upper window that was lighted, and shook his fist.

It was time to look at that upper window. Through it was seen a four-post bed: a nurse or other servant in an armchair, evidently sound asleep; in the bed an old man lying: awake, and, one would say, anxious, from the way in which he shifted about and moved his fingers, beating tunes on the coverlet. Beyond the bed a door opened. Light was seen on the ceiling, and the lady came in: she set down her candle on a table, came to the fireside, and roused the nurse. In her hand she had an old-fashioned wine bottle, ready uncorked. The nurse took it, poured some of the contents into a little silver saucepan, added some spice and sugar from casters on the table, and set it to warm on the fire. Meanwhile the old man in the bed beckoned feebly to the lady, who came to him, smiling, took his wrist as if to feel his pulse, and bit her lip as if in consternation. He looked at her anxiously, and then pointed to the window, and spoke. She nodded, and did as the man below had done; opened the casement and listened—perhaps rather ostentatiously: then drew in her head and shook it, looking at the old man, who seemed to sigh.

By this time the posset on the fire was steaming, and the nurse poured it into a small two-handled silver bowl and brought it to the bedside. The old man seemed disinclined for it and was waving it away, but the lady and the nurse together bent over him and evidently pressed it upon him. He must have yielded, for they supported him into a sitting position, and put it to his lips. He drank most of it, in several draughts, and they laid him down. The lady left the room, smiling good nights to him, and took the bowl, the bottle, and the silver saucepan with her. The nurse returned to the chair, and there was an interval of complete quiet.

Suddenly the old man started up in his bed—and he must have uttered some cry, for the nurse started out of her chair and made but one step of it to the bedside. He was a sad and terrible sight—flushed in the face, almost to blackness, the eyes glaring whitely, both hands clutching at his heart, foam at his lips.

For a moment the nurse left him, ran to the door, flung it wide open, and, one supposes, screamed aloud for help, then darted back to the bed and seemed to try feverishly to soothe him—to lay him down—anything. But as the lady, her husband, and several servants, rushed into the room with horrified faces, the old man collapsed under the nurse's hands and lay back, and the features, contorted with agony and rage, relaxed slowly into calm.

A few moments later, lights showed out to the left of the house, and a coach with flambeaux drove up to the door. A white-wigged man in black got nimbly out and ran up the steps, carrying a small leather trunk-shaped box. He was

met in the doorway by the man and his wife, she with her
handkerchief clutched between her hands, he with a tragic
face, but retaining his self-control. They led the newcomer
into the dining room, where he set his box of papers on the
table, and, turning to them, listened with a face of consternation at what they had to tell. He nodded his head again
and again, threw out his hands slightly, declined, it
seemed, offers of refreshment and lodging for the night,
and within a few minutes came slowly down the steps, entering the coach and driving off the way he had come. As
the man in blue watched him from the top of the steps, a
smile not pleasant to see stole over his fat white face.
Darkness fell over the whole scene as the lights of the
coach disappeared.

But Mr. Dillet remained sitting up in the bed: he had
rightly guessed that there would be a sequel. The house
front glimmered out again before long. But now there was a
difference. The lights were in other windows, one at the top
of the house, the other illuminating the range of coloured
windows of the chapel. How he saw through these is not
quite obvious, but he did. The interior was as carefully furnished as the rest of the establishment, with its minute red
cushions on the desks, its Gothic stall-canopies, and its
western gallery and pinnacled organ with gold pipes. On
the centre of the black and white pavement was a bier: four
tall candles burned at the corners. On the bier was a coffin
covered with a pall of black velvet.

As he looked the folds of the pall stirred. It seemed to
rise at one end: it slid downwards: it fell away, exposing
the black coffin with its silver handles and nameplate.
One of the tall candlesticks swayed and toppled over. Ask
no more, but turn, as Mr. Dillet hastily did, and look in at
the lighted window at the top of the house, where a boy
and girl lay in two truckle beds, and a four-poster for the
nurse rose above them. The nurse was not visible for the
moment; but the father and mother were there, dressed
now in mourning, but with very little sign of mourning in
their demeanour. Indeed, they were laughing and talking
with a good deal of animation, sometimes to each other,
and sometimes throwing a remark to one or other of the

children, and again laughing at the answers. Then the father was seen to go on tiptoe out of the room, taking with
him as he went a white garment that hung on a peg near
the door. He shut the door after him. A minute or two
later it was slowly opened again, and a muffled head
poked round it. A bent form of sinister shape stepped
across to the truckle beds and suddenly stopped, threw up
its arms, and revealed, of course, the father, laughing. The
children were in agonies of terror, the boy with the bed-
clothes over his head, the girl throwing herself out of bed
into her mother's arms. Attempts at consolation followed—the parents took the children on their laps, patted
them, picked up the white gown and showed there was no
harm in it, and so forth; and at last, putting the children
back into bed, left the room with encouraging waves of
the hand. As they left it, the nurse came in, and soon the
light died down.

Still Mr. Dillet watched, immovable.

A new sort of light—not of lamp or candle—a pale ugly
light, began to dawn around the door-case at the back of the
room. The door was opening again. The seer does not like
to dwell upon what he saw entering the room: he says it
might be described as a frog—the size of a man—but it had
scanty white hair about its head. It was busy about the
truckle beds, but not for long. The sound of cries—faint, as
if coming out of a vast distance—but, even so, infinitely
appalling, reached the ear.

There were signs of a hideous commotion all over the
house: lights moved along and up, and doors opened and
shut, and running figures passed within the windows. The
clock in the stable turret tolled one, and darkness fell again.

It was only dispelled once more, to show the house front.
At the bottom of the steps dark figures were drawn up in
two lines, holding flaming torches. More dark figures came
down the steps, bearing first one, then another small coffin.
And the lines of torchbearers with the coffins between them
moved silently onward to the left.

The hours of night passed on—never so slowly, Mr. Dillet thought. Gradually he sank down from sitting to lying in

his bed—but he did not close an eye: and early next morning he sent for the doctor.

The doctor found him in a disquieting state of nerves, and recommended sea air. To a quiet place on the east coast he accordingly repaired by easy stages in his car.

One of the first people he met on the sea front was Mr. Chittenden, who, it appeared, had likewise been advised to take his wife away for a bit of a change.

Mr. Chittenden looked somewhat askance upon him when they met: and not without cause.

"Well, I don't wonder at you being a bit upset, Mr. Dillet. What? Yes, well, I might say 'orrible upset, to be sure, seeing what me and my poor wife went through ourselves. But I put it to you, Mr. Dillet, one of two things: was I going to scrap a lovely piece like that on the one 'and, or was I going to tell customers, 'I'm selling you a regular picture-palace-dramar in real life of the olden time, billed to perform regular at one o'clock A.M.'? Why, what would you 'ave said yourself? And next thing you know, two justices of the peace in the back parlour, and pore Mr. and Mrs. Chittenden off in a spring cart to the county asylum and everyone in the street saying, 'Ah, I thought it 'ud come to that. Look at the way the man drank!'—and me next door, or next door but one, to a total abstainer, as you know. Well, there was my position. What? Me 'ave it back in the shop? Well, what do *you* think? No, but I'll tell you what I will do. You shall have your money back, bar the ten pound I paid for it, and you make what you can."

Later in the day, in what is offensively called the "smoke room" of the hotel, a murmured conversation between the two went on for some time.

"How much do you really know about that thing, and where it came from?"

"Honest, Mr. Dillet, I don't know the 'ouse. Of course, it came out of the lumber room of a country 'ouse—that anyone could guess. But I'll go as far as say this, that I believe it's not a hundred miles from this place. Which direction and how far I've no notion. I'm only judging by guesswork. The man as I actually paid the cheque to ain't one of my regular men, and I've lost sight of him; but I 'ave the idea that this part of the country was his beat, and that's every word I can tell you. But now, Mr. Dillet, there's one thing that rather physicks me. That old chap—I suppose you saw him drive up to the door—I thought so: now, would he have been the medical man, do you take it? My wife would have it so, but I stuck to it that was the lawyer, because he had papers with him, and one he took out was folded up."

"I agree," said Mr. Dillet. "Thinking it over, I came to the conclusion that was the old man's will, ready to be signed."

"Just what I thought," said Mr. Chittenden, "and I took it that will would have cut out the young people, eh? Well, well! It's been a lesson to me, I know that. I shan't buy no more dolls' houses, nor waste no more money on the pictures—and as to this business of poisonin' grandpa, well, if I know myself, I never 'ad much of a turn for that. Live and let live: that's bin my motto throughout life, and I ain't found it a bad one."

Filled with these elevated sentiments, Mr. Chittenden retired to his lodgings. Mr. Dillet next day repaired to the local Institute, where he hoped to find some clue to the riddle that absorbed him. He gazed in despair at a long file of the Canterbury and York Society's publications of the parish registers of the district. No print resembling the house of his nightmare was among those that hung on the staircase and in the passages. Disconsolate, he found himself at last in a derelict room, staring at a dusty model of a church in a dusty glass case: *Model of St. Stephen's Church, Coxham, Presented by J. Merewether, Esq., of Ilbridge House, 1877. The work of his ancestor James Merewether, d. 1786.* There was something in the fashion of it that reminded him dimly of his horror. He retraced his steps to a wall map he had noticed, and made out that Ilbridge House was in Coxham Parish. Coxham was, as it happened, one of the parishes of which he had retained the name when he glanced over the file of printed registers, and it was not long before he found in them the record of the burial of Roger Milford, aged seventy-six, on the eleventh

of September, 1757, and of Roger and Elizabeth
Merewether, aged nine and seven, on the nineteenth of the
same month. It seemed worthwhile to follow up this clue,
frail as it was; and in the afternoon he drove out to Coxham. The east end of the north aisle of the church is a Milford chapel, and on its north wall are tablets to the same
persons; Roger, the elder, it seems, was distinguished by all
the qualities which adorn "the Father, the Magistrate, and
the Man": the memorial was erected by his attached daughter Elizabeth, "who did not long survive the loss of a parent
ever solicitous for her welfare, and of two amiable children." The last sentence was plainly an addition to the original inscription.

A yet later slab told of James Merewether, husband of
Elizabeth "who in the dawn of life practised, not without
success, those arts which, had he continued their exercise,
might in the opinion of the most competent judges have
earned for him the name of the British Vitruvius: but who,
overwhelmed by the visitation which deprived him of an
affectionate partner and a blooming offspring, passed his
Prime and Age in a secluded yet elegant Retirement: his
grateful Nephew and Heir indulges a pious sorrow by this
too brief recital of his excellences."

The children were more simply commemorated. Both
died on the night of the twelfth of September.

Mr. Dillet felt sure that in Ilbridge House he had found
the scene of his drama. In some old sketchbook, possibly in
some old print, he may yet find convincing evidence that he
is right. But the Ilbridge House of today is not that which
he sought; it is an Elizabethan erection of the forties, in red
brick with stone quoins and dressings. A quarter of a mile
from it, in a low part of the park, backed by ancient, stag-
horned, ivy-strangled trees and thick undergrowth, are
marks of a terraced platform overgrown with rough grass.
A few stone balusters lie here and there, and a heap or two,
covered with nettles and ivy, of wrought stones with badly
carved crockets. This, someone told Mr. Dillet, was the site
of an older house.

As he drove out of the village, the hall clock struck four,

and Mr. Dillet started up and clapped his hands to his ears. It was not the first time he had heard that bell.

Awaiting an offer from the other side of the Atlantic, the dolls' house still reposes, carefully sheeted, in a loft over Mr. Dillet's stables, whither Collins conveyed it on the day when Mr. Dillet started for the seacoast.

VOODOO DEATH

GREGOR ROBINSON

It was past midnight and we had finished our business, but Irish whisky and a steady rain, both rare in the islands, kept us late. Mrs. Hamish had cleared the dinner dishes and gone to bed. Now the whisky bottle stood almost empty on the table between us and we sat silent, listening to the gurgle of the water running down the roof and into the concrete cistern beneath the floor. The rain seemed to be letting up—it was difficult to tell with that sibilant rush, the drumming on the window panes; I was half hypnotized—but still it drowned the sound of the surf below. I was planning to walk home along the path which wound through the scrub growth above the beach; it was the shortest route from Burnett's house back to the village. I waited for the rain to stop.

"Not so much the rain as the night you have to be careful of," said Burnett. "Voodoo," he added, with exaggerated dark meaning. "Feeding the *loa*."

I told him I wasn't afraid of the dark. I wasn't superstitious.

"All the same, easy to get lost out there." He gestured towards the black window. "The paths crisscross and twist back on one another. Before you know it, you wind up in the bush at the other end of the island. Completely lost. Zombie country." He grinned. I didn't. He said, "Tell you what: when the rain lets up, I'll get Tommas to drive you home."

Tommas was one of the Haitian refugees. He lived in a

wood hut on a corner of Burnett's property, in return for which he did a little work around the plantation. Tommas would resent being roused in the middle of the night to drive me home—he was sullen at the sunniest of times— and I preferred to walk. But there was little choice, for Burnett had begun the laborious business of cleaning his pipe; soon he was filling it with fresh tobacco. He said:

"I ever tell you about Taff?"

There was no need to answer; Burnett was on his way. Sitting there with a day's growth of beard and his foul pipe, he looked like an old sailor, the kind who, if you saw him at a bar, you'd give a wide berth. The bright gleam of his blue eyes made him look a little off. But he was a director of the bank, and Healey had advised me to humor him. Several times a year Burnett flew to Montreal for board meetings, a different person there, I supposed, in his grey suit and tightly knotted tie, than he was here. If he had a story to tell, I was the one to listen: an employee's obligation. He was a widower and he liked to talk. In Montreal he had this reputation—rather fierce. But living alone in the islands had made him garrulous and a terrible gossip. I poured myself more whisky, just a drop, the one I had declined a moment before. In fact I had heard snatches of the Taff story; it was almost island myth.

"Taffy, everyone called him," Burnett said. "He was an Englishman. Came out to see about starting up some kind of school here. Actually, I had met him in London several years earlier, through my squash club—he still had the damn tie, used to wear it to the Yacht Club on Saturday nights. In England he had been a schoolteacher for a time, then some kind of businessman. Direct sales and patent medicines, that kind of thing; you didn't want to go into it too closely. He seemed to think I could be of some help in this school project of his. He was here maybe six or seven months altogether, but it never came to anything. He was like you, not afraid of the dark, said you could never get lost.

" 'Whatever happens, you come to the sea,' he used to say; 'all you do is follow the coast. One way or another, you come to a pier, somebody's house. Then you're home free.' "

"Something in that," I said.

Burnett continued, ignoring my comment.

"Said he didn't believe in voodoo either, of course, made a great point of it. Called it mumbo-jumbo, the going into trances and so forth, a religion for the ignorant. After all, he was English. 'The Brits are down to earth. Unhysterical,' he said. 'Sensible people. You saw it in the Blitz, old boy.' Who was going to argue with that?"

"Did he actually call you 'old boy?' " I said.

"All the time," said Burnett. "Hexing, spells, the pointing of the bone, whatever you call it—he didn't believe in that either."

"Do you?" I asked. I knew it was all nonsense.

"No," said Burnett, "or rather, I don't like to say. It's like the Holy Ghost, the Trinity. What's all that supposed to mean? You tell me. But here it's in the air. Even the villagers more than half believe, and they're not Haitian. Mrs. Hamish, the housekeeper, you saw her, she's a sensible woman. But talk to her on Christmas Eve, or New Year's. She won't leave the village those nights, and I know what she means. On those nights you can hear the drums from the center of the island wherever you go. If you interrupt the ceremony, the *hougan* will throw a curse." He looked at me, pausing for effect. Then he said, "Have you ever seen a zombie?"

"Only on the *Late Show*," I said.

"You know the fellow Touissant who sweeps the sidewalk in front of the hotel, cleans up the garbage bins?"

I laughed. "Slow," I said, "not a zombie. Mentally backward. He's lucky he lives in the islands. In a big city, he'd be out on the streets."

"Touissant used to work on a forest plantation on Great Abaco," Burnett said. "After the place closed he wandered around in the scrub behind Marsh Harbour. People gave him food. Then one of the refugees saw him, fellow from the north, near Cap Haitien. Said he knew Touissant, that he had died several years before. No one would have much to do with him after that; that's when Madame Grumbacher at the hotel brought him over here."

"What do you think?" I asked.

"It's not what I think," said Burnett. "It's what happens. The *hougan* throws a curse and the victim gets sick and dies."

"Do people actually get sick and die?" I asked.

"Of course people get sick and die. All the time. Always will. Nothing to do with voodoo. Plain illness or maybe poison, that's what Taffy used to say. He'd researched it."

Taffy sounded sensible to me.

"Sensible," said Burnett, "but he had a weakness."

"Who doesn't?" I said.

"He liked to gamble. People on the island didn't notice it at first. I certainly didn't. Gamblers are like alcoholics, you know; they hide their addiction. When Taffy was first here he used to travel a great deal, almost every week. He said it was to talk to people about the school, financial people and so on, government officials. But it was always to places like Grand Cayman and Free Town, places where they have the casinos. Easy money.

"The school plan of his should have given us a clue: he kept changing the notion of what the thing was for. At first it was supposed to be art and drama, something Taffy was interested in—he had even joined the Strawboaters, who perform in the Methodist Chapel; did a very nice Boris Karloff in *Arsenic and Old Lace*. Then he started talking about the project as some kind of science school, a center for human studies, like that place they have over on Andros. Learn all about plants, he said. Finally it was anthropology, which was logical because Taffy was something of an anthropologist himself. There would be field trips to remote places, to see how the backward people live, examine the connections with Africa and so on.

"But the real purpose was money. Whatever else the school was for, it was going to make pots of money. 'Snob appeal, old boy,' he told me. 'A place for rich people to send the brats. Broken homes. We'll get them from all over—the States, Britain, Latin America.' He wanted me to invest, so I heard all about it; of course he knew I was con-

nected with the bank. The pitch was get rich quick. I believe he collected quite a lot of money.

"Anyway, it turned out he had visited every casino in the
West Indies. Then he started gambling here on the island—
perhaps they didn't want him elsewhere, I don't know.
There's a game at the Majestic Hotel on Saturday nights
when the dart league plays; he got into that, but it was
hardly enough action for a real gambler like he was. He
asked around—at the pool room at the Riverside, at the marina, down at the government pier. Word got out. One day
Ti-Paul approached, the fellow who works on the ferry,
asked Taffy if he would like to play down at Annie's
place."

Burnett had my interest. Annie's was at the far end of the
island, at the mouth of a broad, shallow lagoon known as
Fish Mangrove. It was where the drug shippers gathered; at
least, that is what everyone in the village believed. If the
wind was low, you could sometimes hear the throaty roar
of speedboats leaving the lagoon in the middle of the night.
I had never been to Annie's place. But it was what I wanted
to hear about: a hint of corrupt romance.

"There's often a big game at Annie's," Burnett said,
"people from Miami, the other islands. The first few nights
Taffy did well, seemed to know what he was doing. But of
course one night he began to lose, which always happens to
gamblers, and he kept playing and playing. He ended up
losing badly. Everything he had, and he had markers down
for fifteen thousand dollars. That pilot was there, Wade,
and he had brought some fellows from Colombia. You lose
to them, you pay. I suppose Taffy suddenly seemed like
only an Englishman schoolteacher, a shabby con man.
Scared. Small time.

"Ti-Paul took Taffy into the back room, to try and work
something out. There was some difficulty. Ti-Paul and
some of the other Haitians run a little loan operation out of
the Riverside, but they couldn't do the whole amount. It
may not seem like a lot to us, but fifteen thousand was too
much for them to raise, and they were nervous. Annie herself came up with about a thousand dollars; she didn't want
trouble at her place. Ti-Paul could raise almost eleven thou-

sand, but, as I say, he was wary about making the loan. That's when they called me on the radiophone."

"You?"

"Tommas was out at Annie's that night, drinking at the bar; he had introduced Taffy to the game after all. He backed up Taffy's claim that he knew me. They called me at around midnight. I agreed to put up the other three thousand; it sounded serious for Taffy—what could I say? Naturally they wanted cash. I had the money in the house; that was before we had a branch of the bank here on the island. Tommas and Ti-Paul came over immediately.

"That was the most I would do. I told them that I knew Taffy, that he had been a businessman in London—stretching a point—that he was starting a school on the island. But I wouldn't take responsibility for his loans. I suppose it was enough that I even knew him because in the end they agreed to lend him the rest.

"Looking back on it now, I don't think Taffy ever had any intention of repaying Ti-Paul. He paid Annie back almost right away—he had his reputation as a gambler and his potential investors to think of, after all. Annie knew people who came by airplane, and that kind of news travels fast—and he managed to pay me a little within a few weeks. But the big debt to Ti-Paul kept dragging on and on. Tommas came to see me about it. Said he had heard if Taffy didn't pay there was going to be a ceremony in the forest; Ti-Paul would throw a curse. Turn Taffy into a slave."

"A slave?" I had to smile.

"A zombie—just what we were talking about. That's the drill, you know. They kill the fellow with magic, then bring him back—the undead—to be a slave. Like Touissant."

"Right." The rain had stopped. I made a move to leave, but Burnett ignored it. He said:

"I asked him if Ti-Paul thought that kind of threat would induce Taffy to pay up. He just shrugged his shoulders.

"But, you see, the threat of sorcery was the way Ti-Paul's operation worked. Everybody knew about it. It was the best means of enforcement they knew; no goons necessary: they only lent to believers. Taffy started receiving messages—a skull and cross drawn with chalk on the sidewalk in front of his house, a couple of bloodied white feathers and a rock thrown through the window, ugly printed notes. He showed a couple of the notes to me. Then a peculiar thing started to happen: people began to ignore Taffy. It began with the Haitians, of course; it's part of the process. They walked past him in the street as though he wasn't there. All the Haitians did it: Madame Dell who does the laundry, Pierre down at the wharf, the fellows at the marina. Ti-Paul no longer harangued Taffy about the loan. The debt was no longer an issue. And it spread to the villagers. They hardly spoke with Taffy, and they spoke about him even less, as though his fate were a foregone conclusion. As for the tourists and expatriates, those of us who were here watched with amazement.

"One morning Taffy opened the door of the little cottage he had rented to find a dead chicken nailed to the frame. The throat had been slit and blood streaked down the wood onto his floor. There was a cross and a circle of white powder on the steps.

"The next day or two Taffy visited all the merchants with whom he had done business. He was settling up his bills— the little ones at least. He paid Drover down at the grocery store. He paid Mrs. Rainy. He paid Madame Dell, who had complained to everyone that he was always weeks behind. He made a great show of it; the whole village saw. I was in town for lunch and I met Taffy at the bar of the Majestic; it was before the tourists and charter yachts had arrived, the time of year when the locals use the place. I had heard about the chicken nailed to the doorway. Mrs. Hamish had told me over breakfast; news like that travels like wildfire. But I was surprised at Taffy's flurry of activity. I asked him what he was up to.

" 'Voodoo, old boy,' he said in a flat voice. 'Afraid I've become a believer.' I thought he looked a little wan. Then he winked. He never offered to pay me.

"One night, less than a week later, I heard a drumbeat from the woods. Mrs. Hamish had just brought in the coffee tray when it began, and she looked up with a frown. As far as either of us knew it was not a religious day nor a special occasion. I strolled over to the garage to speak with Tommas. He was not a believer but he respected those who were, and he usually knew what was going on. Not this time. The drumming was closer than usual; it seemed to be coming from the trees out beyond my tennis court, above the beach path. I suggested we go and have a look.

"We followed the drumbeat into the woods—it was in fact much farther back than it sounded—until we saw light wavering through the trees. The light became brighter. We saw storm lanterns hanging from branches around a little clearing. There was a fire in the middle of the clearing, and a figure dancing around the fire, beating the drum and shaking a bone rattle. In the woods nearby there was movement, people approaching quietly through the flickering darkness, attracted like us, by the drums and fire.

"When we had crept to within about twenty-five feet of the fire, Tommas held out his arm and whispered, no farther. We were part of a silent circle among the trees, watching. I could see the figure by the light of the fire, dancing in a kind of trance, humming a low drone. A woman advanced from the shadows into the circle of light, dancing to the rhythm of the drum. She moved rigidly, like a person of wood. Her face was frozen, her eyes wide, and she howled. Another woman came into the circle, then a third. Ti-Paul put the drum down. He kept up the guttural humming.

"Near the fire was an old oil barrel cut in half, the kind they used to make steel drums, and a neat pile of broad green leaves and tiny bones. Ti-Paul put the leaves and bones into the oil drum, then began beating them with a stick. One of the possessed women picked another stick and began beating along with him. When the contents of the drum had been pounded into powder, the *hougan* bent down and picked something from the ground. He held it high above his head. It was a doll-shaped bundle of sticks, around which was knotted Taffy's Racquets Club necktie. A *paquet*. There was a howl from the silent circle in the woods. Ti-Paul hurled the *paquet* into the oil drum. The women continued beating with their sticks; they pulverized that little bundle. Ti-Paul threw the whole works into the fire with a burst of flame and a wild shout.

"Taffy was in the clinic two days later. He had been off the island and was in the air over the Berry Islands when the first symptoms appeared. He began to feel faint and nauseated. His skin was cold and moist, his pulse became very rapid."

"The symptoms of severe shock," I said, "continual adrenal overload. Fear. I have heard of such things after a car crash."

"Why did it hit him at that particular moment?" Burnett said. "He did not know when the magic was being done, or if it had been done."

I had no answer for that.

"By the time he went into the clinic here that evening, he was coughing. His blood pressure was very low, his red blood count high, he had lost weight. He asked for me. Naturally I went to see him. By that time he was having great difficulty breathing. Said something about the box, something about its working right. Delirious, I'd say. Then he passed out.

"By morning Taffy was dead. A mysterious ailment, but it was no mystery to the Haitians. Ti-Paul was a *hougan*. Taffy was buried the next day. It was late summer, and they don't keep bodies long around here. There was a little service at the Methodist Chapel where Taffy had done his acting. I heard that there was another ceremony in the woods that night, a kind of mourning ritual, meant to guide Taffy safely into the land of the dead. Too bad about Mr. Taff, people in the village said. You could be sure that they would not fall behind on *their* payments to Ti-Paul."

Burnett paused to relight his pipe.

"You're telling me they killed him with voodoo?" I said.

"You have nothing to worry about. You're not a believer."

"Is the body still in the graveyard?"

"They say not, of course," said Burnett. "Lives in the bush somewhere, hidden away. I haven't the slightest idea. You walk home through the scrub tonight, you might see him."

It had started to rain again. Burnett rose from his chair and went over to the walkie-talkie that connected him with the out buildings. A few minutes later I said good night and climbed into the back of the Jeep.

Bouncing along the gravel road, I thought about the story of Taffy. There was something wrong. The delirious comments? Perhaps. He had known something was up—Burnett said he had looked wan, yet he winked. Why the wink? Taffy was a con man; he had come to the islands to make money. In the rear view mirror I saw the flash of Tommas' bright eyes.

"You know anything about a fellow called Mr. Taff?" I said.

"What do you want to know?" said Tommas.

"Is he a zombie?"

"No such thing." I had felt like a fool asking the question, and his answer made me feel it more. Tommas had had a couple of books of poetry published in St. Lucia—a refugee who wrote. He was used to fending off the idle curiosity of people like me. I was a banker. I rephrased the question.

"Is his body still in the graveyard?"

Tommas did not answer right away. Then he said,

"You still writing, Mr. Rennison?" Tommas had come to see me when I had first come to the islands.

"Stories only, Tommas. And reports for the bank. No poetry." I supposed I was still a disappointment. Tommas shrugged his shoulders and looked away, now considering. Then he said:

"You want to see Mr. Taff?"

I nodded. Tommas slowed the car to a stop, then threw it into reverse.

"We're going to see him now?"

Tommas didn't answer; by then we were turned around and headed south. We drove past the gates to Burnett's long gravel driveway, past the narrows where the Atlantic almost touched the sea, past the fork in the road that led off towards the cove and Annie's place. We turned off several times and soon were driving over rough and rocky tracks between the trees. We drove away from the ocean, away from the cover of the sea grapes and the warm rustle of the palm trees. The weather had quickly changed as it does in the tropics; from being fast-moving clouds came the night sky. At the side of the road, the white ironwood and quicksilver bushes looked deathly pale in the light of the half-moon. This was a part of the island to which I had never been, and the trees were ragged and taller than any I had seen. The moon was soon lost behind a tangled skein of scraggly branches. We lurched to a sudden stop.

For almost half an hour we scrambled on twisting paths. The going was hard. The islands are made of coral rock—the detritus of tiny sea creatures not so different from those that still lived at the edge of the growing reef—and everywhere that wind and rain had worn the stone away, rough growth had gained a foothold. We walked between that growth, over pitted, jagged rock. I could feel the thin rubber of my moccasins being sliced at every step. It was impossible then to know that we were on an island in the tropics. Burnett had been right: it was easy to become lost. I stopped to catch my breath. The luminous dial on my watch showed the time to be quarter to two.

"Not much farther," said Tommas. He pointed. Through the trees I saw light.

I had heard about the Haitian refugees whom no one knew, those who lived in the interior of these out islands, but I had never seen them. I saw now that the places where they lived were not even huts but leantos of gum wood and spindly pine. There were a couple of fires and several lanterns around the edge of the camp. Silent figures watched us.

Tommas said a few words in French. We were led through the ragged village to a large hut, at the opposite end of the clearing from where we had entered. Taffy sat on a wooden bench outside the hut. He was round-faced, pink, short, and balding; his steel-rimmed glasses glinted in the light of the crackling fire. He wore what must have once been a fine linen suit, now tattered, grey, and stained. His mouth was slightly open, and there was a raised streak of fleshy skin along his right temple, the badly healed scar of a wound. I had heard about this kind of mark: the wound of a coffin nail. Yet he didn't look alarming. There was nothing strange about him until we tried to speak.

"Mr. Taff?" I said.

Nothing.

"Taffy? I am a friend of Burnett's." He stared straight ahead, the same empty look about him. He was like an autistic child. Around us a group of Haitians watched. Someone spoke in Creole.

"They say he sleeps most of the day," Tommas said, translating.

"I am a friend of Burnett's," I said to Taffy, keeping it up—trying to engage him. "I am with the bank."

I thought I detected a flicker, but there was nothing. No change in the blank look. I turned to Tommas.

"What happened?" I asked him.

"He was called back from the dead the night after he was buried. Ti-Paul brought him here."

"Where is Ti-Paul?"

"Back in Haiti," said Tommas. "Came into some trouble with the believers."

There was a stirring behind us. Taffy was looking up. His lips moved.

"The box . . ." His voice was a raspy whisper. Filled with sudden energy, he rose and ran toward me; with his hands outstretched he lunged for my throat. There was sweat on his chin, a feral look of madness about the eyes. They grabbed him and he was immediately still; the frenzy vanished, and Taffy turned his stare once more to the ground. He said nothing more.

Driving home, Tommas said:

"He knew about the magic, how they do it."

"What happened?" I asked.

"He was trying to fool the spirits."

As a part of my job I traveled to Nassau every other week to visit with the regional head office, to give my paltry reports on Caribbean country analysis: who had oil; who had sugar; how the refineries were doing; estimates of political stability—that kind of thing. (We never mentioned drugs, which was where most of the money came from.) I also occasionally flew to Miami. Coming home from those trips, I generally stopped off at the branch across the channel to chat with Healey. He supervised all the out island branches.

I told him about Taffy. I had at last met a zombie.

"No way," said Healey. "He knew the whole rigmarole. They do it all with plants and the blood of sea creatures, mashed up bones, you know, stuff like that. Taff told me."

"Plants?"

"Right on. Like an anesthetic. It puts you out for a few days, makes you look dead. They put you in the cold, cold ground. Then the brothers come and dig you up. 'Course, you wake up down there, you go sort of mental. A lot of them never recover, especially if they really think they've been brought back from the dead. Walk around slack-jawed, know what I mean? But Taffy was no Haitian. He knew all about it."

"How did you know Taff?"

"Came in here trying to get money. Said he was onto a pharmaceutical breakthrough. Then it was some school, money for a nature camp or something. Pipedreams. He had a safety deposit box downstairs."

The box. "Is it still there?" I asked.

"Suppose so," said Healey. "You know, another fellow was in here a few months ago asking about Taff's money. Skinny black guy. Didn't tell him a thing, of course. Bahamian bank law."

It was strictly against the rules, but Healey opened the box. We found about fifty-five thousand dollars. Also notes on various types of plants, meticulous notes, in Taff's handwriting. He must have done them in London before he came out. There was a description of the symptoms: respiratory difficulties, weight loss, hypothermia, and hypotension. The poison was topical; it was placed in a white powder which was laid across the victim's doorway and, like drugs for seasickness, was absorbed into the bloodstream through the skin.

"They were in cahoots," I said. "It was a way for Ti-Paul to get the money he was owed. Taffy probably planned it that way from the beginning—even the losing at gambling. An they held the ceremony close to the village—where people like you and the others would hear it and investigate. After that I think it became a question of who was cheating who."

This was several days later, Saturday lunch. Burnett and I were eating conch fritters and drinking Beck's beer at the Poolside Bar of the Majestic.

"You're saying it was a scam—they were in it together?"

"They must have been. Taff had to be certain he would be dug up. Only Ti-Paul could know it was a fake. Taff would be dead, killed for gambling debts, even buried—and those from whom he had wheedled capital for his school scheme would be out the money for good. Like you *are* out the money for good. When he was brought back from the dead, he would make his way to Marsh Harbour, get the money— which had all been converted to cash and put into the safety deposit box—pay off Ti-Paul, and vanish. But something went wrong. He was given too much of the drug. He suffered from lack of oxygen down there—I don't know exactly."

"The trouble with you," said Burnett, "is that you're too removed." He was annoyed. I had forgotten how much he loved the islands and his fantastic stories. "Too analytical."

"How's that?" I asked.

"You've been in banking too long. You have an explanation for everything. All this business of topical poisons and comas. I tell you, there are two worlds: the scientific and the spiritual, religious—call it what you like. At some point, those worlds cross over. It's like the Catholic Mass. When does the wine become the Blood of Christ? It all depends on what you believe. You're quite right, I said he winked. But that was bravado. He looked terrible—and this was well before any illness. I think he half believed even then. Faith is everything—like fear. What Taffy doubted was not voodoo but science. Perhaps he believed he could cheat death. You never can. Forget about overdoses of poison or lack of oxygen. He is what you saw."

"What's that?" I said.

"The living dead."

Burnett had been in the islands too long. He believed in voodoo death. I knew that what I had seen in the woods was the wretched victim of a botched murder.

BLACK WIND

BILL PRONZINI

It was one of those freezing late-November nights, just before the winter snows, when a funny east wind comes howling down out of the mountains and across Woodbine Lake a quarter mile from the village. The sound that wind makes is something hellish, full of screams and wailings that can raise the hackles on your neck if you're not used to it. In the old days the Indians who used to live around here called it a "black wind"; they believed that it carried the voices of evil spirits, and that if you listened to it long enough it could drive you mad.

Well, there are a lot of superstitions in our part of upstate New York; nobody pays much mind to them in this modern age. Or if they do, they won't admit it even to themselves. The fact is, though, that when the black wind blows the local folks stay pretty close to home and the village, like as not, is deserted after dusk.

That was the way it was on this night. I hadn't had a customer in my diner in more than an hour, since just before seven o'clock, and I had about decided to close up early and go on home. To a glass of brandy and a good hot fire.

I was pouring myself a last cup of coffee when the headlights swung into the diner's parking lot.

They whipped in fast, off the county highway, and I heard the squeal of brakes on the gravel just out front. Kids, I thought, because that was the way a lot of them drove, even around here—fast and a little reckless. But it wasn't kids. It turned out instead to be a man and a woman in their late thirties, strangers, both of them bundled up in winter coats and mufflers, the woman carrying a big fancy alligator purse.

The wind came in with them, shrieking and swirling. I could feel the numbing chill of it even in the few seconds the door was open; it cuts through you like the blade of a knife, that wind, right straight to the bone.

The man clumped immediately to where I was behind the counter, letting the woman close the door. He was handsome in a suave, barbered city way; but his face was closed up into a mask of controlled rage. His eyes looked like a couple of smoldering embers.

"Coffee," he said. The word came out in a voice that matched his expression—hard and angry, like a threat.

"Sure thing. Two coffees."

"One coffee," he said. "Let her order her own."

The woman had come up on his left, but not close to him—one stool between them. She was nice-looking in the same kind of made-up, city way. Or she would have been if her face wasn't pinched up worse than his; the skin across her cheekbones was stretched so tight it seemed ready to split. Her eyes glistened like a pair of wet stones and didn't blink at all.

"Black coffee," she said to me.

I looked at her, at him, and I started to feel a little uneasy. There was a kind of savage tension between them, thick and crackling; I could feel it like static electricity. I wet my lips, not saying anything, and reached behind me for the coffee pot and two mugs.

The man said, "I'll have a ham-and-cheese sandwich on rye bread. No mustard, no mayonnaise; just butter. Make it to go."

"Yes, sir. How about you, ma'am?"

"Tuna fish on white," she said thinly. She had close-cropped blonde hair, wind-tangled under a loose scarf; she kept brushing at it with an agitated hand. "I'll eat it here."

"No, she won't," the man said to me. "Make it to go, just like mine."

She threw him an ugly look. "I want to eat here."

"Fine," he said—to me again; it was as if she wasn't

there. "But I'm leaving in five minutes, as soon as I drink my coffee. I want that ham-and-cheese ready by then."

"Yes, sir."

I finished pouring out the coffee and set the two mugs on the counter. The man took his, swung around, and stomped over to one of the tables. He sat down and stared at the door, blowing into the mug, using it to warm his hands.

"All right," the woman said, "all right, all right. All right." Four times like that, all to herself. Her eyes had cold little lights in them now, like spots of foxfire.

I said hesitantly, "Ma'am? Do you still want the tuna sandwich to eat here?"

She blinked then, for the first time, and focused on me. "No. To hell with it. I don't want anything to eat." She caught up her mug and took it to another of the tables, two away from the one he was sitting at.

I went down to the sandwich board and got out two pieces of rye bread and spread them with butter. The stillness in there had a strained feel, made almost eerie by the constant wailing outside. I could feel myself getting more jittery as the seconds passed.

While I sliced ham I watched the two of them at the tables—him still staring at the door, drinking his coffee in quick angry sips; her facing the other way, her hands fisted in her lap, the steam from her cup spiraling up around her face. Well-off married couple from New York City, I thought: they were both wearing the same type of expensive wedding ring. On their way to a weekend in the mountains, maybe, or up to Canada for a few days. And they'd had a hell of a fight over something, the way married people do on long tiring drives; that was all there was to it.

Except that that *wasn't* all there was to it.

I've owned this diner 30 years and I've seen a lot of folks come and go in that time; a lot of tourists from the city, with all sorts of marital problems. But I'd never seen any like these two. That tension between them wasn't anything fresh-born, wasn't just the brief and meaningless aftermath of a squabble. No, there was real hatred on both sides—the kind that builds and builds, seething, over long bitter weeks or months or even years. The kind that's liable to explode some day.

Well, it wasn't really any of my business. Not unless the blowup happened in here, it wasn't, and that wasn't likely. Or so I kept telling myself. But I was a little worried just the same. On a night like this, with that damned black wind blowing and playing hell with people's nerves, anything could happen. Anything at all.

I finished making the sandwich, cut it in half, and plastic-bagged it. Just as I slid it into a paper sack, there was a loud banging noise from cross the room that made me jump half a foot; it sounded like a pistol shot. But it had only been the man slamming his empty mug down on the table.

I took a breath, let it out silently. He scraped back his chair as I did that, stood up, and jammed his hands into his coat pockets. Without looking at her, he said to the woman, "You pay for the food," and started past her table toward the restrooms in the rear.

She said, "Why the hell should I pay for it?"

He paused and glared back at her. "You've got all the money."

"I've got all the money? Oh, that's a laugh. *I've* got all the money!"

"Go on, keep it up." Then in a louder voice, as if he wanted to make sure I heard, he said, "Bitch." And stalked away from her.

She watched him until he was gone inside the corridor leading to the restrooms; she was as rigid as a chunk of wood. She sat that way for another five or six seconds, until the wind gusted outside, thudded against the door and the window like something trying to break in. Jerkily she got to her feet and came over to where I was at the sandwich board. Those cold lights still glowed in her eyes.

"Is his sandwich ready?"

I nodded and made myself smile. "Will that be all, ma'am?"

"No. I've changed my mind. I want something to eat too." She leaned forward and stared at the glass pastry container on the back counter. "What kind of pie is that?"

"Cinnamon apple."

"I'll have a piece of it."

"Okay—sure. Just one?"

"Yes. Just one."

I turned back there, got the pie out, cut a slice, and wrapped it in waxed paper. When I came around with it she was rummaging in her purse, getting her wallet out. Back in the restroom area, I heard the man's hard, heavy steps; in the next second he appeared. And headed straight for the door.

The woman said, "How much do I owe you?"

I put the pie into the paper sack with the sandwich, and the sack on the counter. "That'll be three eighty."

The man opened the door; the wind came shrieking in, eddying drafts of icy air. He went right on out, not even glancing at the woman or me, and slammed the door shut behind him.

She laid a five-dollar bill on the counter. Caught up the sack, pivoted, and started for the door.

"Ma'am?" I said. "You've got change coming."

She must have heard me, but she didn't look back and she didn't slow up. The pair of headlights came on out front, slicing pale wedges from the darkness; through the front window I could see the evergreens at the far edge of the lot, thick swaying shadows bent almost double by the wind. The shrieking rose again for two or three seconds, then fell back to a muted whine; she was gone.

I had never been gladder or more relieved to see customers go. I let out another breath, picked up the fiver, and moved over to the cash register. Outside, above the thrumming and wailing, the car engine revved up to a roar and there was the ratcheting noise of tires spinning on gravel. The headlights shot around and probed out toward the county highway.

Time now to close up and go home, all right; I wanted a glass of brandy and a good hot fire more than ever. I went around to the tables they'd used, to gather up the coffee cups. But as much as I wanted to forget the two of them, I couldn't seem to get them out of my mind. Especially the woman.

I kept seeing those eyes of hers, cold and hateful like the

wind, as if there was a black wind blowing inside her, too, and she'd been listening to it too long. I kept seeing her lean forward across the counter and stare at the pastry container. And I kept seeing her rummage in that big alligator purse when I turned around with the slice of pie. Something funny about the way she'd been doing that. As if she hadn't just been getting her wallet out to pay me. As if she'd been—

Oh, my God, I thought.

I ran back behind the counter. Then I ran out again to the door, threw it open, and stumbled onto the gravel lot. But they were long gone; the night was a solid ebony wall.

I didn't know what to do. What could I do? Maybe she'd done what I suspicioned, and maybe she hadn't; I couldn't be sure because I don't keep an inventory on the slots of utensils behind the sandwich board. And I didn't know who they were or where they were going. I didn't even know what kind of car they were riding in.

I kept on standing there, chills racing up and down my back, listening to that black wind scream and scream around me. Feeling the cold sharp edge of it cut into my bare flesh, cut straight to the bone.

Just like the blade of a knife . . .

SUMMER EVIL

NORA H. CAPLAN

The drive, almost obscured by flanking bridal wreath, lilacs and forsythia, followed one boundary line of the property to a stone building that was once a barn. Between that and the house was a boxwood hedge pruned to a height of six feet.

The house was built in the early 1830's. It was a small, two-story cottage of red brick with a slate roof and huge central chimney. Weathered green shutters framed the windows and recessed front door. Beyond the swell of pin oaks and pines sheltering the site lay Sugar Loaf Mountain. And beyond that, a hazy suggestion of the Catoctin range.

From the moment they first saw the house, Phyllis had a watchful feeling about it. As if she expected some major obstacle to prevent their buying it. But the price was incredibly within their means; Ben had no objection to driving thirty-five miles into Washington; and the county school Kate would attend had a fine reputation.

One night shortly after they'd moved in, Phyllis and Ben were sitting on the steps of the back porch, watching Kate gather grass for a jarful of lightning bugs, her bangs damp with concentration. The sun had almost gone down, and there was a faint mist rising from the creek that crossed the back of their land. The air seemed to be layered with both warmth and coolness, pungent with sweet grass and pennyroyal.

"I'd feel a lot easier in my mind," Phyllis said to Ben, "if we'd discover even one thing wrong about all this. People like us just don't find one-hundred-twenty-five-year-old homes in perfect condition for twenty-three thousand."

Ben folded the sports page and leaned back against her knees. "It's pretty far out here, and most families wouldn't consider a two-bedroom house." Then he added dryly, "Besides, I've never liked the way old houses smell. I noticed it about this one, too, right off."

"I've told you a hundred times, it's the boxwood. That's what the smell is, not the house, darling. Anyway, you'll have to get used to it. I have absolutely no intention of getting rid of that hedge. Mrs. Gastell said it's as old as the house."

Ben grinned as he turned and looked up at her. "Then would you at least trust me to spray it? There are spider webs all over the stuff."

"You'd better check with that nurseryman first, just to be sure. What's his name . . . ?" Phyllis pulled a letter from the pocket of her jamaicas and glanced through it. "Newton. He's just this side of the bridge in Gaithersburg."

"Who's the letter from? The old lady?" Phyllis nodded. "What'd she have to say?"

"Oh, nothing much. Just that she's getting settled, and she thinks she'll like Florida. Every other word is about her granddaughter. I guess the real reason she wrote was to remind us to put in a new furnace filter this fall. A few other things like that." Phyllis frowned. "There's a part here at the end I couldn't quite figure out."

She handed Ben the letter.

He scanned the page and then handed it back. "What's so mysterious about this? All old people take a proprietary air about everybody's else kids. Personally, I don't know why she's so worried about the creek. It's not more than a foot deep. There's no danger of Kate's getting drowned. And I haven't seen any snakes down there—not up to now, I haven't."

"Well, it's not only what she said in the letter. It's the way she's acted about Kate since she saw her. Almost as if she wouldn't have sold the house to us if she'd known we had a child. But I'm sure I mentioned Kate to her the first time we came out with the agent."

Ben lit a cigarette. "Maybe she thought Katie would tear up the place."

"No, it wasn't that. In fact, several times I told her how we've taken Kate to all kinds of museums and historic homes, and how she's always been careful with valuable old things. But Mrs. Gastell hardly paid any attention at all to me. She kept saying Katie shouldn't be allowed to wander all over the place by herself."

Ben shrugged. "Mrs. Gastell's seventy years old. People her age think we give our kids too much freedom. That's all she meant."

Their daughter had abandoned the lightning bugs and was now making hollyhock dolls, lining them chorus-fashion across the brick path to the grape arbor. Her shorts were grass-stained and the soles of her bare feet were already seasoned a greenish-rust. Ben reflected on her a moment and then he said, "I guess it will be hard on Katie, being alone so much now. It might be a good idea to get acquainted pretty soon with the people around here."

Phyllis leaned her elbows on his shoulders. "That's the trouble. Nobody on this road has children her age. But it's only six weeks until school starts. And in the meantime there's plenty around here to keep her occupied. The two of us can start all kinds of projects. I can't describe what a wonderful feeling it is, not to have people running in for coffee all day long or the phone ringing every ten minutes. Everybody knows this is a toll call, thank goodness. Maybe now I can start on the book."

Ben stood up abruptly. "No, you don't. Not after what you went through with that last story. Remember, you promised me you wouldn't do a thing for the rest of the summer."

She took his hand. "I didn't mean anything soon. I only meant now that we've moved. I promise not to write a word until we're all settled and Kate's in school." She called to the child, "I'm going to start your bath now, so don't be long."

"In a minute," Kate said automatically. "Daddy, come here. I made seven pink ones with white hats, and seven white ones with pink hats and . . ."

Phyllis smiled, and went into the kitchen. She turned on the brass lamp over the round pine table. The planked floor gleamed with a fresh coat of wax. It was a low-ceilinged room, full of early morning sunshine and pine-shaded in the afternoon. Women years before her had stood at her window and cleaned berries, kneaded bread, stamped butter with a thistle-patterned mold. Perhaps the room had given them moments of completeness, as it gave her now when she poured milk into a brown earthenware pitcher and set it beside a bowl of tawny nasturtiums.

Then as she was slightly bent over the table, one hand on the pitcher, Phyllis had the sensation that this room, the whole house, had an inexplicable fullness. That the very atmosphere had absorbed a century and a half of other lives. It reminded her of an incredible camera she had once read about—one that recorded, through heat radiations, images from the past, that were of course invisible to the naked eye. There was something about this house that seemed to retain, at times even emanate certain . . . presences. And it was not a feeling that came from any conscious attempt to visualize previous occupants. Somehow this thought disturbed her.

She let go the pitcher and went into the bathroom. The sound of water rushing from the faucet partially distracted her from whatever had bothered her and she dumped half a jar of bubble soap into the tub. Kate would love her extravagance.

The following day the Reverend Mr. White, rector of St. Steven's Church, called. He had the same cheery roundness of a Toby jug, smoked good Havanas and produced a box of licorice cough drops for Kate. Before he left, he told Kate to bring her parents to church Sunday. It'd be a good way for her to make new friends, too.

Until the mail came at eleven, Phyllis had planned to spend the afternoon with Kate, repainting her doll shelves. But she received a letter from her agent. *Woman's World* was interested in her revised manuscript, but they had decided the climax was still weak. She felt a familiar, obsessive pressure to get the work finished as soon as possible.

"I'm sorry, darling," she told Kate after lunch. "But I'm going to have to type for a while."

Kate's gray eyes clouded. "I got everything ready out on the back porch."

"I know, but I'd be all on edge if I tried to do anything before this gets done. You run on outside now. Take your dolls down to the arbor. Or ride your bike."

"Couldn't I start painting anyway? I'd be careful."

"You'd have the whole porch smeared up and get paint all over your hair. Remember what happened the last time I left you alone with a paintbrush?" She pushed Kate away gently. "Go on, now. I'll try not to be long."

Phyllis had already taken the cover off the typewriter. She didn't hear Kate leave the house and walk down the path to the creek.

Whether it was because she hadn't written for weeks or because it was hard to concentrate in new surroundings, the story just wouldn't come off right. Before she started the third draft, she looked at the clock. Five-thirty, and she hadn't even taken the meat from the freezer. Then she remembered Kate. Phyllis called upstairs and didn't get an answer. She went out on the porch. Kate wasn't in the arbor. She called louder.

Finally, from under the willows beside the creek, Kate appeared. She ran toward the house, pigtails flapping wildly. Phyllis hugged her. "I was beginning to get worried. Didn't you hear me calling and calling you?"

Katie's face was vibrant. "We were playing. Is dinner ready?" She pulled away from her mother and threw open the screen door.

Phyllis followed after her. "By the time you get washed and set the table, it will be." As she was searching the refrigerator for something to fix in a hurry, she thought of what Kate had said. She asked curiously, "Were you playing with someone?"

Katie turned toward her with a handful of silver, and her eyes glowed. "Her name's Letty. She's just my age. Seven and a half. Only her birthday's in December. I guess that makes her a little bit older."

Phyllis sliced some cheese. "Where does she live?"

"I don't know," Kate said. "But she showed me how to make a cat's-cradle. It's a trick you do with string. Want me to show you?" Her fingers were still grubby.

"Young lady, you were supposed to wash your hands."

"I did."

"Well, take another look. And use plenty of soap this time."

She heard Ben pull into the drive. She hoped he was in a good mood. As a rule, he didn't like grilled cheese sandwiches for dinner.

Kate didn't mention her doll shelves the following day. Right after breakfast, she told her mother that she was going down to the creek. Letty might be there. In a way, Phyllis was glad. She could have the morning free to work without any twinges of guilt over Katie's having nothing to do. She wrote until noon.

Katie came in long enough to wash down a peanut butter sandwich with lemonade. Then she wanted to be off again, telling her mother before she left, "Letty said she might have to go into Washington City tomorrow to visit her aunt. So we're trying to finish our doll house this afternoon. Can I take her some cookies?"

Phyllis wrapped a handful with a paper napkin. A phrase Katie had used reverberated queerly. Did Letty mean her aunt lives in Washington, D.C.?"

The girl stuffed two plastic cups into a paper bag. "I guess so. Letty says she loves to go there. Her mother always packs a lunch and they stop off by the canal locks to eat. I asked her if I could go, too, but she said there wouldn't be room." Kate filled the thermos with milk. "What's a gig, Mommy?"

Phyllis hesitated. "It's some kind of carriage, I think. Why?"

Kate started past her. "Oh. Well, I'd better go now."

Phyllis caught at her arm. "Look, why don't you bring Letty up here to play? You'd have lots of fun, showing her all your things. I feel funny about the two of you being down there all alone."

"Why do you feel funny? You could hear us if anything

happened." Then she said evasively, "Letty's kind of shy. I already asked her to come inside, but she won't. She said her mother wouldn't like it."

Phyllis snapped, "What does her mother think we are, anyway? I never heard of anybody being so . . . so provincial."

Katie squirmed. "Letty's not like that. She's nice. Honest, she is."

Her mother released her. "All right, but don't go any farther away than the creek."

Perversely, now she wished Katie weren't so wrapped up in this other child. She felt like taking a break herself. It would be nice for the two of them to work in the garden or bake something special like eclairs. There weren't any excuses now for not being with her daughter as much as she liked. Phyllis poured another cup of coffee. She stared at the white linen curtains in the living room gently breathing in, then out against the low sills. Finally, she went back to the typewriter.

Later, she decided to walk down to the creek. She could hear Kate chattering away. When she pushed aside the trailing willow branches, she saw only her child.

Kate looked up. "Hi. Letty just went over to the woods to get some more ferns. See, we're making a rock garden . . ."

Eddies were still swirling in the stream from a recent wading, but Phyllis couldn't detect any movement among the trees beyond.

For a time, Kate was eager to tell her mother and father all about Letty. Gradually, however, she divulged less and less. She sensed that something about her friend made her mother uneasy.

"I'd swear this child was all in her imagination," Phyllis told Ben one night as they were getting ready for bed. "But she's really there . . . or was, until I show up. I mean, the things they do together are really there. Like checkers and doll dishes and scrapbooks."

Ben surveyed his face in the mirror. He leaned closer. "More gray hairs. 'Will you love me in December as you do in May'?"

Phyllis put down her face cream. "Haven't you been listening?"

He turned around. "Sure, I have. It just seems to me that you're the one with the imagination, not Kate. This friend of hers is all right, I guess. From what I gather, her folks must belong to some kind of offbeat religious sect or something. You know how strict they are with their kids. They're pretty slow about taking up with outsiders, too."

"I never thought of that." Phyllis massaged her face.

Ben got into bed and folded his arms behind his head. "Why don't you take Kate into town tomorrow? Have lunch at Garfinckel's and go to a movie."

She turned out the light. "Maybe I'll do that if I can tear her away from Letty."

He pulled her into the curve of his arm. "See, you're tired of country living already. All I had to do was mention town, and you're ready to go."

She didn't rise to the bait. Her voice was unsure. "Nothing's ever the way you think it's going to be." A car passed on the road. Then except for the frogs down in the creek, there was no sound other than the soft brush of a pine bough against the window. Phyllis moved closer to Ben. He seemed to be asleep already, and she wouldn't wake him just to say she was afraid, for no particular reason.

The trip to town had to be called off. Kate was listless the next morning and complained of a headache. Phyllis was almost relieved. Now she could insist on Kate's staying indoors. She walked with Ben to the car.

"I don't think it's anything serious," she said, "but Kate is running a fever so I'll call the doctor. The Warrens told me the name of a good pediatrician near Poolesville."

He kissed her, and turned on the ignition. "Give me a ring after lunch. I'm sorry about today, honey. It would've done you both a lot of good to get away for a change."

She smiled. "I don't mind. Kate and I can watch TV and I'll make something special for lunch."

But Kate was irritable all day, and her fever rose that afternoon. She talked about Letty incessantly. She was obsessed with the idea that Letty might never come back. By the time the doctor arrived, Phyllis was exhausted. He reassured her, "I think she's getting German measles. I've had a dozen cases within the last week. Just give her aspirin and keep her in bed for a few days."

He was right. By Tuesday Kate was almost well. Phyllis remembered a dinner party she'd promised they would attend Wednesday. She wanted to cancel it, but Ben said, "Kate's all right now. Why don't you ask Mrs. Warren to come over and watch her. You told me she'd offered to sit for us."

Phyllis agreed reluctantly. Just before they left, she told Mrs. Warren, "Please call us if anything comes up. I feel uneasy about leaving her."

The older woman propelled her toward the door. "Go on and enjoy yourselves. I brought up six children. Katie and me'll make out just fine."

It was almost eleven when they returned. Mrs. Warren was asleep, completely erect in the wing chair. Phyllis tiptoed over to her.

The woman's eyes flew open. She got up hastily. "Didn't even hear you come in," she said. "I'm so used to going to bed at sundown, I must've dozed off."

"I'm sorry we've kept you up so late." Phyllis glanced up the stairs. "How's Kate?"

"Not a peep out of her since I tucked her in."

After Ben drove off with Mrs. Warren, Phyllis went upstairs. Just as she reached the landing, she saw the light go out under Kate's door. Before she even entered the room, she was sure something was off-balance. "You're playing 'possum,' missy," she whispered in the dark. The child didn't answer. Phyllis turned on the bedside lamp.

Kate's eyes were enormous. Her mouth fixed in a tight unnatural smile. She lay rigid, the covers pulled up to her chin.

Phyllis sat down on the bed. "What's the matter, honey?" She touched Kate's forehead. It was cool.

"I'm all right." Kate flinched under her hand.

She folded back the sheet and blanket, and said lightly, "Well, you'll smother, all bundled up like that."

Kate fumbled at the collar of her pajamas, but Phyllis

saw what she was trying to conceal—a string of red beads. She took Kate's hand away, and inspected the strand. It was coral, curiously strung in an even pattern of six large, then six small beads. "Where did you get this?"

The child avoided her eyes. "Letty gave it to me. She said it'd keep me from getting the pox."

"Keep you from . . ." Phyllis drew in her breath sharply. *But all the doors had been locked and there were screens on the windows.*

Kate took one of her braids and rolled the rubber band on its end back and forth between her thumb and forefinger. "Letty was afraid you might get mad at her. But all we did was play. I promised to sleep late tomorrow." She added as Phyllis stared dully at her, "Look what Letty made for me. Isn't it neat?"

Phyllis took the paper doll. It was crudely drawn, but there were certain significant details. The hair wasn't penciled in exaggerated curls; it was shown parted in the middle and knotted on top. Even the features were strange. There had been no attempt, obviously no knowledge of how to indicate mascaraed eyelashes or a conventionally full, lipsticked mouth.

She turned it over. There was printing on the back. It appeared to be an advertisement of a sale, probably livestock. The paper was cheap rag that would yellow quickly, but it was now crisp and white, the type starkly black. Then she saw two words that formed part of the doll's shoes. *Healthy wench.* She felt nauseous as she realized that this wasn't a handbill for a cattle auction at all.

Phyllis could only asks, "Where did Letty get this paper? Was it something she found in an attic or . . ." She faltered, then repeated, "Where did she get this piece of paper?"

Kate took the doll from her and smoothed down the upward curl of the slippers. Quite easily she said, "In town. Last week. A man in the market was passing them out to everybody. Letty's father got her a whole bunch to draw on. She gave me some, too. Look."

But Phyllis knew that a sheaf of slave auction circulars and a nineteenth-century paper doll and a coral talisman were not enough to convince Ben. No matter how much evidence were presented to him, he would never accept the fact that there could be no scientific explanation for Letty. Nor would anyone else. Except perhaps Mrs. Gastell.

The real significance of the episode, though, was that Letty had ventured into the house for the first time. Having once achieved this, she would become more and more sure of herself until . . .

From that night on, Phyllis resolved never again to mention the name Letty or refer to her in any way—at least not to Kate. She thought that if she refused to accept Letty's existence, eventually Kate would, also. She tried to keep her daughter occupied as much as possible. But if she took a shower or tried to write a letter, Kate slipped down to the creek. Always, Phyllis would discover her alone, with a look of annoyance on her face that Letty and she had been interrupted.

"We'll just have to move, that's all," Phyllis told Ben finally. "I can't keep this up much longer."

He handed her a tall gin and tonic. "I still think you're making too much out of this whole thing. You know what vivid imaginations kids have. This is probably just Kate's way of compensating for the lack of other children to play with. I don't doubt at all that Letty is real to her, but for you to accept her as some kind of ghost is . . ." Ben took her hand and rubbed it between his. "It's unhealthy, honey."

There was no sensation of warmth in her hand. She said tonelessly, "Yesterday I found . . . There's a grave in St. Steven's churchyard. It's hers . . . Letty's. She died of smallpox in 1844. She was only eight years old."

Ben studied the slice of lemon drifting sluggishly around the bottom of his drink. She was too numb even to speculate on what he was thinking.

Indirectly, it was Mr. White who provided a solution. Phyllis had invited him to dinner one night in late August. Afterwards they went out to the back porch, and he lit a panatella. The aroma of it blended with the smell of wild honeysuckle from the woods. He began a discussion on ancient rites of the Church. One that he mentioned pricked Phyllis into complete awareness. *Exorcism. The driving away of evil spirits.*

She leaned forward. "Mr. White, would it be possible for such a rite to be performed now . . . in the present day?"

Ben spoke up. "Phyllis, I don't think . . ."

Mr. White removed his cigar. "There's nothing the matter with a question like that at all. In fact, exorcism has always fascinated me. The last case I remember reading about occurred . . . let me see . . ."

Phyllis interrupted, "But could it be practiced now? Could you . . . could any clergyman perform it?"

His eyes behind the silver-rimmed glasses grew very thoughtful. "A great deal of evidence must be presented to prove that such an act should be performed. It is a very serious step. There are certain dangers involved."

She said clearly, "But exorcism is possible."

"In very rare instances, yes."

It could have been the very stillness that made Phyllis certain that Letty had heard and understood.

After Ben had left the following morning, Kate lingered at the table, slowly eating the last crumbs of a blueberry muffin. With her eyes still on the plate, she said to her mother, "What's exorcism?"

Phyllis's instant reaction was, "How did you happen to ask that?"

The child lifted her face. She went on in the same carefully controlled tone of voice, "If you exorcise somebody, does it hurt?"

Her mother stooped and held her close. "Of course not, darling. It's just a ceremony, a very serious one that has to do with driving away . . . something harmful. Who told you . . ."

Kate interrupted, looking directly into her eyes, "And they'd never come back? The person you make go away?"

Phyllis nodded. "We hope so."

Kate was silent a moment and then she said matter-of-factly, "But you don't have to worry about Letty anymore. She's already gone away."

Without further explanation, Kate reached for another muffin and went into the living room to watch the nine o'clock cartoon show. Dumbfounded, Phyllis arose from beside her chair, and crossed the room to the doorway. For a time she stood there, watching Kate's profile. But the child was absorbed in the program, nothing else.

A few days before school began, Mrs. Warren dropped by with a little girl. She called into the kitchen, "Anybody home? I brought somebody for you to meet." She put an arm around both Kate and the other child. "This here's Judy Davis. She's the daughter of my new dairyman. I been telling her all about you, and how you'll be taking the school bus together."

The two children sized each other up, and then Kate said, "Want me to show you some of my dolls?"

That evening as Ben was helping her with the dishes, Phyllis glanced through the window to the grape arbor where Kate and her new friend were engrossed in coloring books. She handed Ben a plate. "Kate's room is a shambles, but I couldn't care less. They've had such a marvelous time all afternoon."

Judy put down a crayon, and blew a wisp of blonde hair away from her eyes. "Wasn't this a good idea? I wish we'd thought of it sooner."

Kate agreed, "Mm-mm."

The other child deliberated over a picture. Then she said, "I think I'll color her breeches green, dark green."

Kate popped her bubble gum in disgust. "Listen, if I can remember to call you Judy, you'd just better learn to say *slacks*. You want to get me in trouble again?"

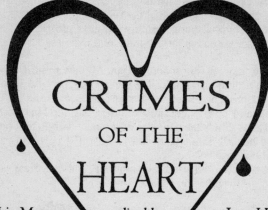

14 ALL-NEW TALES OF DEATH AND DESIRE FROM TODAY'S TOP MYSTERY WRITERS

CRIMES

OF THE

HEART

Lia Matera   edited by   Joan Hess

Nancy Pickard   Carolyn   Margaret Maron

P. M. Carlson   G. Hart   Dorothy Cannell

Susan Dunlap   Carolyn G. Hart

D. R. Meredith   Sharyn McCrumb

Audrey Peterson   Jeffery Wilds Deaver

Marilyn Wallace   Barbara D'Amato

__0-425-14582-4/$9.00